THE LOVE
OF HER LIVES

The perfect uplifting story to read this summer
full of love, loss and romance

C.J. CONNOLLY

JOFFE BOOKS

Joffe Books, London
www.joffebooks.com

First published in Great Britain in 2024

Cover art by The Brewster Project

ISBN: 978-1-83526-547-5

For anybody who seeks a better life —
or has ever simply wondered "what if?"

JUNE, THIS YEAR

Countless billions of stars.

Each one of them with the potential to give life to planets, just as our own Sun gives life to Earth. An infinite universe, with infinite possible solar systems and, within them, infinite life forms. Unending versions of ourselves, over and over again, in every possible permutation of our lives.

Infinite possibilities . . .

Above me, the inky sky twinkles with shimmering pinpricks of light — although nowhere near as many as if I were outside the city. It's a clear, warm night, but Chicago's light pollution isn't helping with my multiverse musings.

Infinite possibilities . . . Infinite lives . . .

Surely there's a killer slogan for our new sportswear account in there somewhere.

Live your best life, maybe? Nah . . . a bit too cliché. Something an influencer would say. For this campaign, it has to be more philosophical. Cerebral.

I place my empty champagne glass on the high-top table beside me, which is wobbling a little on the uneven patio tiles, and type "Infinite possibilities" and "Infinite lives" into the Notes app on my cellphone. Twenty stories below the glass barrier I'm leaning against, the evening traffic is now relatively quiet. It's nearly eleven, and our agency's summer party is gradually winding down.

I turn back to face the sliding doors that lead into our office lounge, and Stephen is pushing through them, two fresh flutes of champagne in hand. He saunters towards me with a wry smile on his face and hands me a glass.

"Hey, Millie. I saw you were dry, which seemed like a desperate situation in need of being immediately rectified." He looks up, past the tips of the tall buildings surrounding our roof terrace. "Finding inspiration in the cosmos? The little of it we can see from here." He takes a swig out of his glass. "Man, I can't *wait* to get out camping next weekend and do some real stargazing."

I take a sip of my own drink, and the bubbles effervesce like a galaxy on my tongue. Our boss, Erin, went all out with the vintage champagne for tonight. I certainly don't need another glass, as the stars above are starting to blur a little, but I can't turn down time with Stephen.

Anything for time with Stephen.

Even though I know that's not good for me. Even though I wish he wasn't what I want.

"That sounds great. I was just thinking some more about a slogan for Vici. They seemed really into our conversation earlier about string theory. I think there might be something there, you know, for the new tagline?" I shrug. "Something about infinite possibilities, or infinite chances. Like, somewhere in the multiverse, there's a version of your life where you've achieved everything you want, including being an awesome athlete or whatever — and with Vici, you can make *this* life that version. Or . . . something."

Stephen nods, still gazing upward, then turns his face down to me. He pushes his black-framed glasses up his nose and smiles. His irises, usually a vivid blue that contrasts with his soft-brown hair, are a deep slate in this low, artificial light. "I love it. Millie MacKenzie strikes again. Yeah, let's brainstorm some phrases tomorrow. Hangovers allowing."

I laugh, then pause for a second as a memory floods over me. "You know, this all reminds me of when we first met — not at work, I mean way back at Northwestern's Orientation Week, when you tried to get me to join the Astrophysics Society. Remember? I really wanted to sit around talking string theory and infinite universes with you and all your nerd buddies, but the meetings clashed with the a cappella group I joined."

He grins again, wider this time, and a thousand stars explode in my chest.

"The Northwestern Notables! How could I ever forget you guys? You were awesome. Oh yeah. 'Maria' . . ." He croons a couple of lines from the *West Side Story* musical we performed, more than nine years and a lifetime ago now.

In the gleam of the patio string lighting, his wedding band glints, as shiny as it was three years back when it was brand new. The stars inside me dim a little.

"Yeah, that group was a lot of fun," I reply. "It's too bad the clubs met on the same night, though. I would've liked to have joined both — then we probably would've been friends at Northwestern. Still . . . we got to know each other here, so no harm done, right?"

Stephen's smile wavers. "I guess." He pauses a moment. "But I wonder what might have been different if we'd been friends earlier? Hung out at Northwestern, you know?"

My stomach flutters a little. "I mean . . . I don't know what would've changed . . ."

That's a flat-out lie.

I know *exactly* what would've happened if we'd both been single when we'd first gotten to know each other. I just know it's wrong to even *think* it, let alone say it out loud to a married man.

I shake my head. "Anyways, it doesn't matter. We met at work later, and still became friends, so it's all good. And I'm sure you wouldn't have wanted your life to go any other way. You've got a great career, a lovely home, you're married, two little kids and another on the way — and you're happy, right? You and Eve?"

He frowns slightly at his drink, then nods, just once. "We're good, sure. It's hard with young kids, because they're monsters who pretty much ruin your life, and now Eve is pregnant again and constantly mad at me about her swollen ankles and not being able to run around after the kids. But we're mostly fine." He screws up his nose. "And we know we're very lucky. I just can't help sometimes thinking about all the what-ifs, you know? Would life have been even better if I'd made this choice, or that choice? If I had chosen Sciences instead of Communications, and gone into research, would that be more fulfilling for me than marketing? If I'd gone into the family business with my dad, would my relationship with him be better? And, you know, about a gazillion other possible life choices."

He lifts his eyes to me, and in them, I can immediately see he's thinking about another what-if. The same one I wrestle with every day.

What if Stephen *had* persuaded me to join the astrophysics club that day? What if *we* had known each other first?

I smile at him, a little sadly. "I get it. I think about the what-ifs of life, too — of course I do. Everyone does, I think. But what good does it do? You have a good life with Eve and the kids, you enjoy your job most of the time, you have a beautiful home, you have your faith . . . Just take the win. I mean, of all the infinite possible life paths you might have gone down, you have a pretty good one. Christ, it could be a lot worse." I stop myself. "Sorry, I didn't mean to blaspheme. I know you hate that." Of the many things Stephen and I have in common, religious belief is not one of them.

Stephen waves the comment away. "That's okay. You're right, I shouldn't be dwelling on this." He taps on the side of his champagne flute. "I've had too much of this stuff. Does me no good." He takes a deep breath, visibly pulling himself together. "And what about you, Millie Mac? You living a good version of all your possible lives? I mean, I know we

4

see each other every day, but I don't know if I've ever *really* asked . . . Are you happy?"

I huff out a slightly hollow chuckle. "Well, I'm lucky in many ways, I guess. Love my job, love my little studio apartment, which is a frickin' steal on the rent. I've got the most wonderful best friend in the world, and a few other really amazing people in my life." I shrug, and look out at the city. "But some stuff . . . isn't so good. My relationship with either of my folks is not the greatest, as you know. I mean, it's tough being an only child of a divorced couple. I haven't spoken to Dad in over a year, and I rarely see my flake of a mother. And I lost the best imaginable surrogate parents. I told you about them, I think, after too much gin at the spring retreat. They died in an awful, totally preventable accident."

He nods, with a sad smile. "I know that's tough for you to talk about."

Shaking my head to stop the tears of regret forming, I turn back to him. His side-lit face, a little long and geeky, has become so beautiful to me.

"Yeah, it really is. And then, of course, there's my love life, which is a total trainwreck. I'm thirty years old, I've only had a couple of short, unsuccessful relationships, because I'm *always* attracted to the wrong men — courtesy of Mom, no doubt. And I don't know if my eye-wateringly expensive therapy is even helping. So, my life is far from perfect. But, again . . ." I sigh, "it could be an awful lot worse. I mean, I'm not a crack addict on the streets."

I look back up to the night sky, and Stephen follows my gaze.

"Do you really think there are all those possible universes, with all the different versions of our lives playing out?" he asks, his voice barely above a murmur.

I take in a big lungful of night air. "I don't know. It's an awfully infinite universe. So . . . maybe?"

And if that's true, then maybe somewhere out there, beyond the stars . . . or somewhere else entirely . . . *somewhere*

5

Stephen and I are together. *We* met first, we took that path, and it's him and me.

But not in this life. Not for me.

Stephen lifts his glass for me to clink against. "Well, then, Millie Mac. Here's to the best version of all our possible lives."

I gently tap my flute against his, and a tiny bell rings out.

"To the version where we're both incandescently happy," I reply, as my heart shatters into a billion pieces.

LABOR DAY WEEKEND, ELEVEN YEARS AGO

"Turn that up!" Bonnie shrieked, her curly blonde hair whipping around her face as she gripped the leather steering wheel.

I laughed, cranking Daft Punk's "Get Lucky" on the radio. It had been our anthem for the summer, which had easily been the best of my life. I'd only met Bonnie in June, at a youth hostel in Santa Monica, but we'd almost instantly recognized each other as a soulmate. Then, when we'd discovered we were both starting at Northwestern University in Chicago in the fall, our best-friendship fate had been sealed.

We chorused into the wind about staying up all night and getting lucky — me tunefully, Bonnie painfully off-key. The late-summer sun beat down on Bonnie's teal convertible as we sped along the shore of Lake Michigan towards Bonnie's family home for the long weekend. Not that it made a difference that it was a long weekend, for us. Neither of us had been doing anything except having fun since graduating high school over a year ago, both enjoying a gap year before university. Bonnie had half-heartedly interned in DC for a while, then spent the summer on the California coast, unnecessarily slumming it in hostels. It wasn't as though her parents wouldn't have paid for a sweet vacation rental, but Bonnie was clearly looking to make new friends.

As was I.

After graduating high school in Indianapolis and deferring my place at Northwestern for a year, I'd taken nine months to travel around Europe, which I spent sitting in cafés and writing mediocre short stories — a trip paid for by guilt money from Dad, who moved back to Ireland following the divorce. After Europe, I'd had an awkward stay with Mom back in Indy — but with her being unemployed and depressed, I needed to get away again before I slipped into my own malaise. Dad was easily persuaded to fund a couple more months of me traveling the West Coast to keep me busy before school.

Thank goodness I did, or I'd never have gone to stay at that Santa Monica hostel near the beach.

I first saw Bonnie, golden curls splayed, sleeping off a hangover in the mock-Spanish courtyard. Snoring gently, with last night's dress hiked way up her thigh, she seemed like my kinda girl. Slightly nervous, I'd taken a chance and grabbed two coffees from the kitchen, bringing one out to Bonnie, who was by then semi-awake from the morning's buzz of activity.

"You look like you could use this," I'd said with a shy smile. "I'm Millie."

"Oh my god," Bonnie gasped, sitting upright on the lounger. "You're an actual lifesaver. Who knew that saints showed up with crop tops and shiny bobs? I don't know you, but I *literally* love you."

We'd barely spent a day apart since. With my poor excuse for a family long imploded, my tiny group of friends from Indy now heading for different universities across the country, and my high-school boyfriend having dumped me just before graduation, I didn't have much of a community. Or anything, really, except for a steady allowance from Dad each month.

It had felt like I had nothing.

Which meant Bonnie was everything.

And now I would be staying with her family for the Labor Day weekend, hopefully longer. I mean, it wasn't like I really wanted to kill another ten days back in Indy before school started. With Northwestern only a half-hour from the

Masons' house in Lake Bluff, and all my worldly goods in a suitcase in the trunk of Bonnie's convertible, it would be way better to stay with Bonnie's family until the dorms opened mid-September. I was so optimistic about this, I'd bought a one-way bus ticket from Indianapolis to Chicago. It felt like I was saying goodbye to that life — and all the pain my parents had bestowed on me — forever. The last thing I wanted to do was get the bus back to Indy again.

So, yeah, underneath the bravado of the song we were singing, I was pretty nervous. I desperately hoped they would all like me. Bonnie's parents, Angela and Frank Mason, were both highly successful — her a family lawyer, him an architect with his own firm. Plus there was an older brother still at home — a Northwestern alum who'd studied theater and was now writing plays. They all sounded a bit intimidating.

Bonnie gave me a sideways glance, no doubt picking up on something being off. She knew me so well already. "You still feeling okay about starting at Northwestern?" she asked, as the music subsided. "I know it's been a weird few years for you, with your folks and everything."

She could always pull me out when I was too much in my own head.

"Are you kidding?" I replied, lightly. "It's gonna be a-maz-ing. You and me living in Goodrich, tearing it up together in our Business Studies class. Plus, bonus! I don't have to listen to you snoring." We'd both snagged singles at the Goodrich House residence, thank Christ. With Bonnie planning on majoring in Political Science and me at the School of Communications, we'd already plotted to take minors in Business so we'd have some classes together. And, as a keen if unpolished writer, I was also doing minors in Creative Writing and Journalism. I figured it didn't hurt to cover all the bases — after all, who knew what future career opportunities I'd get, or which path I'd want to go down?

"Uhm, yeah, and all the booooyyyys," Bonnie drawled. "Why do you think I'm not gonna be staying at home with my folks, even though they live so close?"

I chuckled. Bonnie's enthusiasm for a fresh batch of guys to go through was unbridled. And, if her antics in both L.A. and Portland were anything to go by, indiscriminate.

"Pur-lease. That's exactly what most of them will be. *Boys*." I shook my head, my dark bob catching across my eyelashes in the wind. "Give me a *man* any day. Like that delicious theater professor I met on the campus tour. Rufus. Oh yes. Rufus Anderson."

"Roooo-fus Anderson," Bonnie crooned in delight. "Ooh, like the famous missionary!" She slapped a hand on the wheel. For all her quirks, Bonnie's American history knowledge was impressive.

I laughed. "If you say so. All I know is he can put me in missionary any day."

We were still giggling as we pulled off the highway and into the largely wooded residential area of Lake Bluff overlooking the water. We meandered down a long street, shaded from the sun by tall trees, and pulled into a gated driveway, where Bonnie reached out and punched a gate code. "Mom's birthday," she told me with an eye roll. "Which, yeah, is also Valentine's Day. I'm always telling Dad to change it."

The metal gates opened with a clang and a judder, to reveal a curved drive sweeping into a modern-build, classical-style house clad in stone, with oval frames in the second-floor dormer windows. My boho mother would've hated it, as would my traditionalist Irish father, but to me it was charming and elegant.

"That's weird — Mom and Dad's cars aren't here," mused Bonnie under her breath as we parked outside the double front doors. There was another car in the driveway, a dark blue Honda, that I raised my eyebrows at. "That's Ben's," added Bonnie.

As I dragged my case from the trunk, Bonnie tried the front door, but it was locked. "I didn't bring house keys with me," she explained, watching me struggle with my wheeled suitcase on the gravel. "I didn't realize my folks wouldn't be home while I picked you up. I never have their house keys with me when I'm here."

I uprighted my suitcase in dismay. I was grimy and tired after my long bus journey from Indianapolis to Chicago. "Then how do we get in? Is there a key under a pot or something?"

"Oh, don't worry. Ben's in. He lives in the basement. We'll just have to go in the side door. Leave that here." Bonnie grabbed my case handle and unceremoniously dragged it up the steps to leave it on the porch. "We'll get it when we come up. Follow me."

Bonnie led me along the left side of the house, down a sloped lawn, to a lower-level side door. "This door doesn't even lock — the frame's gotten warped, so you can always get in this way." Bonnie gave it a hard tug, and it opened with an unexpected rush of air. She stepped silently aside for me to enter ahead of her into the relative gloom, from which guitar music was clearly audible. "Starlight" by Muse, that was it — some acoustic guitar version. Through the open living space, I could see right through to sliding doors that led beneath an upper deck onto a pool terrace, with Lake Michigan shining in a slice of silvery teal beyond.

The music stopped abruptly. "Jesus. Who the fuck are you?" came a low, gruff voice to my right. I started out of my skin and turned.

It had come from a guy wearing nothing but a pair of white boxer briefs, sitting on the couch, a guitar resting against his bare chest. He ran a hand through his tousled, dark-blond hair and frowned at me.

"Relax, loser," said Bonnie from behind me, turning on the overhead light. "This is Millie. I told you she was coming to stay. Christ, Ben, you couldn't have gotten dressed today?"

"Oh. Uh . . . hi. Sorry." He put down the guitar and stood, seeming even more underdressed than before, as he stuck out his hand. "Ben, Bonnie's brother."

I shook it timidly, my neck flushing with heat, trying to look anywhere other than the vast expanse of toned, tanned man-chest in front of me. Jeez, he was tall — well over six feet. Probably a whole foot taller than me.

"Uh, hi. Sorry to disturb your playing. Nice to meet you." I turned in desperation to Bonnie. "We should go up? Grab my case from the porch?"

"Sure." Bonnie playfully whacked her brother's shoulder with the back of her hand. "Put some clothes on, slob. We're having pizza when Mom and Dad get back from wherever the hell they are."

"Mom's still at work, Dad's shopping," Ben replied. "For pizza, and supplies for the Labor Day party. Something about getting a cake to celebrate our guest's arrival." He turned to me and smiled disarmingly, his mouth stretching wider than I'd expected. "See you at dinner."

My stomach did a little flip. "Er, sure. See you then."

Lowering my head to hide the blush forming on my cheeks, I followed Bonnie past the couch. My glance caught on a cute, if slightly kitsch, framed print on the wall with cursive script writing that read "*Home is not a place, but a feeling.*"

With my pulse still racing, Bonnie led me up a set of stairs to the main floor and showed me to the guest bedroom, which I took in distractedly.

Well, this was a new development.

Bonnie had never mentioned to me that her brother was *hot*. Not once.

Well, okay — it might've been weird if she had.

But still.

JUNE, THIS YEAR

My window is open all the way down as I make the exit onto Highway 94, my hair blowing so wildly across my eyes, it's almost dangerous. My little red runabout was pretty crappy when I bought it from a used car lot two years ago, after getting my promotion to Senior Digital Marketing Manager at Magnolia. And now the air-con has finally given up trying.

Keeping my eyes on the highway, I reach for the cell on its mount and hit speed-dial for Bonnie on speaker.

She answers with a high-pitched squeal that takes me back to when we were first friends, driving up this highway together. "Happy Friday sunny long weekend! And I've finally got the weekend off!"

I laugh. "For once! I can't wait to finally hang with you this entire weekend and not have you at the store the whole time." I have to raise my voice over the sound of the wind rushing past my ears.

"Yaaass, girl! Where are you right now?"

I roll the window up a little to hear her better. "Heading up 94. But Google says there's traffic ahead, so I'll be maybe forty minutes."

"Okay, that's good," she replies. "I'm still stuck at the store, waiting on some inventory to be delivered. It was supposed to be here at five, so hopefully any time now. If you beat me to the house, you can let yourself in through the basement side door."

A long-ago memory of Ben playing guitar, younger and clean-shaven back then, and shirtless, jumps unbidden into my mind.

"Gotcha. I have some of that good red wine. Is Ben joining us?"

"I don't think so, but he didn't say," Bonnie replies. "I think something's going on with that woman he started seeing. Shelley? The daycare assistant."

Ugh, right. I'd heard about him going on a few dates with some daycare hottie.

"Just us two then, even better," I reply, covering my disappointment. I mean, it's always fun when Ben's around. "Unless, of course, that cute guy from the bakery finally texts you, like he promised. I realize I might have competition for your attention if that happens."

Bonnie scoffs, in the way she does when she cares about something but wants to make it seem like she doesn't. "Paul the pastry chef? I'm not holding my breath on that one. He's too good to be true."

"Well, he's a fool if he doesn't," I reply. "Okay, I'll see you in a while, I guess. You won't be late, will you?"

"Ten minutes behind you, absolute max. And there's already a cold bottle of white in the fridge — you can open that first."

I smile. Bonnie's ten-minute estimations tend to be more like a half-hour, at best, but that's okay. I'll have some cold wine to keep me company.

"Cool beans. I'll see you at the house." I hit end call, and roll the window down again. The highway is busy, and the air is hot, but I don't mind. It's very nearly summer, it's a three-day weekend, and I'm spending it with my best friend in the world.

I really need this break. It hasn't been the best week, honestly. This morning, I got an email telling me my annual lease won't be renewed on my apartment — my cute little

14

downtown studio where I've lived for years and that I love — which means I have to find a new place in a very expensive city by the end of July. Which totally sucks.

Added to that injury, since my slightly inebriated talk with Stephen at the office party last week, I've been feeling pretty down. It's been kinda awkward. The following day, as promised, we'd brainstormed slogans for the Vici account — but he'd barely looked me in the eye the entire time. He seemed to be feeling a bit guilty about the implications we both made in our what-if conversation. Which is only natural, of course. He's a devout Catholic, married with kids, and he let himself slip in a moment of tipsy wistfulness.

In the week since, we've laughed much less than usual, and spoken to each other much more formally — mostly about work, plus the habitual morning and end-of-day exchanges. And today, he took the day off for a four-day camping weekend with his wife and kids.

One thing is for sure — a conversation like that won't happen again.

Not in this life.

Yes, I really need Bonnie and that cold bottle of wine.

It's another fifty minutes by the time I've made it through the traffic to Bonnie's house in Lake Bluff. I tap in the memorable gate code and pull up in front of the house. Unsurprisingly, Bonnie's car still isn't in the driveway, and I don't have a front door key, but I can probably let myself in through the basement.

A growl of hunger tightens my stomach. I have zero faith in Bonnie being ten minutes behind me, so I'd better order some food. It's a busy Friday night, and it always takes forever to arrive out here. I quickly ping Bonnie a text.

Should I get the dim sum ordered?

She responds within moments.

You know it! Get the usual, and add the new chicken pot stickers they have. Yum. :P

15

Chuckling gently, I order a selection of dumplings and spring rolls from our usual delivery app, optimistically adding extra servings just in case Ben shows up, after all. I mean, leftovers are always good, too.

Now there's just the small matter of breaking into the house. I grab the red wine, leave my overnight bag in the car, and descend the steep sloping lawn that leads to the basement's side door.

A wave of nostalgia floods over me. That first time I ever came here, when I had also entered through this side door . . . that weekend changed my life. I'd already gained Bonnie as my new best friend, but the way her parents and brother also embraced me into their lives had cemented our bond into something unbreakable. The weekend gave me a new family — one that I came to love deeply.

If only we hadn't later lost Ange and Frank in such a senseless way.

If only we hadn't asked them to be on the road that night.

I shake off the thought, and place my hand on the slightly rusty door handle. That memory again. First meeting Ben, who'd been living in the basement since graduating. What had he been playing on his guitar when we'd surprised him in his underpants? Something that was super popular back then. "Starlight," that Muse song, that was it.

I chuckle to myself — and at younger, grungier Ben — and hum the tune as I give the door a tug. The frame is even more warped than ever, and it's stubborn.

I give another, harder, tug on the door. This time, after a moment of resistance, it gives in with a whoosh — almost like a vacuum seal has broken, and the basement can breathe again.

Still humming Ben's guitar riff, I step into the dark, unlit space, closing the door behind me, and head towards the stairs that lead up to the kitchen. Bonnie has left the stairway light on — which is unlike her, given her zealousness for switching off all unnecessary lights and electrical devices. But at least I can see.

What's weirder, though, is the unmistakable, delicious smell of Chinese food emanating from upstairs.

Maybe Ben decided to join us for the weekend, after all, and he was way ahead of us in terms of ordering dim sum? I didn't see his car in the drive, but he often parks on the street to leave space for me and Bonnie.

I climb the steep staircase and push my way through the door at the top, calling out, "Ben? Is that you?" as I enter the kitchen.

I stop. The kitchen looks . . . *nothing* like when I last saw it. Different cabinets, in tan wood rather than white, and a different color on the walls, dark taupe instead of cream. An array of food in large dishes all over a black counter, and a bunch of fancy-looking countertop appliances. A red wall calendar with some beautifully scripted Asian characters on it.

And, through the archway, in the dining area . . . a group of people, a family, sitting around Bonnie's dining table.

Chopsticks frozen in mid-air, rice dropping, as they stare at me in evident shock and disbelief.

And it's not Bonnie's simple, rustic, long dining table, but an oval table with elaborate carvings.

Then, the woman of the group — presumably the mother — screams.

Immediately, it's mayhem. The mother is screaming, the kids begin whimpering, and the man at the head of the table stands and starts shouting at me in something that could be Mandarin or Cantonese or maybe something else, waving his noodle spoon aggressively.

I hold my hands up. "Hey, hey, I'm sorry! I'm sorry! I'm Millie, I'm Bonnie's friend. Bonnie's friend?" The mother stops screaming, although she doesn't seem to understand what I'm saying. "I'm here to see Bonnie. Who *are* you?" The kids, three of them and all probably under ten years old, begin to quiet down, but are still staring at me, wide-eyed.

The man takes a step forward towards me and yells something that I don't understand. My hands are still raised in compliance.

17

What the *fuck* is going on? Who are these people, and what the hell are they doing having dinner in Bonnie's house? Which doesn't even look like Bonnie's house?

"Okay, okay! I don't know what's happening, but I'm gonna call Bonnie, we'll get it straightened out, okay?" I don't know why I keep speaking English at them — clearly they're not understanding me. I pat down my jeans back pocket for my phone, but it's not there — I must've left it in the car. Shit. "Okay, I'm gonna go get my phone, it's in my car, I'll call her, okay?"

Not okay, apparently. The man is still yelling, and he's getting louder, and he's taking more steps towards me. I look at the youngest girl, whose gorgeous little face has a fat tear on its cheek, and it breaks my heart to be scaring her.

"I'm sorry," I repeat, holding up my hands again. "I'm gonna go outside until this is all straightened out with Bonnie. She'll be here soon." I back away towards the front foyer, which is painted in a deep plummy red rather than its usual gray-blue, and let myself out of the heavy wooden door, my heart racing.

What in God's name was *that*?

I look around for my crappy car, but it's not in the driveway. Instead, there's a very nice black Audi and a bright red Tesla parked out front.

I hear a shout from behind me — the man has followed me to the front door to ensure I leave.

"I'm going, I'm going!" I tell him. I gesture around me. "I can't see my car!"

He yells something else and throws his arm towards the gate — a very clear, get-the-fuck-out-of-here gesture. I raise my hands once more, and make my way to the gate. I hit the release button on the side and it clangs open. I escape as soon as the gap is wide enough, and run a little way down the road until the gate is closed again.

My heart is pounding so hard I can hear the blood in my ears.

What the hell just *happened*?

I have to get a hold of Bonnie.

Taking deep breaths, as controlled as I'm able, I pat my back pockets again for the missing phone. I'm not wearing a jacket, so the only pockets I have are in my jeans.

Hold up. I wasn't wearing these white jeans before.

I don't even *own* any white jeans.

The side pocket has the lump where I put my car keys — at least I have those, even if I can't remember where I parked my car. I thought I'd parked it in the driveway? I remember punching in the gate code.

I pull out the car keys — and they're wrong, too. Not my car keys — somebody else's. There's a VW logo on the fob, and a set of house keys I don't recognize.

Okay, this is getting really fucking scary. My head is starting to swim, my vision increasingly blurry.

I crouch on the grass verge of the residential street, my face between my knees, like I used to as a kid when I was feeling panicky about Mom and Dad's fights. I blow out big breaths.

In for four. Out for eight, slowly.

Just breathe. Then I'll be able to think.

In for four. Out for eight.

When my pulse has slowed a little, I lift my head.

Okay, let's figure this out. Bonnie's house . . . doesn't appear to be her house anymore. Bonnie still hasn't shown up. I don't have my car, or my phone, or any stuff with me. Apart from these keys.

Well, if these keys are all I have, maybe I can use them. Maybe I can find a phone to use.

I scan the street. It's largely devoid of street parking, given that the houses are mostly gated with driveways and parking space on the property. But there's a cluster of parked cars a little further down. I walk towards them, and start looking at the logos on the front. The third is a green VW Golf.

My pulse quickening again, I lift the VW fob, point it at the car, and press the unlock button.

Beep. Clunk.

The unmistakable sound of a car unlocking.

One mystery solved, a whole bunch more to go.

I'm nervous to climb inside, given that it's not *my* car —
but there must be a reason I have these keys. I take another
deep breath, open the door, and get into the driver's seat.

Perhaps I can stay in here, in this safe, lockable envi-
ronment, until Bonnie comes home. I can still make out the
home's gated entrance from here, so I'll see when Bonnie
pulls up in her bright yellow Nissan.

Assuming she *does* pull up.

Given that there's a random family living in her house,
and her house doesn't look at all like her house anymore . . .
I have a pretty bad feeling that maybe she's not coming.

What the hell is happening? Have I . . . slipped into
some kind of impossible parallel universe where Bonnie
lives . . . I dunno, somewhere else?

But that's ridiculous. Impossible.

A sharp spike of fear and loneliness, painfully familiar
ever since I was an only child with constantly battling parents, stabs at my chest. The truth is, if I don't have Bonnie,
I don't really have anyone. Nobody in my life who cares if I
live or die, apart from a useless mother who drives me crazy.
Okay, sure, I have a couple of other friends from work. And
of course there's Ben, who's someone I can rely on to be
there for me, no matter what. It's really only been since I
had him and Bonnie in my life that the terror of being alone
has been gone.

Maybe I should go back to the city and find Ben. After all,
I am sitting in a car that I could drive there. But no . . . he'll
be at the theater, busy with his play. He'll think I've lost my
mind if I show up there and tell them this nonsensical story.

Perhaps this car holds some clues as to what the hell
is going on. I turn to the passenger side. A black purse I
hadn't noticed before is on the seat. I grab it and, ignoring
my qualms about invading its owner's privacy, open it and
tip the contents onto the passenger seat.

A phone — thank Christ! — and a pink leather wallet, along with the usual purse detritus of pens, lipstick, plastic-wrapped tampon, notebook, business cards, tube of hand cream, and tissues. I grab the wallet first, and open it to find out who owns this mysterious car.

Inside is a clear plastic window with a driver's license behind it.

My driver's license.

My own face staring out at me, and my own name. Emilia MacKenzie, in clear type.

The credit cards, too. All four in my name — two with banks I've never used. Various shopping loyalty cards, all in my name, none that I'm subscribed to.

I flip over the business cards that fell out. No names or companies that I recognize. But the moisturizing cream for dry hands is my favorite brand — has been since I was a teenager.

My stomach churns horribly. I might just throw up in the immaculate interior of this weird VW.

Gulping down air, I pick up the phone, which is in a chic navy-blue case. It's already turned on, but the screen is locked, with a flower background. I look up to the camera at the top, and it recognizes me.

This is *my* phone. It unlocks through facial recognition.

Except I've never seen this phone before in my life.

I immediately open the text messages to find my last conversation with Bonnie, to check that our text thread is normal, before I call her.

But there's no text conversation with Bonnie. Her name isn't even in this phone. Nor is Ben's.

There's a bunch of text interactions with someone called Chris, who texts most days, about mundane but strangely intimate stuff, like what groceries to get and what time we should meet somewhere. And a host of other people whose names I also don't recognize.

This is really, *really* fucked up.

I'm starting to panic again. I force myself to rest my head on the wheel and breathe myself out of it.

In through the nose for four, out through the mouth for eight — slowly, measured. And again. And again.

I try to gather myself. Okay, so I can't contact Bonnie from this phone. But I know where her interiors store is, in the commercial center of nearby Lake Forest — it's only a five-minute drive from here. She might still be waiting there for her inventory.

With at least a minor plan in place, I begin to feel a little better. I put my phone on the mount on the dashboard, in case I need to follow a map at some point, or in case she calls me when I'm driving. I start up the car, pull out of the parking space, and shakily drive past Bonnie's gateway. Fortunately, at least, there's no sign of the family calling the police on me.

I drive to the stretch of retail outlets in Lake Forest's center and look for Bonnie's tiny storefront, which is always hard to spot. It's a couple of doors down from the European desserts place that she always makes me go into, to get her a cream puff. This time, her little store is even harder to find, and I slow to a crawl, craning my neck to see the name above every store. Surely it's where that bagel shop is? Why have I never seen that bagel place before?

I brake, check there's nothing behind me, and reverse slowly, scanning the names above every door. At the end of the block, I drive forward past every store once again.

Yep. Bonnie's store isn't here, and there's a little bagel shop in its place.

Okay.

This is worst-case scenario.

But I'm not going to panic again. I'm not. I'm not. I can do this.

What *can* I do?

I can go home. Fuck it. I'm giving up, and I'm going back to the city. Back to my cute little rental studio, where I feel safe. I can figure all the rest of this out later. If and when I manage to track down Bonnie, I can tell her everything that happened, and she'll just have to understand.

I take a right after the shops towards I-94, and put my foot down on the gas and speed up as I approach the highway. But I don't normally drive from Lake Forest, so I'm not sure where the intersection is.

I press the side button of the cellphone mounted on the dash, and it jumps into life. I speak clearly. "Siri, give me directions to home."

"Okay. Calculating directions to home," the Siri voice replies. "In one mile, take the next left and join Interstate Highway 94."

Okay, that makes sense. The intersection is still a bit further ahead.

I glance at the map that has come up on the phone.

There's something wrong. Another thing that's wrong.

Yes, Siri is taking me south down I-94. But then the blue route line runs *way* past Chicago, round the bottom of Lake Michigan, and all the way to New Buffalo — nearly a two-hour drive from here.

My cellphone thinks I live in *New Buffalo*.

But I've never even been there.

That's the last thing I think before the grass side verge and a huge green hedge come to meet me.

MID-SEPTEMBER, ELEVEN YEARS AGO

"You know, it's really a lot of fun. I joined as a freshman myself, last year, and now I'm the society president. And you really don't need to be majoring in Sciences to join. We have members of all kinds — a lot of philosophy students, for example. And I'm not studying sciences either, I'm a Comms major."

The brown-haired guy with the glasses was definitely giving me a convincing pitch at the Astrophysics Society stall. Plus, he had the bluest eyes behind those lenses. And I'd always loved learning about and debating the universe and the cosmos, and pondering the vastness of it all. Even if, as a Communications major myself, it wasn't my specialty.

But I'd just come from the Northwest Notables A Cappella stall, and they'd been equally convincing. I was dying to get back into singing after more than a year. Choir had been one of my greatest joys in high school — and a much-needed escape from the fights between my parents at home, until they divorced.

Problem was, both of the groups met Tuesday nights.

"I'll have to think about it," I told the brown-haired guy with a smile. He grinned back, clutching theatrically at his heart as if wounded by an arrow, and backed away. Soon his attention was caught by the next prospect. I stepped away and made room for a pair of nerdy-looking guys in sweater vests who had been clamoring for my spot at the stall.

Dammit, it sucked that my top two extracurricular choices were on the same night. Maybe there was another vocal harmony group. But I'd really liked the people on the Notables booth, and could imagine singing with them. Maybe becoming friends.

"Deep in contemplation, I see."

A low, newly familiar voice behind me. I turned with a smile.

"Ben! What are you doing here?" I reached up to give him a slightly awkward hug — awkward because he was so much taller than me, and because the hug had clearly caught him off guard. Also because I'd seen Ben only two days ago, when he helped me and Bonnie move into our university dorm, so a hug was probably overkill.

But even in that slightly stilted moment, his strong arms definitely felt good around me.

No.

I absolutely could *not* think of Ben that way. Developing a crush on Bonnie's brother would be disastrous. He was entirely off-limits, and nothing could ever happen — not if I didn't want to risk my friendship with Bonnie, and my newfound closeness with the entire Mason family. I had to think of him as a good friend — nothing more.

We pulled back, a little bashful. Ben was dressed in a crisp pale-blue shirt that looked great against his tan. It was the most put-together I'd seen him in the two weeks since we met.

"I was just dropping off more clean laundry for Bonnie, under Mom's instructions," he said with a laugh. "And no, I'm not going to be her regular laundry errand boy. I was heading into the city, so it was on my way."

"I figured you looked like you were going somewhere. Hot date?" I joked, then instantly regretted it. My cheeks burned a little. Hopefully it would just look like I'd caught the sun.

"Actually, yeah," Ben replied, unflustered. "A girl I knew from high school recently got in touch, now that she's back from Stanford. We've seen each other a few times over the summer. I'm taking her for a birthday dinner in the city."

"Oh." I wasn't quite sure what to do with this information. Why hadn't Bonnie mentioned Ben was *seeing* someone? "Well, that's great. Have an awesome time." I turned to leave, but he caught my arm.

"What about you?" he asked. "You joining any of these clubs?"

I glanced back to the astrophysics table, where the brown-haired guy was looking over at us. "I think so. I just need to decide between astrophysics — which, as you know from our firepit and s'mores conversations, I love talking about — or a cappella, which I want to get back into. Both groups meet on the same night, which sucks."

Ben followed my gaze to the astrophysics guy, who quickly turned away. "Well, I also know from our firepit and s'mores nights that you hold a hell of a harmony line, and you have one of the warmest alto tones I've heard in a while. So my vote would be singing. Not that you're looking for my advice, of course." He waggled his eyebrows.

I chuckled. "I guess you've seen the Notables perform — at least its previous members, when you were at school here?"

"Oh yeah," he replied, "loads of times. They're a lot of fun. They've even gone to some international a cappella conventions. I got to know some of the previous members when they sang in a Performing Arts department recital night, alongside a short play I was doing. That would've been . . . my junior year of Theater Studies, I guess."

Despite Ben in all his tanned, six-foot-four manliness standing in front of me, an image popped into my mind. The dazzling smile and salt-and-pepper beard of the theater professor I'd met on the spring campus tour.

"You must've studied under Professor Anderson, when you were here?" I asked, feigning innocent curiosity. "He showed us the theater when I visited earlier this year."

"Yeah, sure, Rufus was one of my main professors," Ben replied, an eyebrow raised. The side of his mouth twitched in a not-quite smile that had a knowing edge. "Very brilliant in many ways. Very charismatic. *Very* popular with the female students, as you can imagine. But also very much attached to Professor Amy Brandon, the philosophy lecturer. They live together."

"Oh, right, no, I mean, I wasn't—" I stammered. My not-sunburn flush deepened.

He chuckled, letting me off the hook. "Anyways, just remember, with the a cappella group, you're working towards something — something you achieve together. Usually there's a big end-of-year performance, plus other smaller gigs through the year, and the possibility of travel. That's a lot more rewarding than simply sitting around talking about the universe with a bunch of know-it-alls." He gave me that wide grin. "In my opinion."

I laughed. "Well, Mr. Playwright-slash-Theater-Director, you would say that, being all about the Big Show. It's already your chosen path."

He nodded, the smile still lighting up his face. "Well, then, Millie, I will leave you to choose *your* path. But make it a good one." He placed a hand briefly on the side of my shoulder, then turned and walked away, his dark-blond head above virtually everyone else's.

Why did I always feel a little bereft when Ben left my presence? And now he had a *girlfriend*. Probably fabulous and confident and pretty.

Ugh.

I shook myself out of it, and turned back to the decision at hand. Ben had a good point about the benefits of joining the singing group. I threw the brown-haired astrophysics dude another quick glance, turned, and headed back to the Northwest Notables stall.

The guy from the choir I'd chatted with earlier — maybe he'd said his name was Chris? — gave me a warm smile as

I approached. "Back again, I see. I thought we'd lost you to the space nerds."

I pulled in a deep breath. "I'd like to audition, please — Millie MacKenzie," I said quickly, before I could change my mind.

JUNE, THIS YEAR

"You okay, miss?"

Someone's arm is reaching in the car door, lifting me back by the shoulder, away from the steering wheel my forehead is resting against.

"You okay? Your airbag didn't deploy," the voice says again. I turn towards it. It's an old guy, maybe in his seventies.

I touch my forehead. It's a little sore, probably bruised, but there's no blood.

"Yeah, I'm fine. I think." I attempt to smile at him. "Thanks for stopping. Uh, I'm not sure what happened."

The old man grins back. "You were a couple cars ahead of me, and you just swerved right onto the verge and into the hedge. Guess it wasn't enough impact for the airbag." He raises his thick, white eyebrows. "D'you know why you drove off the road?"

I look ahead of me to see the hood of the green, not-really-mine VW Golf encased in a thicket of hedge. Parked on the grass next to my car is a beat-up old pickup, presumably belonging to my rescuer.

"I . . . uh . . . dunno. I got distracted for a second, I guess, looking at the map on my phone. Next thing I knew, I was in the hedge."

New Buffalo.

That's what happened. Siri's map telling me I live where I don't live.

Bonnie's house, inhabited by a random family who were shocked to see me there.

Bonnie's store, disappeared, replaced by a bagel shop.

None of my friends listed in this weird navy-cased cellphone that's still in its holder on the dash.

"If you're feeling okay, you wanna try to back out of the hedge, and get back on the road?" asks the old guy. "Doesn't look like there's much damage, other than some scratches to the paintwork." He steps back from the car and closes my door.

I nod. Not that I know where I'm going, anymore.

"Sure," I tell him, with more certainty than I feel. The car's engine is still running, so — with a trembling hand — I put it in reverse and pull slowly out of the hedge, straightening on the grass verge. I roll down the window. "Thanks for stopping — I'll be fine," I tell the old man. "Have a great evening."

"You take care now," he replies with a wave, ambling off to his truck.

I wait for a pause in traffic, then pull out onto the road, still a little shaky. In a few moments I'm at the I-94 intersection, so I turn left to head into Chicago. Siri is still telling me to go "home" to New Buffalo, but that's not where I live.

I have to go to *my* home.

I tap "End Route" and, after forty-five minutes of pretty unsteady driving, I pull up outside my building. I don't have my usual keys with me, so I have no fob to get into the underground parking garage. Instead, I find a spot in a nearby side street and park hurriedly, too far from the curb.

Keys. That's my problem now — I don't have my own building and apartment keys on me either. Just the set that has the Golf car keys and a weird set of house keys that presumably belong to somewhere in New Buffalo.

Maybe I can get Graeme, my next-door neighbor, to buzz me in. He's got a spare key to my studio in case of an emergency. And this definitely qualifies.

I punch the # for the building's buzzer directory, and hit it three more times to get to the twelfth-floor units. Graeme's name is there, as usual, for 1205.

But mine is not. Instead, the electronic directory reads, "Johnson: 1206" where it normally reads "MacKenzie: 1206."

This is ridiculous. I punch in 1205, and wait as it beeps. "Hello?" It's Graeme's voice.

"Graeme? It's me, Millie. I, uh, lost my keys and need to get into my place. You still got my spare?"

A pause. "Sorry. Who is this?"

My stomach drops. "Millie. Millie MacKenzie. Your neighbor, next door."

Another silence, longer this time. "Uh. I don't remember a Millie in the building. Are you new? And no, I don't have your key."

"Graeme. It's me, it's Millie." I'm trying to keep the panic out of my voice, but it's bubbling up. "I live right next door in 1206. I gave you my spare—"

"I'm sorry, I don't know any Millie." Graeme's voice is ice-cold through the intercom. "Jake and Savannah live in 1206. I can't buzz you in. Have yourself a nice evening." The intercom beeps, and is silent.

Fuck.

Some random couple are living in my unit, and Graeme has no idea who I am.

I'm really in . . . in an *alternate reality* of some kind.

The panic that was bubbling up spills out of my mouth, and I find myself emitting a wordless shriek of horror and frustration into the street. A woman and her child on the sidewalk stop, alarmed, and cross to the other side to avoid me.

I've become *that* person. In a matter of a few hours, I've gone from a relatively happy, albeit imperfect, person with a good job and friends, to the disturbed weirdo that people avoid on the street.

A disturbed, friendless, apparently homeless weirdo.

I stare down at the set of keys in my hand. Okay, maybe not *entirely* homeless. After all, these house keys open a door somewhere.

Maybe there will be answers in New Buffalo. I don't really have much choice but to go and find out.

Back in the Golf, I reset Siri to "home" from my current location, and follow her instructions to drive south out of Chicago, along the lakeside highway, and out of Illinois into the northwestern corner of Indiana.

The evening sun is lowering to my left as the highway gradually turns northeast, through Burns Harbor, Michigan City, and Michiana Shores. Just before I get to New Buffalo, I drive over another state line into Michigan, entering the Eastern Time Zone, and my phone's clock jumps forward an hour. By this time, the shadows are lengthening and the light is a golden shimmer through the trees and low buildings.

"*Take the next left onto Harbor Isle Drive,*" Siri instructs me, and I turn down a narrow street leading to the water. "*Your destination is on the right.*" I pull up next to a row of gray-shingled, white-trimmed townhomes overlooking a gorgeous marina. A boardwalk runs next to them, with a white-painted pagoda at the central junction with the outstretched dock leading out to the marina itself. Beyond a parking lot, a set of bigger homes in the same gray-and-white style are jutting right out over the water, partly held up on stilts.

Wow. This place is beautiful.

But which one is — supposedly — mine?

Maybe Siri knows. "Siri, what's my home address?"

"*Your home address is set to Unit 17, Seashore Mews, Harbor Isle Drive, New Buffalo, Michigan.*"

Huh. Thanks, Siri.

I park in what looks to be a residents-only parking lot, hoping I haven't taken somebody else's regular spot, grab the black purse, and lock up the car. Unit 17 seems to be one of the smaller townhouses to my right. I step along the boardwalk until I find it, and pull out the set of keys as I reach the white front door.

What am I going to find inside?

I pause, my hands trembling so violently the keys are jangling a little. The low sun casts my shadow on the door, which has a large picture window next to it. A window that has thin, gauzy curtains obscuring the interior from view . . . but there's definitely a light on inside the house. And, now that I can hear over my own racing heartbeat, soft strains of music are coming from inside too.

There's already somebody in there.

Should I knock? Or just try the keys?

I have to know if these keys open this front door. I just *have* to.

Very quietly, and with my stomach pitching, I slip the key into the lock, and turn. It clicks open with ease. I put my hand on the door handle and pull it open.

My heart in my mouth, I step into a little enclosed vestibule. Ahead of me, hanging from an adorable row of hooks with anchors painted at each end, is my own denim jacket that I've had for more than ten years, the one with the patch. Below the coats is a row of shoes, including two pairs of my own that I also recognize.

This is definitely my house. Some of this is *my stuff*.

I reach out for the jacket and trace my finger along the hand-stitched seam, uneasily. It gives me little comfort to see such a familiar item in a house I've never been to before. Especially given that next to my jacket is a man's sports coat. And at my feet are two pairs of men's shoes — dress shoes, and sneakers.

So, who the hell is already here? Do I live with a *guy*, in this insane version of reality?

I quietly open the door to the front living area. The space smells like roast chicken and garlic. The room is small but pretty, with a loveseat couch in front of the modern fireplace, and a small dining table next to a pass-through into a kitchen at the back. To my right is a narrow set of stairs leading upwards.

"Hello?" I call out, my voice weirdly high-pitched and wobbly.

"Hey." A man's voice, warm and familiar. "You're late. Where did you get to? I'm sorry, I was so hungry, I had to eat already."

A dark, male head pops round from the side of the kitchen wall, with a friendly, open face, beaming widely at me, teeth bright. A face I know very well, but haven't seen since the end of my final year at Northwestern.

Chris.

My long-ago ex-boyfriend, Chris — someone whose heart I broke — is in a house that I now appear to share with him, in New Buffalo. And he's cleaning up the kitchen and acting like it's the most normal thing in the world.

He looks exactly the same . . . maybe a little older around the eyes. But the same soft, very short, curly hair; the same doleful, puppy-dog, chocolate eyes. The same adoration in them, with just a touch of melancholy.

His smile disappears when he realizes I'm staring at him and saying nothing. "Mill?" he says, taking a step towards me. "What happened? Why are you so late home?"

I shake my head. I have absolutely no idea what to say to him in this moment.

Chris comes forward to meet me, and raises his hand to my forehead. "What did you do?"

I touch my forehead — I'd forgotten about the bruise. It's probably turning darker by now. I look up at Chris. "I got in an accident." My voice is small and weak.

He pulls me towards him in a gentle hug. "Oh, honey. Are you okay?"

I nod into his shoulder, and feel my body breaking down into sobs. Once they start to come, I can't stop them. I'm shuddering against Chris' chest, silently, tearlessly. My knees buckle a little and he gently lowers me to the couch, still holding me. That's when the tears start. A torrent of tears, and an embarrassing amount of mucus, floods out of me. He hands me tissue after tissue, keeping me close, his arm around my shoulder.

I weep for my terror and panic at how utterly wrong this world is. I weep for my lost friends, and my lost home.

And I weep for how carelessly I treated Chris when we were together. I was never in love with him, but he was a sweet guy who deserved way better.

I blow my nose one last time, and look up at him. How on earth did I end up living with him, in this upside-down world? We were in the vocal group at Northwestern together for three years, and we'd dated nearly a year before I ended things with him. Things between us had been kind of awkward, after that, but he'd graduated a year before me so I never saw him again.

Clearly that wasn't the course of events in this version of reality.

Chris is still holding me, kind and patient. He strokes my hair, and pulls back to look at my face. "Can you tell me what happened?" he asks, gently.

I blow out a big breath, and shake my head. "I ran off the road. I was . . . distracted by my phone, I guess, and didn't realize I was swerving to the right. The car's fine, I only ran into a big hedge, but I bumped my head on the wheel."

I scan the living room. On each side of the fireplace is a set of shelving with books, potted plants, and framed photos. Mostly photos of the two of us, it seems, on various vacations. And is that—?

Chris interrupts my thoughts. "My sweet girl. I'm just glad you're okay, and that you didn't total the car." He smiles, pats me on the leg, and rises from the couch. "You hungry? I can make you a plate."

I nod, realizing it's past eight and I still haven't eaten dinner. The world in which I should be sitting on Bonnie's lake-view deck, drinking wine and giving her the last spring roll, seems a million light years away.

Bonnie. What happened to her? Is she waiting for me? But no, she can't be — at least, not at the Lake Bluff house, with that family there. Am I still friends with her in this weird reality?

And how did I end up living here, with Chris, of all people?

Chris brings me a plate of chicken, broccoli, and potato salad, and sits with me as I eat it greedily at the small dining table.

"Where did this accident happen?"

I swallow. "Just near the intersection before I got onto 94." That's true, at least. That highway runs all the way from near Lake Bluff to New Buffalo. He doesn't need to know I was closer to the former when it happened.

Chris nods, absorbing this, a frown line between his brows. "And there was a hedge that stopped you? At your usual intersection? I can't picture a hedge there at all."

Crap. My story obviously has holes in it. "Uh, no. I'd taken a detour, so it wasn't my usual route. That's why I was distracted, I guess — asking Siri for the best way home."

Chris examines my face, seeming to accept this. "Well, that's a nasty bruise — it's getting good and purple. I hope you don't have any whiplash. How about I run you a bath after you finish dinner — soothe any aches and pains?"

I smile at him through another mouthful of chicken. He always was so thoughtful.

"That'd be great." Maybe I can get him to give me some more clues about our life together first. I touch my sore forehead. "I gotta admit, I'm feeling . . . weird. Kind of headachey, and confused. After the accident, I couldn't remember how to get here, and had to get Siri to direct me home. I'm . . . not remembering a lot of stuff."

"Shit, Millie," Chris replies, his nose crinkled in concern. "Maybe you have a worse head injury than it seems. We should get you checked out."

Hospital is the last thing I want right now. I'd end up getting admitted to a psych unit.

"I'm sure I'm fine," I reply, hurriedly. "Just feeling a bit shaken and mixed up." I pause as an idea strikes me. "I know what will make me feel better. Why don't you tell me the story of how we decided to live together, from your perspective?" I take another bite of dinner, trying to act casual.

Chris pulls his mouth down at the corners, clearly skeptical. "Oh-kay," he replies slowly. "From my perspective . . . yeah, I guess that could be slightly different from your memories. Sure." He looks above my head, perhaps at the photos on the shelves behind me. "Well, I guess after our off-and-on

36

relationship at Northwestern, and then with you being in Asia for so long after that—"

What? I've *never* been to Asia.

"—I wanted to give you the security you'd never really had at home, right? So when you got that job at Magnolia, and seemed to be settling back into Chicago, and we got back together, it just made sense that we'd live together. I mean, you didn't really even know anyone else in the city anymore."

I didn't *know* anybody? What about Bonnie, and Ben?

My mind jumps back to the navy-cased cellphone. Their numbers weren't in it. Seems like I'm really not friends with them in this version of reality.

"I guess you needed me, and I still loved you," Chris continues. "I was just so happy, living with you in our first place downtown. And then when we saved for this place, you were so excited to be living on the marina — and you were getting, I guess, the stability that you hadn't had growing up. It's made me so happy to give that to you." He smiles at me as I scrape my plate. "Is that any different than how you remember it?" He rises, holding his hand out for my dish, eyes shining and full of love.

"Uh, no," I lie. "That's about it."

Only my job at the agency, Magnolia, is the same — and that through sheer coincidence, probably. Everything else is different. Everything.

Chris washes my dish in the kitchen as I rise, slowly, from my seat. A bath is a pretty great idea about now. It will calm me, soothe my nerves, help me think. Not that I can think my way out of this impossible situation.

I turn to the wall of shelving behind my chair. Me and Chris in sunny locations, and one of us in New York. And the biggest framed print of all . . . a wedding photo.

Me, in a white dress, elegant and strapless. Chris looking handsome in a black tux, his dark skin contrasting with my ivory paleness. We're in a garden somewhere I don't recognize.

We're *married*?

I check my left hand for a wedding or engagement ring that I might not yet have noticed. Nothing. And I'd have seen them, anyways, while I was driving.

"Hey," I call out to Chris, feigning nonchalance. "Do you remember where I left my rings?"

He emerges from the kitchen, wiping his hands on a towel. "You really have hit your head. We put them back in the box for safekeeping — you said you'd get them resized tomorrow, remember? Now you can stop pretending they aren't too big." He grins at me. "The box is on the dresser. But if you don't feel like going to the jewelry store tomorrow, I can do it."

"Oh," I reply. "Right. Yeah, of course. Thanks. That would be great."

He throws the towel through the kitchen pass-through, and gives me a kiss on my cheek. "I'll run that bath. Lots of bubbles."

"Perfect."

As he goes upstairs, I stare back at myself, smiling uncertainly in my wedding dress, Chris beaming beside me.

How in the world did we get from my version of events, in which I was always half-in and half-out of my relationship with Chris, to a world where we are married? It seems impossible.

I examine it closer. Do my eyes look kind of dead in that photo, like I'm going through the motions, but not really there? Or am I imagining it?

I study the rest of the collection of memories. They're all cheerful images of vacations and festive holidays, but they have this weird look of royalty-free stock photography. "Image search: happy, interracial young married couple." Like everything is posed for effect. But maybe it just feels that way because this isn't my life.

"Hey, honey, your bath is ready!" Chris calls from upstairs. I'm pulled out of my musings and make my way up the narrow staircase. A small landing leads to a main bedroom with a large dormer window and in-built closets, and another open door reveals a small second bedroom with a skylight and an office desk. The third door is a bathroom, also with a sloping roof, and a clawfoot tub full of aromatic bubbles.

Chris squeezes past me on the landing, planting a gentle kiss on my temple, just beside my bruise, before heading back down the stairs. I undress in the bathroom — after locking the door behind me — and slide into the steaming bath.

I'm grateful for the comfort of the warm water and lavender foam, but my mind is reeling.

What is *happening* to me?

Like a weird version of grief, I'm getting hit by waves of overwhelm that crash over me and then recede. In moments, everything feels surprisingly normal, given that I've been catapulted into the wrong version of my life. Maybe like some kind of muscle memory of existing in this world — this body is accustomed to being here, after all, even if my own mind isn't.

But at other moments, like now, I'm suddenly nauseous with fear about being ripped from my world, my home, the people I love and who love me. And the terror that I'll never be able to go back. That there *is* no going back.

I close my eyes, and sink further into the water, my nose just above the bubbles. Maybe everything will be fine. Even if I can't figure out how to get home, maybe I'll be okay here. After all, this seems to be a good life, right? At least it's safe, and warm. Cute home, adoring husband. Like I told Stephen the other night, things could always be so much worse.

But this isn't *my* life, so it's impossible to imagine being fully happy here. I can't even imagine ever truly falling in love with Chris, given my experience of our relationship.

How had our relationship changed so much that I ended up marrying him? He'd mentioned earlier we'd been "off and on" through Northwestern, and that I'd gone traveling for a long time. And that I didn't really have anybody but him.

That I needed him.

Is that why I married him? For some reason, I'm not close to Bonnie or Ben in this weird timeline, so maybe he really was all I had. Maybe I was just forced to settle because I had nobody else in my life. Then again, it's possible that those circumstances changed everything for me, and I grew to really love him, and we're happy together. Or, at least, the Millie who married him is happy.

But I'm not her. And I'm not sure I could ever be happy, living out my days with Chris — no matter how great he is.

The question is, am I stuck here forever, or is there a way home?

MID-NOVEMBER, TEN YEARS AGO

I twisted in my white university-issue bedsheets, which were damp from our perspiration. I unstuck the sheet from my bare thigh, and draped my leg over his, pushing my torso into the side of his body. I rested my head on his broad shoulder and traced a fingernail delicately down the smattering of hair over his chest.

"Picking out the grays, are we?" he muttered into my hair, a smile in his voice.

I lifted my face to his. "Far too many to pick out, unfortunately." I touched my lips to his mouth, briefly. "But fortunately, I like my men older."

"Hey," Rufus said with a laugh, feigning offense. "I'm only thirty-seven. I'm not that old."

"Well, I've just turned twenty, so *technically* you could be my fa—"

Rufus shut me up with a kiss. "*Don't* say it. Or if you do, you'll get a paternal spanking. I can be very strict in my punishments. Just ask the drama group."

I pulled back to grin at him. "I don't think I'd mind that kind of punishment at all."

He laughed, but untangled himself from my embrace to sit up on my tiny twin bed. Thank God I'd gotten a single room again this year. It would've been almost impossible to maintain our secret relationship if I'd been sharing.

Well, not that it was exactly a relationship. Not while he was still living with the beautiful philosophy professor. *Amy*.

But I got it. Rufus and Amy had been together forever, over a decade, and he couldn't leave her — she needed him. Given all her mental health problems.

Plus, considering relationships between students and professors were very much frowned upon, it's not like we wouldn't have had to be secretive anyways.

"I have to go," Rufus said, swinging his bare legs off the bed and pulling his boxers and black pants over his pale skin. "If I stay any longer, everyone will be back from the Black Friday party and I won't be able to escape without being spotted."

What he didn't add, I silently observed, was that Amy would be expecting him home before midnight, knowing he was at a student party. Still, it wasn't even eleven p.m. yet.

He pulled on the black sweater he'd been wearing for the residence party, as one of only a handful of faculty considered cool enough to be invited to the all-black theme party. It wasn't actually Black Friday today — that was two weeks away — but as everyone would be home for Thanksgiving on the day, the party was traditionally held in mid-November instead. Just for the hell of it.

Everyone was still in the downstairs lounge, with not a soul to be seen in my fifth-floor corridor as I stuck my head out of the door, pulling a robe tightly around me. "Coast's clear," I told Rufus as he gathered his winter coat. He gave me a quick, slightly apologetic kiss on the cheek, muttered, "I'll text you," and slipped quickly across the hallway into the stairwell that nobody ever used except in fire drills. Lucky my room was right there, otherwise he'd be taking a huge risk if he had to navigate even a short length of the residence corridor. There would be serious questions asked if he was discovered upstairs. It was dubious enough that he was attending a student party — but at least that could be explained away with a laugh.

I wondered, not for the first time, whether Rufus had wielded any influence on my room placement this fall semester. He was pretty friendly with Ted in housing services, after all. But surely he wouldn't have exposed his motives in that way? Maybe it was just luck.

Still, despite my room's convenient exit route, we'd inevitably been taking massive risks ever since we'd started sleeping together in the spring semester. There were always just so many damn people around.

Our affair had started with a flirtation at a party before my freshman-year winter holidays, when he'd finally noticed me. The Notables had been invited to join the theater department's lavish festive gathering, to entertain students and faculty for an hour or so with holiday songs, in exchange for access to what was widely acknowledged as one of the best parties on campus. It was held on stage after the drama group's closing performance of *It's A Wonderful Life*, and it was truly like having a Christmas party in George Bailey's Bedford Falls home, with the Notables singing carols from the steps of the wide, garlanded staircase.

Rufus, leaning against the fireplace mantel like the master of the house, had grinned up at me as we sang, not once taking his eyes off me. Of course, his partner Amy wasn't there. Amy seemed to never be at these kinds of events, despite Rufus being at the very center of the university's theater galaxy.

After we'd all drank a lot of mulled wine, he'd approached me in the corner between the enormous Christmas tree and the darkness of the wings. We'd been so deep in conversation about music and movies, we hadn't even noticed the party winding down. Eventually, after a few raised eyebrows, I had to accept a friend's offer of a ride home to my dorm. There were only a handful of people left, it was snowing outside, and it would have looked suspicious if I hadn't accepted.

But the spark had been ignited, and I knew it wouldn't take much to start the flame. I'd known the danger, how utterly dumb I was being, but still I'd encouraged it. With the Notables now honorary members of the theater department, our singing group was regularly invited to the larger events. Each time, Rufus and I made eye contact and flirted, subtly but relentlessly, and eventually there was another post-show party at the theater, just before spring break.

This time, after a lot of drinks and even more flirting, I'd stayed behind with Rufus, slipping into the wings with him as the last partygoers gathered themselves and arranged rides to residences. The excuse was that he'd give me a ride home, but we both knew that there was more to it. As Rufus was shutting the theater down, I waited alone on the stage, which this time was barren save for some large, plain blocks that had variously served as beds, tables, and desks in the minimalist play that had just closed.

Rufus had left a single spotlight on me, before he joined me on the stage, silently unbuttoned my dress, wordlessly removed my lace underwear, and fucked me senseless on the hard fiberglass surface.

Ting-ta-ding.

I was brought back to the present with the sound of a text. I closed my dorm-room door, tugged my robe belt into a loop, and flipped my phone open.

Aww. He was missing me already.

But it was from Bonnie.

> *Where RU? You disappeared and it's like Night of the Living Fucking Dead in here with everyone all in black and drunk as hell. You didn't go to bed already?*

> *Sorry, Bon. I'd had too much tequila and wasn't having fun anymore. Looked for you to tell you but couldn't see you. Catch you for breakfast. Try to have fun! Night xoxo*

That part about looking for her before leaving wasn't true, of course. Rufus and I had deliberately, separately, slipped away around ten p.m. to go up to my room.

44

I hated lying to Bonnie. Absolutely hated it. But I was giving her the gift of plausible deniability. At least, that's what I kept telling myself.

It didn't make me feel any better.

* * *

After the Black Friday party, I only had to wait a week before the next social event at which I knew Rufus would be there. I'd washed and blow-dried my dark hair until it shone, spritzed on some light fragrance — I had to smell great, but didn't want to be trying too hard — and donned a deep blue sweater that was a little tighter than usual. Kinda sexy, but not too much for a night of casual drinks after a rehearsal.

The Notables wouldn't normally be invited to random post-rehearsal drinks, given we weren't performing in this year's holiday show, a period murder mystery. But the invitation, unexpectedly, had come from Ben — to both me and Bonnie.

Having taken a year after graduating to write a play, Ben had persuaded his former professor Rufus to allow him to intern as a stage manager for a year, and Rufus had promised to consider Ben's play for production.

Which meant that Ben was now around for *all* the theater group stuff.

Great, right? After all, I adored Ben. I adored the whole Mason family.

But I didn't know how to feel about Ben being around Rufus so much, and attending the parties. I felt like Ben would . . . what? *Smell* me on Rufus?

It turned my stomach to think of Ben, and by extension, Bonnie, finding out about our affair.

Bonnie and I were already on our third margaritas in the bar — our fake IDs doing an effective job of presenting us as a year older than we really were — by the time the cast and crew showed up at 9:30. Ben immediately sat beside us, giving both me and his sister a warm hug and enthusiastically introducing Bonnie, who hadn't hung out with the drama crew before, to all his friends.

That was one of the things that was great about Ben. No pretense of playing it cool, of not adoring his sister. He was so sweet.

Rufus, devastatingly handsome in a turtleneck sweater, his salt-n-pepper hair a little longer and curlier than usual, showed up as one of the last of the group — much to my dismay. All the seats near me and Bonnie were now taken, which meant I'd have a hard time getting any conversation with him tonight. Unless I got up to go to the restroom, then managed to "lose" my current seat to someone else, and sat near him instead . . .

Then I noticed the redhead he'd walked in with wasn't a cast member. It was his partner, Amy, the gorgeous but — according to Rufus — severely depressed philosophy professor.

Amy *never* came to these social things. What was she doing here?

He had his arm around her waist, and was murmuring something in her ear as they entered and looked around the bar for a seat. Amy looked up at him with clear, shining eyes, and he beamed back at her.

Shit.

Rufus resumed scanning the room, and eventually locked eyes with me. His expression visibly dropped. He clearly hadn't been expecting to see me there. He gave me an unreadable expression, just for a moment, then ushered his partner to the other end of the long table. He sat on the same side as me, on the banquette facing the room, so I couldn't even catch his eye again.

A clenched ball of something dark lodged in my stomach. This is what it felt like to have an affair, to be lying to everyone around you, and for your lover to be lying to his partner. It was the first time I'd really felt it.

I stayed quiet the rest of the evening, hating being there, but for some reason not wanting to leave. Maybe because I didn't want to let Rufus off the hook, make it easy for him.

And because I ached for him. For his attention. A secret smile, even just a flirtatious glance. I'd gotten so used to him making me feel like I was the only woman in the room, like he couldn't take his eyes off me, no matter how wrong it might be. Now I felt invisible, a ghost.

I had to communicate with him somehow. But a visit to the restroom, including some prolonged hovering near the doorway and pointed gazes in his direction while I was standing chatting with someone else, yielded no results.

On my return, I sat back down at the table, frustratedly downing my fourth drink way too fast. Ben was mid-flow in a story about a show he'd been in as an undergrad, with several female cast members hanging on his every word. He seemed to be enjoying himself. Bonnie, more observant, gave me a puzzled look, but turned back to her conversation with the lighting guy.

It was no use — I'd have to text Rufus.

I tried to play it cool.

> *Hey handsome. Are you ignoring me? I hope not!!*
> *Meet me by the accessible restroom at exactly 10:30.*
> *I'll go wait there a few minutes earlier. ;) M xox*

No reply.

But then, maybe he couldn't reply, with *her* right there. He'd probably just say nothing and come to the bathroom.

At 10:27, I excused myself again and headed for the restrooms. I fixed my lip gloss in the women's mirror, then stepped back out into the corridor next to the accessible washroom. But 10:30 came and went, according to the clock on the wall, as did 10:35. I'd foolishly left my phone on the table, so I couldn't send another text to see where he was. I waited ten full minutes before I could no longer reasonably stay hanging out suspiciously in the restroom corridor, and returned to the table. By this point, I was almost shaking with frustration and hurt.

I sat heavily, and slurped down the last of my drink. Bonnie and Ben, sitting opposite me, were now the only ones left on our section of the table.

Why were they staring at me like that?

Ben broke the silence.

"You got a couple of texts."

Oh *shit*.

My flip phone was open on the table. Open to the text messages, displayed in big, easy-to-read type for all to see.

"We didn't mean to look," said Bonnie, her expression severe, "but it was doing that annoying beeping and I thought it might be important."

I glanced down at my phone. Two replies had come in since I'd been away from the table.

RUFUS CELL [10:29PM]
So sorry, sexy girl. You know I can't with Amy here. I'll make it up to you, I swear. Let's meet up off campus sometime soon. A whole night in a city hotel, just us. I'll make an excuse to be away. Just can't talk tonight.

RUFUS CELL [10:32PM]
Miss you and your sweet pussy. You know I'm crazy about you, right? xo

Fuuuuccckkk.

I couldn't even look up from my phone at my two most important people, who were silently bearing down the harshest imaginable judgment on me. I shook my head and stared at the cardboard coaster on the table instead.

"Life's Good on Bright Side!" the coaster's logo mocked, its happy, illustrated couple sipping on Bright Side coolers on some tropical beach. I picked at its corner with my fingernail, separating the damp fibers.

"I'm so sorry," I finally said, my voice tiny.

Bonnie sat back in her chair with an audible sigh. "Seriously, Mill? A *professor*? And a married one at that? What the hell are you—"

"He's not *married*," I objected, pathetically. "Just . . . you know. Cohabiting."

"Oh. Well." Bonnie had a mean, sarcastic tone I hadn't heard before. "That's totally fine, then."

"I'm gonna fucking kill him." Ben's voice was uncharacteristically dark. I looked up at him, but he was glaring furiously down the long table at Rufus, who was laughing loudly.

I reached my hand out toward Ben, but he ignored me. "Please. Don't do anything, or say anything. Let's just go, okay? I've had too much to drink anyways. Take me and Bon back to the dorm?"

Ben finally turned to me, an unrecognizable fire in his hazel eyes. His gaze met mine, and the fire smoldered a little. "He's an asshole. And you're a goddamn idiot."

"I know." I shook my head, and a tear dropped unexpectedly from the corner of my eye. I brushed it rapidly away and rose, grabbing my winter coat. "I know. Let's go."

I gave Rufus a backwards glance as we left the bar, and he graced me with a flash of a look in return. A tiny, sheepish, fraction of an apology.

We were silent on the return back to the dorms, with me in the back of Ben's car, no words coming to me that wouldn't make this situation worse. It had never been awkward to be in their company before.

Had I just screwed up my best friendships ever?

In the rearview mirror, Ben scowled as he pulled up outside our residence. I opened the door to the frigid November night and got out without a goodbye, as Bonnie got out of the passenger seat. As I was closing the door, he said one thing.

"Swear you'll end it."

The door slammed before I could even respond. Ben drove off, the exhaust pushing great plumes of steam in the night air, leaving me and my best friend in a deep, heavy silence.

JUNE, THIS YEAR

There's my best friend. Big smile, blonde curls, and lashes for days. But this formal corporate headshot doesn't really look like *my* Bonnie. Too stiff, too buttoned-up. And where did she get that power-suit blazer? It's nothing like the pictures I took of her when we were setting up her website and social media profiles.

I examine Bonnie's LinkedIn entry. Economic Development Officer at Chicago's City Hall. *Really*? It's a world away from her career as I know it, as the owner of A Bonnie Home interiors store and design consultancy. Sure, she'd studied Political Sciences at Northwestern, but she'd never really liked it, and she'd far preferred the Business Studies class we'd taken together. She'd confided in me about her dream to have her own business someday, and I'd encouraged her. When her parents had died, she got a chunk of inheritance and I pushed her to take the plunge.

Has my influence in Bonnie's life been so significant that it altered her career path from what it otherwise would have been?

I tuck my legs underneath me on the living room's little couch, finding a more comfortable position with my laptop. It's weird how relatively relaxed I feel in this marina-side townhouse, given that it's been less than twenty-four hours since I found myself in the wrong universe, married to an ex I haven't seen in years. It's almost like there's some psychological muscle memory that remembers this place — at least the version of me it is truly home for.

It's as though I'm both her, and not her.

Back to the task at hand — figuring out this new life. I've already checked out my own LinkedIn profile, and it's mercifully not too dissimilar to that of my regular life. Instead of my internship at Frank Mason's architectural firm after university, I had a couple of years in South-East Asia, where I apparently worked in "hospitality" at various resorts, before coming back to the city and landing the same job as I have in my real life, at Magnolia Marketing and Advertising.

I guess some things were meant to be.

I've also checked Stephen's profile, and he is also my colleague in this world. But his cell number isn't in this phone, unlike in my life. So it seems we're not as close. Probably because I'm also married, and therefore presumably haven't been crushing on him for years.

There are more people to investigate, too. My mind lingering on the Masons, I type "Ben Mason" into the LinkedIn search bar, and Ben's profile pops up. A cool black-and-white picture of him, unusually clean-shaven, and a list of his theatrical accomplishments. Currently, it seems, he's General Manager of the Lookingglass Theater downtown — a pretty sweet gig. But it doesn't look from his resumé like he's directed a lot of his own plays — he's more on the management side.

Last time I saw Ben, which was a couple of weeks ago, he was celebrating the hugely successful run of his latest play that he'd written and directed — a "whydunit" murder story about a toxic, competitive artists' retreat, which had gotten critical acclaim in all the reviews. But that doesn't seem to exist in this world.

I can understand different influences inadvertently changing the course of people's lives and careers. Maybe me being able to help Ben get his first play staged at Northwestern was what kickstarted his playwriting-directing career in my world. Or maybe it was something else entirely — a totally different course of events.

But what I can't figure out is why I'm not close with Bonnie and Ben in this reality. Did something happen that caused us to stop being friends? Or was I never close with them?

Maybe my email history will tell me. I've got archived emails dating back at least fifteen years, as I'm so horrible at clearing anything out, and I'm guessing that's true here, too. My email address is the same in this world, so I'm able to log in and check to see if Bonnie and I were ever friends.

I find a host of messages between us, dating back from eleven years ago, the summer she and I met — most of them very similar to what I remember. Arranging to stay with her family that first Labor Day weekend. Various emails about starting Northwestern. Dozens, into the hundreds, of messages over the next year or so, all aligning with what I remember. Talking about social stuff, evenings out with Ben, weekends with the whole Mason family.

So, we *were* friends in this world, too. I blow out a slow breath of relief.

But wait. After the Christmas of our sophomore year . . . no more emails. Just one from me in the Sent box, asking her to please call me back and saying that I was very sorry. That's all. No reply. That seems to be our last correspondence.

What in the world *happened* to us?

I pull myself back to the present, and check the clock on the mantel. It's not yet two p.m., and Chris is out all day — first getting my engagement and wedding rings resized, and then to visit his parents and stay for an early dinner. He was so kind to me last night — treating me with care after my accident, picking up on how traumatized I was feeling. Although, of course, he had no idea just how messed up I was feeling. Giving me space as we went to bed in the cutely decorated bedroom, he'd even said I didn't seem like myself. I had almost laughed at that. If only he knew how true it was.

He won't be back until at least eight or nine, so I've got five hours to do some detective work.

More than anything, I want to call Bonnie — to meet her for a coffee, try to figure out what went wrong with our friendship. But I don't know how to contact her, and it's a Saturday, so she won't be at City Hall. We're not even friends on Facebook, and she doesn't have an Instagram profile. I could send her a Facebook friend request, or a DM, but she's hopeless with social media — at least the Bonnie I know is — and I suspect she wouldn't see a message for days. I've no idea if her old email address still works, but I doubt it.

What about Ben? He'd know what happened between us. I don't have his personal number either, but it's much more likely that he'd be at work on a Saturday, as GM of a theater.

I look up the number for the Lookingglass Theater, and call it from my cell. A woman answers, quicker than I was expecting.

"Uh, hi. I'm trying to get a hold of your General Manager, Ben Mason. Is he there?" My voice is high and shaky.

"Sure, let me put you through to his office," the woman replies. "One second."

Crap. What am I going to say to Ben when he answers? "Hi, this is your sister's ex-bestie Millie, except I'm in a parallel universe and I'd like to know why we're not friends anymore?" Why the hell didn't I spend at least a couple of minutes thinking this through?

"Hello?" Ben's voice. Low, gentle, unmistakable.

"Huh-hi," I stammer. "This is . . . this is Millie. I mean, Millie MacKenzie. I . . . uh . . . I guess it's been a while and I wondered—"

"*Millie*? Shit." Ben's tone rises by an octave. "It's been forever. I didn't expect to hear from you again. Wow. How've you been?"

"Uh, yeah, uh, great, I guess." Thank God he can't see the vivid red flush all over my neck. "Yeah, it's been a long time. And look at you, managing a theater. That's awesome."

A pause. "Yeah, yeah, thanks," he replies. "Wow. After all this time. What prompted you to call?"

I have to come up with a story, and fast.

"Well, erm . . . it's like . . . I had this thing happen to me . . ." Crap, this isn't going well. "So, it was, like, an accident. Yeah, I had a car crash, and I hit my head—" inspiration is now striking me — "yeah, I hit my head and I have some longer-term memory loss. And I wanted to call Bonnie, but her number isn't on my phone, and it seems like we're not friends anymore, but I can't remember anything that happened between us to make us fall out. I was hoping you could help."

A sharp intake of breath. "Wow, Millie, I'm sorry. That sucks. I'm glad you weren't hurt worse, though." He pauses again. "I mean, sure — I guess I could fill you in. I'm about to go into a stage crew meeting and then I have some stuff to do. But I can take a break between, say, four and five. I could call you back, if you're free then? Or, I dunno, we could meet for a coffee or something. Where are you?"

I nod, even though he can't see me. "I'm in New Buffalo. It's . . . it's where I've been living. But I can get downtown by four — that'd be great. Meet you outside the theater?"

"Sounds good," he replies. "I'll see you then."

I spend the next half-hour making myself look presentable, changing into a white linen shirt and a cute pair of lemon-yellow shorts I found in the closet upstairs, and some tan sandals that were by the front door. I check the time — 2:32 p.m. — plenty of time to get into the city for four p.m.

But hold up. I'm an hour ahead in New Buffalo. It's only 1:32 p.m. in Chicago.

Jeez. As if it wasn't bad enough dealing with traveling to an alternate universe, I've now got to deal with time zone differences? That's almost worse.

And it means I've got an extra hour to kill. Then again, it's always easy for me to do that — for my gap year, I spent nine months in Europe doing nothing but kill time in cafés, mostly by writing stories. And, now that I appear to be in the

54

presumably unique position of being a multiverse voyager, I should be able to come up with some decent new material.

I check around for a notepad and pen, and it hits me that there is already a notebook in the black purse I found in the Golf yesterday. I grab the purse from the vestibule by the front door, and pull the notebook out.

It's full of scribblings. Jammed with ideas for stories, snippets of poetic sentences, bullet points of a plot about a young woman traveling through Asia. Maybe inspired by this Millie's real life experiences. After all, she's had a different life path from me over the past decade.

Looks like this version of me also enjoys creative writing, and has probably been more diligent than me about pursuing it. Maybe I can kill my extra time in a café in the city, and add some of my own ideas to hers in the notebook today. That'd freak her out, if she ever gets back to her own life.

I chuckle, and pack the notebook back into the purse. Deciding against writing a note for Chris — I should easily be back by 7:30, if I leave the city at five — I grab the keys to the green Golf and head out to the highway.

In the city, searching for a parking spot, I'm ridiculously nervous. I mean, I've seen Ben recently — but *this* Ben hasn't seen me in years, and I don't know how he'll be with me. Plus, the truth is, I've never really hung out with Ben on our own much. We were almost always with Bonnie, our common denominator, and being together just the two of us would have been weird, given that one of us has pretty much always been in a relationship. Not that a man and a woman can't be platonic friends outside of a relationship, of course. It just never really felt like we were separate *buddies*, without Bonnie around.

In fact, the only time I've fully hung out with him on our own was the night he and I went to see that cover band play at Howl at the Moon. Which had been kinda . . . new, for us. And we were having a really great time together. But then I ran out on him, because Stephen had texted that he needed me to troubleshoot some work crisis.

I don't even remember what the emergency was. But I'll never forget the expression on Ben's face when I left him alone in the bar. A look of sheer disappointment. I guess he was disappointed in me for being into a married man, and bailing on our night to help him.

I eventually find an overpriced parking spot just off Michigan Avenue, and head around the corner to a café that I've been to several times before. I take my latte to a window seat and pull out the notebook, reading through this Millie's notes again before starting to add my own jottings and questions about multiverses and alternate lives, tying the thoughts back into my conversation with Stephen on the roof terrace.

How could this . . . *impossible* thing happen? Then again, it's clearly not impossible, since it's happening to me. The multiverse is evidently real — I'm living proof of that. But what *is* it?

Do our lives split off into new realities at every moment of minuscule choice or circumstance? Is every single possible permutation of my life being played out in an infinite number of realities — and the same goes for every person who ever lived?

And if that's the case, how is it that I somehow flipped from one reality to another? That's the thing that seems impossible — much more so, to me, than the existence of alternate realities. What caused me to step into the wrong one?

It happened at Bonnie's house, I know that much. One moment I was texting with her about dim sum in the driveway, the next I'm stepping through the basement door and I find myself in the same house, but belonging to someone else, in the wrong reality.

So, then, is it the basement that is some kind of multiverse travel hub? But no, I was already in the wrong world, the *moment* I stepped into the basement — thinking back, it didn't have the Mason's couch or wall art, and it already smelled of that family's dinner.

Maybe the basement door itself, then? Like a doorway to another world? But why would such an incongruous door be my own personal multiverse portal?

Maybe it's because I'm about to meet him, but Ben springs to mind. I'll always associate him with that basement, as I first met him in that room, more than a decade ago. The weekend I was welcomed into the Mason family.

Perhaps that's it — a life-defining moment is enough to create some kind of soft spot between worlds. And if you go through that soft spot again . . .

I get so absorbed in my notepad scribblings that I don't look at my phone again until 3:52 p.m. Shit — now I'm gonna be several minutes late to meet Ben. By the time I've hurried the six blocks, he's already standing on the steps by the main doors of the old, castellated building the theater is housed in — always an incongruous sight among the gleaming towers of downtown Chicago's Magnificent Mile.

Staring down at his phone, Ben doesn't see me approach and it gives me a moment to assess him. His dark-blond hair is much shorter and neater than the last time I saw him, and he's unusually clean-shaven. Why is that? Surely my compliments in our regular lives about how much his beard suits him haven't made *that* much of a difference? But then again, the difference is probably due to something else entirely. Maybe in this life, he's dating someone who doesn't like a beard.

Of course, he's still objectively very handsome without it — more chiseled, even — but less like the man I know. More like a manager, less of an artist.

"Ben."

He looks up as I come closer and gives me a tentative smile.

"Millie, hey. Good to see you. You're looking well."

We hesitate, then give each other a slightly awkward side-hug.

"Sorry to keep you waiting — I got a bit sidetracked."

"No problem. You wanna grab a coffee to go? It's such a beautiful day — I figured we could walk and talk. I just gotta be back by five."

"Sounds good."

As we turn to step down to the street, Ben runs his left hand through his thick hair. No wedding ring. Interesting. At least that means he didn't end up marrying that god-awful girlfriend he was with for all those years. Although, who knows, maybe they're still living together.

He makes some small talk as we walk — perhaps slightly nervously — about his theater's current production, and asks me about my marketing job as we line up for iced coffees from the Starbucks beneath the John Hancock tower. Thankfully I can answer his questions, as my job is the same as in my world — it seems like it's about the only thing that's consistent. I resist the urge to ask him about his own playwriting, given that his LinkedIn profile suggested he hadn't seen as much success there as I know him for.

When we emerge into the sunshine with our drinks, he leads me further north up Michigan Avenue. I know him well enough to know where he's taking me without having to ask — towards the Oak Street Beach park, and then along the lakefront path. He's been regularly walking, running, and riding this trail ever since I've known him.

How are such insignificant things still the same, yet entire friendships have changed?

"You said you've lost some of your memories, including what happened with my sister, right?" he asks me, eventually, after we've hit the beach and are heading south along the waterfront. The late-afternoon sun is hot, and the beach and path are packed with families and tourists enjoying the long weekend.

I nod through a slurp of my iced coffee, while stepping aside to give space to a passing rollerblader. "Yeah, some things are pretty hazy. I was wondering . . . what can you tell me about why she and I are no longer friends — at least from your perspective? I only have patchy memories from that time."

He pauses for a moment, narrowing his eyes against the dazzling sunlight. "You really hurt her, Millie. Over that whole thing with Rufus, our theater professor. You do remember *him*, right?"

Oh, fuck. I've been hoping not to ever think about that guy again. I behaved so badly back then, and I hadn't even stopped seeing Rufus even after Bonnie and Ben found out. In truth, after that night, I'd slept with Rufus on several more occasions, and it had only stopped because of something totally out of my control.

My neck flushes red. "I remember him, yes." My voice is small, almost lost over the sound of music and chatter from those around us. "But I don't remember falling out with Bonnie about it."

"Right. Well, we found out that you guys were . . . involved, and I made you swear you'd end it. My sister and I both thought you'd done the right thing, and it was over. But that Christmas, Bonnie saw you with him in a bar downtown, when you'd told her you were going to be staying with your mom over the holidays. She was totally crushed that you'd lied to her." Ben takes the last sip of his drink, as if stalling for time to figure out what he'll say next. "Honestly, she was never able to forgive you for it, and the trust was totally gone. I guess, after that, you just drifted apart. Which meant that I also didn't get to see you again." He looks sideways at me. "It was a kinda shitty move on your part, Millie."

My stomach sinks, and the drink in my hand suddenly seems cloying and sickly. I throw the rest in an overflowing garbage can, trying to make sense of this information.

How can that have happened? Sure, I remember that Christmas, very clearly. Things had been a little strained with Bonnie, after she'd found out about my affair with Rufus around Thanksgiving, but we were generally fine. I'd made holiday plans to stay in Indy with Mom, in an attempt to rebuild our relationship somewhat. But Mom had canceled on me last minute, as usual, in favor of some new love interest. Unexpectedly alone for the holidays, I'd met Rufus for a festive drink downtown and we'd stayed a night at the Allegro Hotel.

But why had I been alone those holidays, and not spending it with Bonnie and her family, given that Mom had canceled? Oh, hold up — hadn't the Masons gone to Florida that year?

I turn to Ben, slowing my walk. "It's all a bit . . . muddy. I have a vague memory of your sister and parents being away on vacation those holidays, but maybe I got that wrong."

He nods, his lips in a slight downward turn. It's weird how much more of his mouth I can see without the facial hair. Maybe the beard has been hiding some of his more subtle expressions all this time.

"Yeah, I can't remember exactly what happened either, but I think that was the last year Mom and Dad went to Florida to visit our grandparents for the holidays. Bonnie . . ." he hesitates, clearly trying to pull the memory out. "I think she was supposed to go too, but managed to miss the flight for some reason, and couldn't get another, so she ended up staying here over Christmas. And she figured you were in Indy, so she had no reason to spend the holidays with you. I remember she was out with old friends from high school the night she saw you with Rufus."

Shit. That's not what happened in my world.

It's all coming back to me now. Bonnie *definitely* made it to Florida to see her grandparents — in my timeline, she still has a photo on her bedside table of her with them, standing in front of their Christmas tree. She treasures that picture, as it was the last time she ever saw them.

But in this world, she missed the flight and never made it there.

Seeing me with Rufus must've been devastating for her in that moment, given she thought I was with my mom, and she was supposed to be with family herself. It must've felt like a monumental betrayal.

"I never *lied* to her," I tell Ben, somewhat pathetically. "I *was* supposed to go visit Mom, and do some damage repair to our relationship, but Mom canceled on me last minute. I didn't even know to tell Bonnie that I was in town for the holidays after all, as she was supposed to be in Florida."

He frowns. "Okay. But you *were* with Rufus that night. And you had let her, let us both, believe you weren't seeing him anymore. That was a lie of omission, at best."

I sigh, looking out over the glittering water, where a couple of jet skis are tearing up the gentle swell. "Yeah. That's true." I pause. "I just didn't want her — either of you — to be disappointed in me. I was making some pretty bad choices back then."

Ben nods, and we walk in silence for a few minutes. The sound of the families laughing together tugs at my chest. Ben seems lost in thought. Then he stops abruptly, laying a hand on my arm, pulling me to an awkward halt. "So, then, you do still remember kind of a lot from back then? I thought you'd lost a bunch of memories to a head injury."

Shit.

"I, er, well, just *some* memories. And you've been very helpful in prompting some others to come back to the surface. I'm grateful. Really."

We're standing in the way of other walkers, so we resume our pace, and Ben changes the subject.

"You said you've been living in New Buffalo? What took you out there?"

Oh, God. Now I have to tell him about Chris. My so-called husband, and the house we live in.

"I live there . . . with Chris. You remember him, from the Notables? We got married this past spring, and bought a cute little townhouse on the marina there. His folks are in Grand Rapids, so I guess it made sense for us to settle there, between Chicago and Grand Rapids. I mean, it *did* make sense to live there."

Ben is silent again for a moment, and I glance at his profile. His eyebrows are raised, and he looks at me sideways. "You're married?" He nods downwards, towards my left hand. "No wedding ring, though."

"Oh. No." I flutter my left hand as if to show the rings' absence. "Chris is getting my engagement and wedding ring resized as we speak."

So, Ben has also been checking out *my* left hand for a wedding ring.

"Well . . . then, congratulations," he says, without much enthusiasm. "I remember Chris, yeah. He was a good guy. I'd heard you were dating, back at Northwestern, after the whole Rufus thing. But last I heard, you'd gone off solo traveling in Asia for a couple of years."

We've reached the Ohio Street Beach park, and Ben leads us past the cute beach café and turns us right, back into the city in the direction of the theater.

"Yeah, I guess Chris and I got back together after I came back to Chicago," I tell him as we descend the steps into the gloomy underpass beneath the lakefront highway. "I've lost a bunch of memories from back then, too," I add, hurriedly, "so I don't exactly recall how that happened. But he's filling me in on a lot of stuff."

My voice is echoey in this enclosed space, giving me a weird, slightly out-of-body sensation. Not that this whole reality isn't a total out-of-body experience.

Literally.

"In that case, it's good that you have him," Ben replies. "I just hope he makes you happy."

"He's a great guy," I say, noncommittal. "He does everything he can to make me happy."

That much I'm sure is true. Whether I'm actually happy in this life . . . who the hell knows? But presumably I married Chris for a good reason.

"What about you?" I ask Ben. "Are *you* happy?" We emerge into the sunshine on Ohio Street.

"Oh, yeah, pretty good," he says. His voice is a little flat, though. "Work is fine, and I like my place. I've been seeing someone new — Lexie. She's Irish, and a lot of fun. No complaints about my life, I guess. I still hang out with my sister a lot — she's still single, just dating around. We always spend holidays together, with our parents being gone." He turns his head sharply to me. "Wait — you do remember what happened to our parents, right? It was a weird time, given that you and Bon were no longer friends at that point. I had to tell you via Facebook."

I pull in a deep breath. It's hard to imagine going through that devastation without Bonnie's friendship, and even harder to imagine not being there for her when it happened.

"I remember that, yeah. It was so awful." I hesitate. "Do you think Bonnie would accept an olive branch from me? I'd love to see her again. Make up for some of that lost time."

Ben screws up his face. "Honestly, Millie, I doubt it. I think there's too much water under the bridge at this point. Probably best that we all move on with our lives. You have Chris, and your great job, and your new home, you know?"

I swallow the lump that's forming in my throat. I can't live here, in this world, with only Chris in my life. He's a sweet man, but a man I barely know anymore, and a man I'm definitely not in love with.

What do I do here, if I can't rebuild my friendship with Bonnie and, by extension, Ben?

"Sure, I get it." I turn my face away so he can't see the tears that are starting to cloud my vision. "Probably for the best that I don't reopen old wounds. But if you feel like telling her that you and I met up, feel free to say I was asking after her and that I'm hoping she's happy. If it won't cause any pain to do so."

We walk for a few moments in silence, and then I stop at the intersection of the side street where the Golf is parked. "My car's down here, and you need to get back to the theater." I pull out my phone to check the time, and it's ten to five. "Perfect timing. It's been great seeing you, Ben." I reach up to give him another slightly clumsy hug.

He squeezes for a fraction of a second, then pulls back. "You too, Millie. You take care." With that, he turns and crosses the intersection, his long legs making easy work of the distance. I watch him walking up the street, and he doesn't look back.

I unlock the Golf, and sit in it for a few minutes, deep-breathing away the threatening tears. I honestly don't know how to live in this world without Bonnie and Ben. They're the only people who feel like home to me, and now I can't see them again. That too-familiar sting of loneliness stabs at me — remnants of my troubled teenage years. The pain that only the Mason family were ever able to take away.

Now I have to drive back to New Buffalo, and have Saturday movie night with my "husband" Chris, and then go to the bed we share.

And then what?

MAY, NINE YEARS AGO

The woots and applause slowly died down, and the house lights came on as audience members began to shuffle out into the warm spring evening. I peered out of the wings to see if the coast was clear to join Bonnie, who'd been clapping wildly in the front row.

"Friends of yours out there?" The soft voice of Chris, a tenor in the Notables, came from behind me. I turned to him with a smile.

"My best friend, Bonnie," I replied. "She comes to everything I perform in. Positively a Notables groupie — I think you met her at the last afterparty."

Chris grinned back, rubbing his hand across his black hair. He cast the briefest of glances out to the departing audience before settling his gaze back on me. "Ah yes, your exuberant friend Bonnie. She's fun. Okay — I'll leave you to it. Enjoy the wrap party tonight."

He gave me a screwed-up parting smile with an almost-wink, and turned to head towards the green room. Beyond him, next to the props table, Rufus was watching our exchange with undisguised curiosity. Waiting until Chris had passed, Rufus gave me a pointed double-eyebrow raise.

I knew what that meant.

It meant, "Are we getting together later, or what?"

I gave him a non-committal single-eyebrow quirk in return. He could wait. It wasn't as though he hadn't kept me waiting a thousand times. I was feeling too fabulous to be messed around by Rufus tonight. If anything happened later, it would be on my terms.

I stepped out onto the stage and down the side steps into the auditorium, where Bonnie was doing a poor job of gathering her snack detritus. I gave her a hug, an empty Cheetos packet crinkling between us.

"I could hear you from the wings, munching those, all the way through 'Tonight,'" I said, pulling back and lightly punching her on the shoulder. "Kind of ruined the romance of the moment. Plus you now have orange Cheeto dust all over your dress."

Bonnie laughed. "Sorry, Mill. If you people will schedule these shows over dinner time, what's a girl to do? I was starving." She brushed herself down, somewhat ineffectually.

I shook my head with an affectionate smile. "Well, you could've waited an hour. They'll be bringing out snacks for the party now."

On cue, several stage hands brought out trays of sandwiches, bowls of chips, and various boxes of cheap wine and beer onto a makeshift bar on the side of the stage. The set was still in street mode as the final scene of the theater group's *West Side Story* production, which had been bolstered vocally by the Notables as chorus. All of us women in the cast were dressed in jewel-tone, short, flowy dresses like the Puerto Rican girls in the original movie, and mine was a flared, sunshine-yellow halter neck. The show was easily my favorite production that I've ever been in, and the final scene — where bad luck and circumstance cause Maria to be too late to save her Tony — never failed to wrench my heart.

As Bonnie went to discard her trash, I ascended the steps to the stage to set out plastic wine glasses. Emerging from the dark of the wings, Ben, who'd been stage managing the production as the final duty of his internship, stopped by the beer crates.

"Uh, hi, Millie." He nodded at me, without smiling. "Great show."

Things had been slightly weird between us ever since that awful moment in the bar when he and Bonnie had seen my texts from Rufus. Ben was still around all the time, mostly in his capacity as theater intern, and he was still . . . pleasant to me. Friendly, even. But something had changed.

Bonnie, on the other hand, had been surprisingly forgiving. "Look, I get it," she'd said to me, a few days after that night. "Professor Anderson is a total hottie. But he's very much taken, and he's never leaving her for you, Mill. Don't be a fool for him." She'd hugged me, my tears dampening her shoulder. "But I still love you."

I hadn't heeded her advice, though. Rufus and I had still snuck in a couple of illicit moments, including a ten-minute quickie in my dorm, and one whole night (our first and, so far, only full night together) over Christmas in a downtown hotel. But that was all. The periods in between getting Rufus to myself — those aching, agonizing stretches — were getting longer and longer. And I was getting tired of waiting between snatches of beautiful moments with a man I wanted so badly but would never have to myself. And I was beginning to fully realize how pathetic that made me.

I smiled warmly at Ben, despite the clear reservation in his face. He was looking great — he'd grown out a beard during his year at the campus theater, and it really suited him. He'd moved from unemployed dude-with-guitar to a capable leader; someone people admired.

He'd turned into a man.

"Thanks. It was a really fun production." I straightened up a row of plastic cups, unnecessarily. "How are you feeling, now your internship is done? Got a plan for what's next?"

Ben pulled some beer bottles out of the crate and set them on top of the bar. "Yeah, I'm hoping Rufus will put on my play this fall semester, and hopefully let me direct. It's that family drama in the ski chalet I wrote a while back, the one I showed you. *A Chill in the Air*. Being a winter-themed show, it should work for a December run. Rufus is reading it right now." Ben flinched with evident discomfort at having to mention Rufus. Clearly, this was still an issue for him.

"Oh yeah — I loved reading that one. Probably my favorite of yours so far. It's really clever. And kinda dark." I smiled at him again, hoping to thaw him out. I hated this distance between us. "I'm guessing you won't need the Notables as chorus for that one."

Ben twisted his mouth. "Sorry."

He turned away as the stage began to fill with cast members for the party. Bonnie emerged from the green room, now fully de-Cheetoed, with vivid red lips. She nudged me aside and poured herself a plastic cup of red wine from a box, sniffing at it suspiciously.

"Have you and my brother finally made nice? I saw you two chatting."

I sighed, pouring myself a white wine, which smelled even worse than the red. "Honestly, Bon, I don't know. He's been very weird with me, ever since . . . you know. He's a harsh judge."

Bonnie winced as she sipped some of her drink. "Well, he's a moral, stand-up kinda guy — we all know that. He *really* didn't approve of what you were doing with—" she checked around for eavesdroppers — "Rufus. Do you know he now calls him Dufus behind his back?" Bonnie cackled lightly. "He totally can't stand having to work with him. But the truth is, Rufus is Ben's best shot at getting a real theater career."

I nodded, grabbing a slightly stale sandwich-quarter to mitigate the acerbic taste of my wine. "Ben told me he was trying to get *A Chill in the Air* staged here next semester. That would be incredible."

Bonnie nodded. "Maybe you could ask Dufus to stage it — assuming you're still on good terms, since you're no longer banging him." She nudged me, not unkindly.

My stomach knotted. I hated lying by omission to Bonnie — and to Ben. I *really* had to end this thing with Rufus once and for all. At this point, I was being a total asshole by keeping our ongoing hookups from my closest friends.

I gulped my wine with a grimace, and topped up the cup. "I can ask," I replied. Maybe this really was something I could do for Ben. Even if Ben never found out that I had helped — as long as he was happy.

Plus, it might ease my conscience a little.

Bonnie had abandoned the nasty wine and was switching to a beer. "Anyways, Ben's been seeing some new girl — Amber — so he'll be busy until September. They're doing a big road trip together this summer, down the East Coast, through the Carolinas and Georgia, all the way to Florida and Key West, then back up via Louisiana and Tennessee. Three months. It sounds amazing."

I frowned, glancing over to where Ben was holding court with some cast members, all of them literally looking up to him. I hadn't heard anything about this *Amber* woman, and they were already at the stage of spending the summer together? Then again, Ben wasn't letting me into his life much these days.

I didn't like it.

"That's awesome," I said with a forced smile. "I'm glad he's found someone."

I battled my way through more of the cheap chardonnay during the evening, keeping in my peripheral vision both Rufus — who, in the absence of his partner Amy, was doing his best to attract my attention — and Ben, who seemed to be studiously avoiding me. By the time the cast and crew started drifting away, wishing each other a great summer, my post-show high had been leached from me. Even my yellow dress looked less sunflower and more sickly under the stage lights.

But still I stayed, and drank. Even after Bonnie had left with the cute lighting guy she'd been eyeing for months, and

Ben and his buddies had said goodbye, I stayed behind. Only one thing could obliterate my unnamed disappointment, and that would be ripping off Rufus's clothes, as well as my own. Getting that rush of pleasure from the skin-on-skin moment.

Yes, I'd give him what he was wanting tonight. Pathetic though I knew it was.

On the way back from a long trip to the backstage restroom, where I had tried to fix my make-up so I looked a little more bright-eyed, I stumbled in my red Mary Janes on a cluster of cables in the wings. A familiar pair of male arms caught me before I fell.

"You okay, beautiful?" Rufus murmured into my hair. "Everyone else has gone. I thought you'd left, too — I was about to go home, heartbroken." He pulled back, stroking my bob from my forehead. "I miss you, sweet girl."

I said nothing. Instead, I grabbed his shirt collar and kissed him, hard and long. He laughed low in his chest, and kissed me back, his tongue exploring my mouth. It was full of promise — I knew very well what that tongue was capable of. Our kissing became more feverish, more frantic. Rufus guided me back towards the props table, pausing in his kisses just long enough to sweep the table clear of some props used in the show, and to lift me onto the edge of the table. He pushed my silky yellow skirt up to my waist, and reached up to pull my lace thong down over my butt, down my legs, and over my shoes. "A thong?" he murmured, amused, between kisses, my underwear dangling from his finger. He dropped it theatrically on the floor.

I chuckled, but didn't answer. Rufus wouldn't comprehend the challenges of visible underwear lines beneath silk dresses, especially under stage lights. Let him think it was all for him.

Rufus unzipped the fly of his bulging jeans, which were a little tight for him at the best of times, and tore open a condom packet that he already had to hand. He slid it on and pushed into me as I lay back on the table with a cry of pleasure. With one hand on my braless, silk-covered right breast and the other gripping the table to stop it being pushed away, Rufus pumped with increasing speed and determination, my ankles crossed behind his waist, my Mary Janes bobbing. We both climaxed quickly, calling out at the same moment, this time unafraid of eavesdroppers in the empty theater. We usually had to be so quiet.

Rufus slumped onto the table beside me with a soft laugh, then rolled over so we lay side by side, legs dangling off the edge. It wasn't the most comfortable post-coital moment we'd ever had, but I'd take it.

I moved onto my side, propping myself up on my elbow to look at him, tucking my bare legs behind me.

"Another great performance," I said, giving him a smile that was more enthusiastic than I felt. The post-coital shame was already starting to creep in. Was it worth lying to my friends *and* committing a form of adultery for a brief moment of gratification? A moment that was already over?

Rufus responded with a belly laugh. "In more ways than one," he replied. He reached up to stroke my cheek. "Seriously, though. I'm really going to miss you this summer. I hope there's another production you'll be in next semester."

I remembered my conversation with Bonnie earlier, and saw my chance. "I don't know . . . maybe. But I also hope you'll consider staging Ben's new drama. I read it last year and I think it's brilliant. Maybe it's time to do a smaller, more serious play? It can't all be musicals and big-cast productions."

Rufus nodded, thoughtfully. "You're probably right. And yeah, it's a great play — the kid has a lot of talent. If you think it's a good idea . . . yeah, okay. I'll tell him yes."

I leaned down to thank him with a kiss to the cheek.

"What the fuck . . . ?"

A woman's voice, broken and strange, from a few feet behind me. Rufus froze, eyes wide. We both turned our heads towards the interruption. Standing in the wings, a bouquet of tropical flowers in her arms, mouth agape, staring at my bare butt, was Rufus's partner Amy.

"Oh, shit." Rufus bolted upright, slid off the table, and quickly turned away to zip up his fly. Cringing with utter mortification, I dropped off the props table and smoothed down my skirt.

I couldn't look at Amy. The poor, poor woman. What a way to find out your partner is cheating. A flood of guilt washed over me, hot and prickly.

Rufus, tucking in his shirt with one hand, was reaching the other towards Amy. "My love. I'm so sorry. So, *so* sorry. I don't know what I was thinking." I raised my eyebrows at this — he was making it sound like this was the only time. "We got caught up in a moment — but I know it was so wrong. It's *you* I love, honey. Only you."

Amy was still rooted to the spot, although the bouquet — no doubt a congratulations on the closing night of the show — was slowly slipping from her grasp. She didn't seem to notice as it tumbled to the floor, the orange bird-of-paradise blooms getting crushed beneath its weight.

Rufus was still rambling. "I swear, my love, she's just a cast member, and I had way too much to drink. There's nothing between us, I promise." He turned to me. "Tell her, Millie. Tell her. That we aren't anything."

I'd never felt more ashamed.

"I'm going to go," I said in a very small voice. "I'm so very sorry." This was directed towards Amy, although I still couldn't look at her. I slipped out of the side door, stumbling on the same cluster of cables as I had on my way in.

I deserved to fall flat on my face and break my nose. I deserved much worse, even.

What in the *hell* had I been thinking?

One thing was for sure, though. It was definitely over with Rufus.

JUNE, THIS YEAR

I'm crawling through Sunday traffic on the edge of the city, my nerves on edge, grateful at least for the air-conditioning in the Golf. It's even warmer today than it was yesterday, and I had gotten a little sunburned on my waterfront walk with Ben. I'd normally turn on some music on a road journey like this — it's nearly a two-hour drive from New Buffalo to Lake Bluff — but my mind is racing, and I need to focus on my thoughts. I'm not even sure exactly what I'm doing.

But I'm convinced of one thing.

That the answers lie at the Masons' old house in Lake Bluff. That it has something to do with the basement, or the door, being a parallel-universe portal.

Of course, I'm aware that the house is currently occupied by a non-English-speaking family who definitely don't want me showing up again, after I intruded on their dinner on Friday evening. But I have to go back and see if I can figure any of this insanity out. Maybe I can get through to the family who live there, and ask some questions. If I can get them to understand me.

Fortunately, Chris is out for the day, golfing with his work buddies. He was all apologies this morning for not spending more of the long weekend with me, promising me that we'd do a hike and a picnic tomorrow, the Juneteenth holiday Monday.

Bless his heart. He's so well-intentioned. Unfortunately, the thought of a hike and picnic with Chris is deeply unsettling. I have literally no idea what to say to this man. I have no shared memories of our relationship, or — more importantly — our love for each other. And I presume the me of this life does love him, otherwise I wouldn't have married him, right? I have to hope that, with all the changed life circumstances I encountered, my relationship with Chris grew and blossomed in a way it never got the chance to, in my world.

After all, wasn't it Ben himself who had persuaded me to end things with Chris, back at Northwestern? And without Ben's influence in my life, given the falling-out with Bonnie, Chris and I had obviously gone on seeing each other.

Maybe the me in this life really is happy.

I wish I could give her life back to her, and go home.

That's the other reason I'm going back to Lake Bluff today. To see if that house really is the key to going home, and getting my own life back. Sure, my life wasn't perfect, given that I'm chronically single and infatuated with a married colleague. But it has Bonnie and Ben in it, and that makes it way better than this version, as far as I'm concerned.

As Chris slept peacefully beside me last night, I was staring at my phone, doing more research. If the house in Lake Bluff is any part of this puzzle, I need to figure out what happened. In this world, Bonnie doesn't live there — presumably because she has a job at Chicago City Hall, instead of her Lake Forest interiors business. With Ben already living in the city, they must've decided to sell the house after they inherited it from their parents. Sure enough, a website offering Illinois property sales history revealed that the Lake Bluff house was sold just under a year later — and hasn't been sold since, meaning Bonnie and Ben sold it to that family I walked in on.

Which raises another significant question. I know what *I* was doing there on Friday night — I was there to see Bonnie, and spend the long weekend with her. But the other version of myself, the one who is really married to Chris, must've driven there, too. Because when I came out of the house and found myself in another universe, her green Golf was parked nearby, and I had the keys in my pocket.

So here's the question. What was Married-to-Chris Me doing in Lake Bluff, if she hadn't been friends with Bonnie in years, and Bonnie didn't even live there anyways? It makes no sense. She should've driven home after work to Chris in New Buffalo, from the Magnolia offices in downtown Chicago. Lake Bluff is in the opposite direction.

What *was* it that compelled me — her — to drive instead to the Lake Bluff house, that warm Friday night?

Was it some kind of call across universes? An undeniable, intrinsic knowledge that our life paths were about to intersect?

And, if that's the case, maybe I can make them intersect again, at the same place. Because right now, all I can think about is finding a way home.

The traffic is starting to clear now, and I'm soon heading northward with speed towards Lake Bluff. I take a right exit to drive via Lake Forest, the community where Bonnie — usually — has her store. In the town center, I slow down to double-check whether it's there in the row of commercial storefronts. Nothing — still just the bagel place.

Okay, then. Time to visit a family who don't speak English and will probably call the cops on me.

I pull up in the same parking spot where I found the Golf less than forty-eight hours ago, leaving my purse and phone on the passenger seat, and tuck my keys in my jeans pocket. Just like last time. With my heart pounding in my throat, I walk up the street to the heavy metal gate that protects the house I know so well.

Shit. The entry code has always been Bonnie's mom's birthday, but the other family have lived here for years, so they must've changed it. I'll have to buzz in . . . but they'll never let me in. Maybe I can pretend I have a delivery? But then they'll know I'm a liar, right away. They have every reason not to trust me.

I don't really know what I'm doing here — I don't have a plan. I tried to come up with one in the two-hour drive up here, and all I came up with was that I'll have to wing it, based on what I see at the time.

The metal gate is curved at the top — high in the middle, but low at the sides. If I stand on this rock, maybe I can see into the drive, and figure out if the family is home. Sweating in my white jeans — which are too heavy for the day but I'm wearing them because I'm trying to recreate Friday's conditions — I clamber up onto one of the large, flat-topped rocks that flank the gateposts. On my tiptoes, I can peer into the gravel driveway.

No cars. Both the black Audi and the red Tesla that were here before are gone. Maybe they're all out on this sunny Sunday.

I throw a glance over my shoulder in each direction, up and down the street. There's nobody around in this leafy, suburban neighborhood — everyone's elsewhere, having fun in the sun.

Now's my chance.

Emboldened by the lack of cars in the driveway, I step down and give the old entry code a test attempt, in case for some reason they never got around to changing it, or figured Valentine's Day was a cute code to keep. But no . . . it doesn't work. Dammit.

Time to go old-school, I guess. Checking again for any onlookers and finding none, I step back up onto the flat rock. The huge middle hinge of the gate is about at knee level, and if I can get a foot-grip on it, that would probably give me enough purchase to swing my other leg over the top. The drop on the other side . . . well, it's not that far down. And I can lower myself slowly. One advantage of being petite — I can hold my own body weight pretty easily.

The execution of my leg swing and drop to the drive isn't as elegant as I'd imagined, but there's nobody around to see it, and I manage to make it down onto the gravel without spraining anything.

Now what? The front door will be locked, presumably, and I definitely don't want to try it. Then again, aren't I recreating Friday night's events to try to get home? In which case, it makes more sense to go in via the basement side door.

I step down the sloping lawn on the left of the house, hoping that the family haven't done a better job than the Masons at fixing this door, which always had a warped frame that stopped it from locking. If they've replaced the door frame and the lock, and the whole house is secure, I've got nothing. I'll have to . . . do what? Drive back to New Buffalo, and live with Chris forever?

I shudder. No. He's adorable in many ways, but . . . no. That's not the life for me.

Determinedly, I give the basement side door a huge yank outwards. To my surprise, it opens easily with a slight rush of air, making me nearly fall backwards.

I'm in. And no alarms are going off, so that's a bonus. Now, though, I'm just an insane person who has broken into a very nice family's home while they're out.

I close the door behind me, blowing out a shaky stream of air. What the fuck am I doing? I've honestly lost my mind. How is any of this going to help my impossible situation?

Get a grip. Maybe the act of going upstairs and letting myself back out the front door will be what takes me home? I mean, probably not. But I'm here now, so it's worth a try.

I step into the basement, past a couch that looks a lot like the one Ben was sitting on, playing the guitar, the very first time I came through that door. My memory is so vivid that strains of music are almost audible in the quiet of the basement.

No, not *almost*. They *are* audible. That's definitely music.

Which means I'm definitely losing my mind. Nobody's home — how could there be music playing?

Unless — *shit* — both the parents are out in their cars, but some of the kids could still be at home, perhaps? Weren't they all too small to leave alone? Maybe there's a babysitter.

I move towards the bottom of the stairs, where the light is leading the way up to the kitchen. I can hear the music louder now. It's definitely not my imagination.

And voices. There are voices there, too, in the kitchen. Not even the sound of kids, more like adult voices. Dammit, the family is home. Just because their cars weren't in the driveway . . . of course that doesn't necessarily mean nobody is home. What was I *thinking*?

I'm rooted to my position at the bottom of the steps, every hair on my body on end, skin prickling. What to do now? Go out the way I came in, and make a break for it, out of the gate? At least I can release the gate from this side. I could be gone before they even realized I was ever here.

A woman's voice, louder now. "Hey, quit that! I'm cutting you a slice." A warm voice. Almost familiar.

And in English, with a local accent.

Now a man's voice, low and gruff. "You want me to bring out the heavy cream?"

"Sure," the woman says.

This is *not* the same family. Or maybe that family is also here, but they have some English-speaking guests? Maybe that's good. Maybe I can still risk trying to get out the front door, and then try to explain myself if I get caught. At least I'll be understood.

Trembling, I make my way silently up the stairs and open the door to the kitchen, just a crack.

That's . . . weird. The walls are no longer the darker taupe of the kitchen as I last saw it, and instead are a rich cream again — just like Bonnie painted them when she renovated the kitchen after buying Ben out of the house. The cabinets are also white again, although a different style than Bonnie's Shaker cabinets. And . . . it's too tidy to be Bonnie's kitchen. The old-fashioned FM radio on the counter is playing some kind of Spanish guitar music.

Plus, if I was back in my reality, the house would be empty, as Bonnie was delayed at the store.

No, I'm not back home in my own world. I know it, right in my core.

I'm in a *new* world — one that's different again.

Which means, I guess, that I'm about to intrude on yet another unwitting family, who happen to have similar décor tastes to Bonnie. Maybe I can just sneak out past them, now that they've left the kitchen — they seem to have gone out on the deck.

I open the door wider, and take a tentative step into the kitchen. I'm gonna have to be quick if I don't want to get caught slipping out of the front door. Although, maybe recreating that action is pointless, anyways, since I'm evidently already in a third universe. Which means, it's not looking like what I'm doing will take me home to mine.

A loud male laugh booms above me. Yes, they're definitely all out on the deck, and there are a couple more voices coming from there, too. That gives me plenty of space to creep past the dining area and beeline it out of the front.

I take a few more steps, trying not to breathe, my runners squeaking ever so slightly on the hardwood floor. As I pass the dining area and its window view to the deck, I can't resist taking a look at the new family who have moved into Bonnie's home. They sound like they're having such a great time.

Two adults with graying hair, a man and a woman, have their backs to the window, facing the lake view.

And at the end of the table, standing to reach a pitcher from its center, is Bonnie.

As real as anything, looking fabulous in a red playsuit and wide-brimmed hat.

I let out an involuntary yelp.

I've made it home, after all!

This really is Bonnie's house, she's merely changed her kitchen cabinets, and she's tidied up because she had some older guests visiting.

But who *are* those people? And how did Bonnie get home so quickly?

At my strangled noise, Bonnie looks up, into the house. Can she see me, through the reflection of the lake on the window? She moves her head to each side, as if to try to make me out.

Suddenly, she sees me. She squeals in excitement and puts the pitcher down with a clatter on the glass table. "Ohmygodohmygodohmygod!" she shrieks, raising both hands. She beckons me to come outside, and my feet follow her instructions. I slowly make my way out to the deck, terrified that all this is a mirage, and I'm about to fall through a hole in the universe yet again.

The sun on the deck is blinding, and the heat intense after the cool interior of the house. Bonnie is hugging me, and I'm hugging her back. "I had no idea you were going to make it, after all! Why didn't you *text* to say you were coming?" She swats me lightly on the arm. "Never mind, you're here now. Have a seat, let's get you a plate."

What? None of that makes any sense.

Bewildered, I turn to see who her older guests are.

Angela Mason, Bonnie's late mother, risen from the grave, gets up out of her chair to greet me.

"We didn't think we'd see you today, honey. What a nice surprise." She gives me a hug.

Frank Mason is beaming at me from his seat beside her.

Bonnie and Ben's dead parents.

Here, on Bonnie's deck.

I try to respond, but no words come out. Instead, I turn to look out at the lake to somehow reorient myself, before looking back to see whether I was imagining them. But the lake is at a weird, tilty angle, like all the water should fall off the edge of the world.

That's when I manage to say something.

"I think I'm going to fall down."

Frank springs to his feet, and manages to guide me as I slump into the patio dining chair at the foot of the table. The deck swims nauseatingly beneath me, and I grip the edge of the table to stop myself falling right off the seat.

"I think she's dehydrated," I hear someone say — Bonnie, or her mom.

"Pour her some of that ice tea."

"Here, put your sunhat on her, she needs shade."

"We need to get her inside where it's cool."

"Lord, she's white as a sheet."

"She's always white, Mom. It's her Irish skin. No wonder she gets terrible sunstroke."

"Not usually *that* white, though, sweetie. She's almost gray."

"She probably needs to eat something. There's nothing to her — all skin and bones." Frank this time.

"Mill, are you okay?" Bonnie has her hand on my shoulder. It's a little darker now, shadier. Oh, I have Bonnie's brimmed hat on. "Can you drink some of this ice tea for me? I think you have sunstroke."

She raises a glass to my lips, and I sip some of the sweet tea and swallow it down. The deck is tilting less now, no longer like a ship in a storm. More like the gentle swell of a paddleboard on the lake. I take a few deep breaths, and look up. Frank and Angela are still there, in person, and definitely not dead.

I open my mouth to speak again, but all that comes out is a sob from right down in my soul, followed by a flood of tears.

"You poor thing!" Angela says, kindly. "You're in a bit of a state, huh? Come now, slowly, let's get you inside."

I let Angela and Bonnie raise me out of my seat unceremoniously by the armpits and guide me into the cool living room. Frank brings my tall glass of tea and a plate with a huge slice of apple pie and a generous pouring of cream, which he places on the coffee table.

"Have you been out in the sun again without a hat?" Bonnie asks me disapprovingly, once my sniveling has subsided and I've sipped some more of the tea. "Seriously, Mill, how many times do I have to tell you? Sunstroke, no joke — remember?"

I do remember. We'd driven in Bonnie's convertible car to this house the very first time I came here, the Labor Day before starting at Northwestern, and I hadn't worn a hat the whole drive. I had terrible nausea and a headache for the next two days. Since then, I've tried to be good — but I hate wearing hats. They always drown me, and they squish my already flat, straight hair.

This time, however, it's not the sunstroke that has me floored. It's the resurrected parents. Two people I loved as much as if they were my own family.

How are they alive?

Unfortunately, I can't exactly ask them that. "Why aren't you dead?" doesn't seem like an appropriate question right now.

Instead, I smile weakly and eat some apple pie. Pretending to get my strength back up is a good excuse not to talk.

Angela sits down gently beside me on the couch. "Honey, sunstroke aside, it's a treat to see you." She pats my knee. "How did your plans change so that you could make it here? Bonnie said you had long weekend plans with that handsome husband of yours, and couldn't make it."

The fork freezes on its way to my lips.

Chris?

I'm back in a world where this is Bonnie's house again, or maybe it's her parents' house, and yet I'm still married to Chris? How did *that* happen?

My mind races. Shit. Maybe that means I still have to go back home to New Buffalo after all. But at least I'm friends with Bonnie again. And the Masons are alive. So . . . that's better than yesterday. But still not great.

"Uh . . . no. Turns out he had his weekly Sunday golf thing with work buddies, so he was busy after all. I figured I'd come up here, since it's such a lovely day. Surprise," I add, weakly.

Frank gives Angela a weird glance. "But, Millie, it's Friday. Do you mean he has a Friday golf thing?"

Friday? No.

It was Sunday afternoon when I left the house today.

I look outside at the long shadows on the deck. The sun is way too low for three in the afternoon, which was the time when I got here.

It's Friday evening, all over again.

"Uh, yeah. Sorry. My brain is addled with this sunstroke. Friday. I meant Friday."

Ten minutes into having the Masons back, and I'm already lying to them.

Frank raises his eyebrows. "I didn't have him down as a golfer. Doesn't he have any Friday afternoon classes? Oh, I guess not in summer, when school is out."

What in the world is Frank talking about? What classes, what school?

I'd looked up Chris' profession during my LinkedIn research, too, and it said he's in pharmaceutical sales — which makes total sense. Nothing about taking any adult education classes, although maybe he chose not to put that on his profile.

Bonnie laughs. "Yeah, Mill, I'm with Dad on that one. Rufus really never struck me as the golfing type."

Rufus?

She said *Rufus*, not Chris.

They think I'm married to Rufus. Oh my God.

I'm now in a world where I married *Rufus*, and the Masons are alive, and Bonnie and I are still friends.

Maybe we're still friends *because* I ended up marrying Rufus — because he and I somehow got together legitimately, rather than continuing our illicit affair.

I look down at my left hand, which is gripping my plate of pie. On my ring finger are a glitzy, slightly ostentatious engagement ring — a large stone surrounded by tiny ones — and a wedding band in a white metal of some kind.

The room is swimming again, so I try not to think about it, and focus on finishing my apple pie while Angela and Frank go outside to clear the table. Bonnie's expression has softened, and she's looking more approving. "I'm happy to see you eating that, Mill. I swear, you're getting so thin."

She's right. My wrists are tinier than I've ever seen them as an adult.

"I've lost weight," I say, dumbly, looking up at her.

"No kidding. Not that you really had much to lose in the first place." Bonnie holds her hand out to take my plate, but doesn't stand with it. She pauses, her eyebrows pinching with that look she gets when she wants to say something serious. She studies my empty plate for a moment, then lifts her eyes to me. "Mill . . . I know you don't like talking about your marriage, but . . . I guess it feels like you've been stressed for a long time now, and I don't think it's just about work. So, when you're ready to open up to me, I'm here." She gives me a pointed gaze, eyebrows raised, and gets up to go into the kitchen.

Stressed?

Yeah, just a little. I don't even understand what universe I'm in.

Apparently one where I'm married to Rufus, the impossibly handsome professor I had an affair with when I was twenty. Which, at the time, in my youthful stupidity, had seemed thrilling and intoxicating — at least to start with. Now, it just seems super sleazy that a professor would sleep with his adoring student while cheating on his partner. Not to mention a really terrible and dumb thing for me to do.

I rise on unsteady legs, and follow Bonnie into the kitchen. Rufus aside, I've got to figure out how her parents are alive and well, and currently laughing on her deck. Or, I should say, *their* deck, since this is evidently still their house. I need to find out what happened the night they died — or didn't die, apparently.

I lean against the counter, watching my best friend stack the dishwasher.

"Hey," I say, attempting nonchalance. "I was thinking on the drive up here about that night at the Va-Va-Voom Diner — do you remember? When we had the fight with Ben about Amber."

Bonnie pauses, still bent down over the plates, her blonde curls obscuring her expression. "Sure," she says, slowly. "I mean, vaguely. Like, we both told him that she wasn't right for him, and he got all shitty with us about it, something like that?"

And then he stormed out and left us, so your folks had to drive on icy streets to the diner to pick us up, and that was when it happened.

"Yeah," I reply. "He got pretty mad about it. Didn't he walk out in a pissy mood and abandon us there?"

"Uh, no, I don't think so." She straightens up and looks at me, eyebrows quizzical. "I mean, I think he might've done, but then came back inside, because I would've been staying at his place that night? I don't really remember — it was years ago. Why do you ask?"

I turn away, pretending to busy myself with putting the bread back into the metal bin, hiding my reaction to this news. This tiny but universe-altering adjustment in our timelines.

He came back. In this life, he came back. We never needed to call the Masons to pick us up. They lived.

I breathe through my racing pulse. "Oh, I dunno," I lie. "I was just thinking about him and Amber, and trying to remember that night — our come-to-Jesus talk with him about their relationship. We were such meddlers."

Bonnie laughs, and resumes cleaning up. "Yeah. Not that it made much difference, given they've been married . . . what? Four years now? And they seem . . . okay. Maybe not deliriously happy, and she and I will never be close, but whatever. She's fine, I guess."

He married her?

Ben ended up actually *marrying* Amber?

Oh, fuck.

Still, I married Rufus, apparently, so I'm not one to judge.

This is all wrong. My knees wobble again, and I pull myself onto a stool at the end of the counter, watching my best friend wipe up crumbs around the toaster.

A rush of need to be honest with Bonnie washes over me. I *have* to tell her. I have to tell Bonnie what's happening to me — I can't go through this alone. And we swore we'd always tell each other everything, no matter what, once we'd made up after the whole Rufus thing at Northwestern. I can't go back on that now.

"Bon?"

"Mmm-hmm?"

I blow out a big breath. "This is going to sound totally nuts, but . . . I'm in the wrong life, Bon. I don't know how it happened, and I know it's impossible, but I walked through your basement door, and then found myself in a life where I was married to Chris, my old boyfriend from the Notables, and you and I weren't friends anymore. Then I did it again and found myself here, in a life where I'm married to Rufus, and you and I are still friends, and your parents are still alive."

She stops wiping the counter at this, but doesn't look up. Her perfectly smooth brow furrows.

I press on. "In my real life, I'm single, and your parents *died* in a car crash that night we were at the diner. *That's* why I nearly fainted outside, Bon. I haven't seen your parents in six years. I've been to their funeral, with you and Ben. We buried them. And I haven't seen Rufus since we ended our affair at Northwestern."

Bonnie turns to me, her face scrunched inscrutably, a blue sponge still in her hand.

"Mill . . . what are you even *talking* about?" She shakes her curls. "The sun really has gotten to your head. You're talking cray-cray."

"I know it sounds totally impossible. It *is* impossible . . . but it's also true. This is not my real life. I'm not really married to Rufus. Not in the . . . reality where I'm from."

She puts the sponge down and comes closer, examining my face. She can always tell if I'm lying to her — or to myself. She places a damp hand over mine on the quartz countertop.

"Mill. I don't . . . Look. I've been worried about you, for a while now. You always refuse to talk about it but, girl . . . I *know* things with Rufus aren't good. And I don't know where all this weirdness is coming from today, but it's clear you're struggling with life right now, and with what's really happening. You could even be, like, *disassociating.*" She squeezes my hand, her gaze flitting between my eyes. "We all love you, and we want you to be okay. I think . . . maybe it's time we got you some help. Right? Will you let us help you?"

Help?

I don't even know what "help" looks like, when you're an apparently delusional person who believes they're from another reality. But it could very likely involve a mental health facility, and I'm not about to do that. Not willingly.

Although, maybe I should. Maybe this *is* all a delusion. I mean, that would definitely make more sense than the reality — or realities — that I seem to be living. Maybe I do need professional treatment.

Still, I won't go down that road without a fight.

I shake my head. "I'm sorry, Bon. I just . . . I don't know what's gotten into me. This sunstroke has me all over the map. I'm tired and confused, is all. I need to get myself home."

I slide off the stool and give Bonnie a shaky hug before she can say another word. Her body tenses for a second, as if bracing herself to argue, then relaxes beneath my tentative squeeze. She's clearly thought better of it — at least for now. I know the last thing she wants is to have to give me some kind of mental health intervention, and now I've given her a temporary reprieve from that duty.

"If you're sure," she mutters into my ear.

I pull back, giving her a weak smile, and she turns away, struggling to meet my eyes. We may still be friends in this life, but there's clearly a rift between us that I can do nothing about. And it seems to have a lot to do with my marriage.

I check my pockets and pull out new, different house keys, and a Honda car fob. In my back pocket is an Android phone in a floral-print case.

A new house, a new life, a new timeline. Some good things in it, like the Masons being alive and Bonnie being my friend, again — and several that are not so good.

One, Bonnie doesn't believe me. And why would she? What I'm telling her seems impossible. Unhinged, even. No, I'm on my own here. Nobody would *ever* believe this story.

Two, I have a new husband to go home to. Again.

And there's no clear way of getting back to my real home. My real life. I'm not sure I'll ever get back there again.

My stomach churns and lurches, and a flood of thick saliva washes the back of my throat. I lean over the side of the counter, and throw up apple pie, cream, and ice tea into the Masons' trash can.

DECEMBER, NINE YEARS AGO

"Congratulations, Ben. It was a total triumph."

"Thanks, Millie." Ben scratched at his beard with a smile that — finally — reached his eyes. He looked a little tired, after what I'd heard was a series of long, late-night rehearsals with the small cast, but he also seemed really happy. I wanted to hug him, but maybe we weren't there yet.

Bonnie did the hugging for me, congratulating her brother on the successful opening night of *A Chill in the Air*, his very first written-and-directed play. Amber, who'd been sitting with us for the performance, waited impatiently for her turn, then flung her arms around Ben's neck and gave him a longer-than-necessary kiss.

I looked away. It always felt weird to see Ben kiss someone. Then again, Bonnie probably didn't like it much either.

Chris ambled over with some drinks, handing one to me and planting a kiss of his own on my temple. I responded with a small smile. Chris was such a good boyfriend. So reliable.

We'd been dating casually since the start of the junior-year fall semester, when the Notables got back to rehearsals for their own Christmas concert, and he'd asked me out to a movie. He was such a refreshing change from my disastrous affair with Rufus. Always there for me, always available, always wanting to do things. Go to dinner, see a downtown exhibit, go for a weekend lakeshore hike, or just spend the day having sex and eating pizza.

So goddam enthusiastic about it all.

I felt a slight wobble in my stomach as Chris and Ben chatted about the play. Bonnie, who'd been working admirably over the past few months to embrace her brother's girlfriend, was listening to Amber talk about her cosmetology course.

I scanned the room where the show's afterparty was being held — this time, a somewhat soulless function room near the campus theater. Rufus had been told by the dean to stop hosting drama group parties inside the theater itself, following the *West Side Story* wrap event earlier that year. Rumor had it that the caretakers had arrived in the morning, and complained to the university administration about sticky wine and beer spilled all over the stage, and even someone's lace underwear left in the wings. The complaint had gotten back to the theater group, and was met with a lot of laughter and wild speculation about whose underwear it might've been. Most of the cast eventually decided it was probably Bonnie's, as she'd been seen getting very close to the lighting manager that evening. Bonnie, graciously, neither confirmed nor denied the accusation.

My cheeks burned with shame every time I thought about it.

As if to compound the humiliation of that memory, I spotted Rufus and Amy, joined at the hip, on the other side of the function room. They were chatting to some university faculty, and Amy was laughing with abandon.

The two of them had clearly worked through Rufus being a liar and a cheat, then.

Rufus had always told me that Amy was severely depressed and isolated, but every time I'd seen her, she'd looked perfectly happy. Aside from *that* night, of course. With the benefit of distance from my affair with Rufus, it seemed increasingly likely that Rufus had simply lied to me in order to gain my sympathy — to make him seem somehow less of a cheat, since he was supposedly unhappy at home. And it had worked. I had, in the early days at least, presumed Rufus would break up with Amy, validating our affair and turning it into a real relationship. That had made it feel less shameful to sleep with him.

In more than a year of sneaking around and lying to others, it had never occurred to me that Rufus might also be lying to *me*. Now it seemed so obvious.

But that was all in the past, and now I had Chris. I was pretty confident Chris would never lie to me.

I turned and gave my boyfriend a winning smile. *Was* he my boyfriend? We hadn't used such terms yet.

Distracted from his conversation with Ben, Chris raised his eyebrows at me. "Yes, ma'am?"

"Oh, nothing. Just glad you're here."

Chris beamed at me. "Me too." He kissed me on the forehead, and something caught his eye behind me. "Oh, there's Andy. I gotta see if he and Bella are still up for the ski trip. Give me ten minutes."

Left alone with Ben, as Bonnie and Amber were still subcutaneous-deep in skincare discussions, I was suddenly awkward again. Ben, bless him, broke the silence.

"How's the latest short story coming along? Weren't you expanding on some of the stuff you wrote on your Europe trip?"

I smiled at him, tentatively. Trust Ben to ask about that. He was the only person in my life who was truly interested in my fairly poor attempts at creative writing — Bonnie and Chris included. Bonnie, for as much as she loved me, didn't really keep track of my hobbies. And Chris, although he was very sweet, wasn't much of a creative guy, and simply let me do my own thing when it came to writing.

"Thanks. There's one that's coming along okay, I guess. About a girl who keeps missing her buses in various European cities, which is driving her crazy, but it turns out that it was meant to be, as it leads her to a guy she likes. Eventually."

Ben chuckled lightly. "Sounds fun. Your character sounds a bit more like my ditzy sister than you, though. Presumably it's not autobiographical?"

I laughed. "No, my own trip to Europe was much less eventful. And the protagonist *is* partially based on Bonnie, I think. I'd definitely say my character is more her than me. But the guy she falls for isn't based on anyone real."

"Not Chris, then?" Ben nodded towards where Chris was talking to some guys. "He seems like a good dude."

I followed his gaze. "He is." I nodded, turning back to Ben. "He's really . . . uh, into me, I guess. Which is super sweet."

Ben raised a brow. "And are you really *into* him? Kinda has to be a two-way street, Mill."

Rude.

"Erm, yes, of course I am. Like I said, he's great."

Ben lifted a hand in defense. "Okay. If you say so." He paused, taking a sip of his beer and scanning the room. "Well, I've said this before, but thank you again. I suspect you were — how can I put this delicately? — *instrumental* in helping my play get produced."

My cheeks flushed for the second time in the past few minutes. "You're very welcome. And rest assured, that phase of my life is one hundred percent behind me."

Ben nodded. "Thank goodness for that. That whole thing was a total shitshow, Mill. And if I'm being honest, Rufus may have been good to me from a career perspective, but he is an asshole of the highest order. You deserve so much better than that — I could hardly stand the thought of you allowing yourself to be treated like that." He visibly shuddered.

"Thanks." I gave him a light arm-punch. "Protective big brother."

I regretted the phrase as soon as it came out of my mouth. Something about the word "brother" felt squishy and wrong.

Ben frowned, and muttered, "That's not exac—" He was cut off as Amber, Bonnie, and, from the other side, Chris, returned to our group all at once.

Chris pulled me close to his side, and tucked a strand of hair behind my ear. "Having fun?" he murmured to me.

Breaking eye contact with Ben, I turned to Chris and gave him a light kiss. "Always, when you're around," I replied.

I chose to ignore the squirmy, unsettled feeling in my gut.

JUNE, THIS YEAR

I'm aware of being awake even before I open my eyes, as the
light beyond my pale-red eyelids is so bright. I squint, opening them slowly, not yet quite sure where I am.

Or, for that matter, which multiverse I'm in.

Industrial ductwork — complete with hard-to-reach
cobwebs — high over my head. Exposed brick walls, punctu-
ated by a row of tall arched windows with distressed, peeling
paint on their frames. But in a trendy way.

Of course — Rufus's downtown loft. Well . . . *our* loft,
theoretically, given that I'm apparently his wife.

I'm lying alone in an enormous, super-king-size bed
with soft brown linen sheets. This place is a super-hip bach-
elor pad that bears very little trace of my — or Bonnie's —
decorative influence. It's as if the me who married Rufus just
moved in and got absorbed into his life.

I had found my way to my new home late last night,
after recovering from my "sunstroke" at finding Bonnie and
her previously dead parents at the Lake Bluff house. After
my failed confession to Bonnie, I'd had to get out of there.

Finding the apartment had initially been a challenge,
given that I couldn't figure out the Android phone or whether
I had "home" set in the Maps app, but I'd remembered

94

Rufus's downtown building from years ago, and found through an email search that my "home address" was the same converted warehouse unit.

Letting myself in at nearly midnight, I'd expected to find Rufus here and wondering why I was late home, just like Chris had done in New Buffalo. But the loft had been empty, with no sign of Rufus.

Just a hand-scrawled note on the concrete kitchen island, saying "*Back in the morning — R.*"

I'd taken the opportunity to poke around, examining the stylish furnishings, the vast black-and-white photographic prints of theatrical productions, and several expensive-looking tabletop sculptures. Nothing that reflects my own tastes, which lean more cute-rustic. It doesn't even look like I live here, aside from my clothes in the closet, some of which I recognize, and my name on some of the mail near the door.

But at least Rufus is someone I already know, so I can anticipate what to expect when — if — he comes home.

And, let's face it, he was always insanely hot.

I have to admit, there's a part of me that's feeling some anticipation at seeing him again. Sure, he was a deeply flawed man back at Northwestern, given he was sleeping with his much-younger student while living with someone else. But in this version of reality, he and I are *married*. The rules are very different now.

If I'm honest with myself, that's why I decided to go "home" to Rufus, instead of taking the Masons up on their offer of their guest room for the night. I just had to see what this version of life is like.

And although it's insane to be in this alternate life, it's not as weird as I initially thought. I mean, I *know* Rufus. I've adored him before. I've *wanted* this life with him.

This version of reality at least feels reasonably safe — not entirely alien.

But what would it be like if I had found myself in a world where I live with someone I *don't* recognize? Would I still have to go home with them, in the absence of any reasonable option? Would some kind of intrinsic muscle memory kick in, and make it easier to be with them, like it did with Chris?

I sit up in bed and swing my legs off the side. The concrete floors are cool beneath my bare feet. I pull on a floral silk robe that isn't my usual style, and pad into the open-concept kitchen-living room, searching for coffee.

As I'm examining the contents of the built-in fridge, a key turns in the front door and it creaks open. I quickly shut the fridge door and pull my robe closed.

Rufus, his hair now considerably more salt than pepper, and sporting an overnight stubble that's also partially gray, is riffling through the mail on the hallway console. I haven't seen him since I graduated eight years ago, and he's now in his mid-forties. He's older, looking tired, but pretty much as handsome as ever. My stomach performs the same flutter it always did when I was twenty.

"Hi," he says, not looking up.

"Uh, hi," I reply. "I'm just making a coffee."

"Mm-hmm. I ground some of the new beans before I went out yesterday — in the jar." He finally looks up at me, but doesn't smile.

I turn away, not wanting my face to betray me as an imposter, as if it might. Hopefully my instinct will take me to the right cabinets to find a mug, and it won't look like I've never been in this kitchen before. Although, what I'm trying to achieve by pretending to be Rufus's real wife, I'm not entirely sure.

A glimpse into the would-have-been, I guess.

I open the cabinet above the coffee machine. Right first time. "Where'd you get to last night?" I ask him, more out of a need to fill the silence than genuine curiosity. I pull out a mug and try to look natural making my coffee.

His voice is low. "Really, Mill? You're asking me that *now*?" A pause. "I thought we had an understanding."

Shit. I've messed up already.

I turn to face him, eyebrows raised. His brow is furrowed, dark. I hold up a hand. "Just making conversation. Sorry if I overstepped."

His expression softens. "That's okay. I accept the apology. You know how I appreciate it when you apologize." He puts his mail and black cellphone on the island countertop, and holds out a hand. "Come here."

I hesitate. What does he want? I'm right in front of him, talking to him.

"Come here," he repeats, quieter, still holding out his hand. His slate-gray eyes tunnel into mine, and a flood of memories wash over me. The greatest sex of my life. My tiny single dorm-room bed, wrapped in white sheets and each other. Rufus screwing me, that very first time, on the fiberglass set on stage at Northwestern's theater, late at night. Him going down on me — the first time anyone had done that — in a downtown hotel room, that one time we spent the whole night together. How I had screamed out with an orgasm like nothing I'd ever experienced before.

With a pull between my legs, I move around the kitchen island to meet him, and he grabs me by my waist, his arm inside my silk robe. This close, his breath is slightly bitter, and he smells of sex.

He always smelled of sex.

His stormy eyes roam my face, and then he yanks me in for a rough, hard kiss. Despite myself, the tug between my legs pulls harder, and the moisture makes itself known. Dammit, I still can't resist the dark lure of this man.

But I'm here now. We're married. And this *was* what twenty-year-old me had most wanted.

I kiss him back, and a chuckle rumbles through his chest. He knows he has me exactly where he wants me. No matter where he was last night.

He slips a long finger into my sleep shorts, and it meets wetness. He moves his kisses down to my neck as his fingers explore me and I writhe against the countertop. With his other hand, he lifts up my T-shirt and puts his mouth against my small breast, circling his tongue.

Jesus.

He laughs again as I gasp aloud, and stops to suddenly pull down my shorts and panties. He kneels on the cold concrete floor, lifting one of my feet onto the bar of a stool, exposing me fully. Then he buries his face between my legs and lets his tongue do the work, one hand still reaching up to my nipple.

As I reach orgasm, crying out, he immediately rises to lift me onto the counter, unzips his fly, and pushes himself into me. He only thrusts maybe a dozen times until he, too, comes with a violence I haven't seen before, his face strained and contorted.

Rufus collapses against me in a move that's both familiar and foreign, shaking his head.

"See what you still do to me?" he mutters.

I know this man well enough to know he's not really looking for an answer. He often used to say that to me, back at Northwestern. "See what you do to me?"

Like it was *me* being so seductive that he couldn't possibly have resisted.

There was a time that I would have found that rhetorical question romantic — a compliment. To be that desired. Now, only now, does it occur to me that it was his way of shifting blame.

Regret for having just had sex with him washes over me, as quickly as the desire had washed over me less than ten minutes ago.

Not for the first time following sex with Rufus, I'm left wondering what the hell I was thinking.

Rufus straightens up, running a hand through wavy hair that's looking a little greasy, his brow set hard once more. I slip off the countertop, lifting my panties and shorts back on and pulling my robe closed.

He pulls his pants up from below his butt but doesn't zip them, and moves away. "I need a shower. Then I'm heading out again — to check on the new set build, since you're apparently so curious about my whereabouts, all of a sudden.

And I'll be gone all night, so don't wait up." His tone is as icy as when he arrived.

Guess he only softens his manner when his dick hardens.

I watch him tread into the bedroom, and listen to the sound of the shower being turned on.

How in the world did I end up being married to this guy, where he chose me over Professor Amy? Maybe this is simply the version of reality where she dumped him for being a cheating asshole, like she should have in my world.

Even if Amy dumped him and he and I ended up in a legitimate relationship, how could I have ignored every red flag to get to the point of marrying him? Bonnie and Ben surely would've advised me against it.

But I also know the answer to that. It's entirely possible that I would have remained blinded by my infatuation for him, and Bonnie and Ben would have known that I would only dig in if they tried to interfere. At least they didn't fall out with me about it, and we stayed friends in this reality.

It seems like the me in this life may *still* be blinded by him — her judgment as poor as mine ever was.

What was that he'd said earlier — that they had some kind of agreement about her not asking where he'd been? Is she just turning a blind eye to . . . whatever he was doing?

Am I — is she — a downtrodden, possibly even emotionally abused wife, trapped in a don't-ask-don't-tell marriage with a serial womanizer? Probably a sex addict?

Something else he'd said earlier is niggling at me, too.

"You know how I appreciate it when you apologize."

Yep, if I'm honest, I remember that about him. Nothing is ever his fault — and he genuinely believes that to be true. Zero self-awareness.

Classic traits of a narcissistic personality disorder.

Why did I never see it before? Rufus is a raging narcissist.

Jesus Christ, *why* did I just let him screw me?

Beside me, on the countertop, his black cellphone pings. I glance at it, then up at the bedroom door. The shower is still running.

I pick up his phone, and a text preview is clearly visible across the top, from someone called Chantel.

Thanks for last night, sexy. Miss you already. See you next weekend when you're back in town. Xoxo

I mean. It was already obvious, but now it's confirmed that the guy is screwing around on his wife. And I just had unprotected sex with someone who slept with someone else mere hours ago, which isn't even safe. Married or not.

This trip down what-might-have-been lane is rapidly becoming an I'm-really-glad-it-wasn't revelation.

I need to get out of here. Even if that means jumping into yet another universe. I can't stay where I'm clearly being cheated on and belittled by my husband.

But what about the Millie who really *is* married to Rufus? I don't know how this multiverse stuff works, but I have to presume that if I step out of this reality, she'll resume her life. And I really don't want *any* version of me to put up with this bullshit. *She* may still be blinded — we all know how hard it is for chronically mistreated women to leave relationships — but *I'm* perfectly able to see this situation for what it is.

Maybe I can try to save her before I leave.

I tap on the text, and it pops open on Rufus's phone, without even a password to protect it. Arrogant shit.

The running water of the shower stops. I don't have much time.

I type a reply into the text field.

Hi Chantel. I don't know if you know that Rufus is married, but this is his wife, Millie. I found your text on his phone. I'm leaving him, so he's all yours, but you should know he's an asshole who WILL cheat on you. And I know he's spending the night with someone tonight, and from your text it's clearly not you. So he's cheating on us both. I wish you luck.

I hit send, then immediately second-guess myself. What if Rufus is also physically abusive, and hurts me — or the other me — for sending that text?

I have to get out of here right now. And I have to find a way to get a message to the other me, in this life, after I'm out of it.

Notes — that's the best way. I always use the Notes app on my phone to jot down ideas and thoughts — maybe she does, too. I can maybe get a message to her that way.

Rufus walks into the kitchen, now dressed in a black T-shirt and blue jeans, running a hand through his wet hair. He looks every inch the cool theater professor.

Shame the man is such a dick.

"You getting dressed today, or what?" he asks, a slight sneer curling his lip. He doesn't wait for me to answer. "I gotta run — I'm meeting the set designer at noon, and she hates it when I'm late."

Female set designer, huh? That tracks.

He grabs his cellphone and keys from the island, walks to the door, and slips on some sneakers. Not even the pretense of a marital kiss goodbye. "See you tomorrow." He lets the front door slam behind him.

Okay. Now I have some space. But hold up — if "Chantel" replies to my text on his phone, he could be back here any second, in a rage. I've got to get out of here, and quick. And I need to make sure the other version of me doesn't ever come back.

Despite desperately needing a shower, I hurry to throw on yesterday's clothes and stuff a bunch of others into a weekend bag, along with a large wash bag of toiletries and cosmetics, the passport from the dresser, and the phone charger by the bed. She'll need this stuff to be in the Honda, if she's going to be able to run.

I'm working under the assumption that she'll find herself outside the Masons' basement door once I've slipped into the next world — if the multiverse shift works again, of course. Hopefully she'll be able to take refuge with the Masons at the Lake Bluff house.

As long as she knows she must.

I grab my own keys and the floral cellphone, pick up a jacket from the hallway closet, despite the warmth of the day — who knows how long she'll be without her stuff? — and slip out of the apartment. I'd parked the Honda a couple of blocks away, so if Rufus is still in the basement parking garage, having discovered my betrayal and stewing in fury, he won't catch me leaving.

I break into a run out of the building and down the street, into the refuge of the Honda. I throw the bag into the back seat and set off, this time knowing exactly where I'm going.

Back to Lake Bluff.

Back to the basement door, and hopefully home. Or maybe, like last time, it'll be yet another version of my life — where who-knows-what will be happening? Hopefully not worse than a sex-addicted, narcissistic husband who I've just spectacularly pissed off.

Driving the familiar highway north out of the city, my racing mind wanders back to that night with Stephen, on our office roof deck.

Infinite universes . . . infinite possible lives . . .

There are literally any number of universes, and versions of my own life, that I could wander into. And yes, the one I'm escaping is not great, given the toxic relationship I'm in. But in reality, it could be even worse. A lot worse. Like I said to Stephen that night, I'm not a crack addict on the streets.

There will be versions of reality where I *am* a crack addict on the streets. And ones where I'm suffering from a horrible disease, or a debilitating condition. One where I'm horribly beaten and abused, worse than anything Rufus would do.

An infinite number of lives so bad that I can't even imagine them.

Every step through that basement door is a monumental risk.

But surely, for every horrible life that's out there, there must be good lives too, right? Better than being with Rufus.

Maybe I can quickly escape the bad ones, knowing that I *have* an escape hatch, and find my way to a good one. And maybe, just maybe, help some of the versions of me who are in a bad spot, bringing my fresh perspective to their lives, before moving on to find a better version.

Because there's one thing that is increasingly gnawing at me, filling my body with a chilling sense of dread.

That I might not be going home to my own world any time soon. If ever.

After all, going back through the door last time didn't take me home, it just took me to another new life. So, given the infinite possibilities, what makes me think I'll ever get back to my own, or even find one that's similar enough not to know the difference? The chances are infinitesimally tiny.

Even if I did find my home reality, how would I know that it was really the one I left? There could be an infinite number of worlds almost identical to mine in every aspect other than a single grain of sand or a blade of grass being in a slightly different place. There could be literally no way to tell if a world is really the one I came from.

Unless I somehow intrinsically *know* when I'm home. But it could take forever for that to happen — if at all.

"*Home isn't a place, it's a feeling.*"

Isn't that what the Masons' poster said?

My chest heaving with a sudden sob, I turn off the highway and onto the Lake Forest road where I crashed into the hedge a few days and one universe ago.

I may never get my real life back. The one where I have a cute little rental studio downtown, and the best friendship in Bonnie, and where Ben isn't disappointed in my choices, and where things aren't perfect, but life is safe and easy.

I pull over onto the verge at the first opportunity, and let the tears come, resting my head on the steering wheel.

If I can't find my home, then what? Keep going through the door until I find one that's good enough?

And why that basement door? Why has it suddenly become my portal to alternate versions of my life? I mean, yes, it's the door I used to enter the Lake Bluff home for the first time, that Labor Day weekend before we started Northwestern. My life definitely changed that day, when the Masons embraced me into their family. I met Ben for the first time when I went through that door. Maybe that's significant.

But another thought is starting to tug at me — something from my conversation with Stephen the night of our office party. Something I'd considered while we were tipsily pondering alternate realities.

Somewhere, we're together.

I lift my head off the wheel.

That's it.

Maybe I shouldn't even be looking to get back to my *home* life. Maybe this is my chance to find a *better* version of my life — the one I've wanted, the one where *I met Stephen first*. Where I said yes to astrophysics club, and joined a different singing group. Where Stephen fell in love with *me*, not Eve. And I never got to know Rufus. Where Stephen and I are together, and happy, right now.

Of course, I've no idea how many versions of reality I might have to go through to find such a life. It could take hundreds. Thousands. Millions. Infinite.

And each time I've gone through the basement door, it resets to Friday evening of the long June weekend.

I may never age.

I may be stuck in an eternal cycle of multiverses, trying to find the one where Stephen and I are happy.

I laugh aloud, despite myself, slightly manically.

I mean, Stephen is a great guy, but after trying about a hundred lives — many of which could easily be much crappier than what I'm used to, and some perhaps even scary — surely I'd give up on him and just stick with something halfway decent to live out my days? I can't keep trying forever, right?

I pull back out onto the road and join the traffic heading towards Lake Bluff. It's weird, but I almost feel better now that I have the beginnings of an insane, ridiculous plan.

Try to find my life with Stephen, while maybe helping out other versions of me along the way. With the caveat that I won't do it forever, and may choose to give up when I find a livable life.

And try not to lose my mind in the process.

Within twenty minutes, I'm parked a few hundred yards down from the Masons' house. I'll have to sneak in without them seeing that I'm back, less than twenty-four hours after I left them. But at least I know the gate code in this world.

One more really important thing to do before I switch lives again. Get a message to the Millie who's married to Rufus to not go back home, and to leave him forever. Who knows if she will listen to me, or believe any of this? But I can surely make her believe that Rufus is furious, as it won't be long before he finds out about the text I sent to Chantel, and he'll be calling and texting to find out where his wife is.

As if to help me out, the phone tinkles in its floral case. A text from Rufus, as I predicted.

Not an expression of rage. Tight, controlled. Almost scarier.

> *Where are you? I need to talk to you. I came back home but you weren't there. Call me asap.*

I blow out a big breath, and hit reply.

> *Hey, I'm out for the afternoon. Didn't think you were coming home today. What's up?*

The reply is almost instantaneous.

> *Where are you? We need to talk about something urgent.*

I need to send him as far away from Lake Bluff as possible. If he gets wind of me coming to the Masons' house, he might arrive here right when a bewildered version of me is left outside the basement door, and take her home to God-knows-what punishment. I need to make up a story to throw him off my scent.

> *Sure! I went out today to visit a friend from work in New Buffalo. She needs me right now — boyfriend trouble. Back in time for dinner if you want to talk.*

Hopefully he hasn't put a tracker on my car and knows I'm lying — presumably not, or he'd already be following me here. He's probably accustomed to a docile, compliant wife, not the rebellious one he got today.

Just one quick reply.

> *Please make sure you are home by then. I'll be waiting.*

Hopefully he'll be waiting a long time for his wife to come home. Hopefully forever.

I open the Notes app on the phone, and find countless notes stored within. Shopping lists, to-do lists, recipes, ideas. Way more than even I use it for. She probably uses this much more than handwritten lists, as the phone can only be opened by passcode or facial recognition. It's probably the only safe place she can record things privately.

There's a directory titled "Mine" with a series of documents inside it.

Lists of dates, with notes next to them such as "out all night" and then sometimes a woman's name next to that. Often with a question mark next to the name.

A list of women's names, with Chantel as the second-last entry, and Nichole — whoever she is — after that. Maybe the set designer?

This world's version of me has been *tracking Rufus's infidelities.*

This gives me some encouragement. Maybe she was already mustering the courage to leave, and was collecting the evidence she would need for a divorce on the grounds of adultery.

I can only hope that's true, and that what I'll tell her today will finally sway her.

I open a new note, and title it "!!READ ME!!" so that it appears at the top of her list of documents.

Dear Millie,

This is the most impossible thing I've ever written, given that it's to me from . . . me. I am also Millie. I am you, only another version of you, who has unwittingly traveled into your version of life, and lived it for less than twenty-four hours.

Yes, the multiverse is a real thing, and there are infinite possible versions of ourselves. But I have no time to go into that now. Just please believe me, and believe this is real. For example, only I could know about the time I was ten years old and stole the money out of the fountain in Briars Park, and then felt so terrible that I later put it all back plus my savings, then Dad was furious I'd spent all my piggy bank money. I never told anyone that. Yes, it's really me. Really you.

I can't possibly explain how all this works. I just need to tell you that there are better lives than the one you are living now. I know that YOU know your husband is a liar, a cheat, and a narcissistic asshole. I don't know how badly he has treated you, but I know it's not good. I don't know why you're still with him, but I do understand his allure, and how he can make you feel like the most amazing person in the world while also being totally worthless and nothing without him. I get that, truly.

But you are strong, and you can leave him. And now you must — he's really mad at me, and therefore you, as I told one of his mistresses that he was married. He's furiously waiting for me — you — to go home, and I don't know what he'll do. You can NEVER GO BACK.

I've packed an overnight bag for you, in the back seat of the Honda, which is parked a little way down the street (in case you read this before you find the car).

Knock on the Masons' front door — Bonnie should be there, too, she's staying there this weekend — and tell them you've left Rufus. They will give you safe harbor. Then, for God's sake, divorce that asshole. You've got a great cache of dates of his infidelities, so I have to believe you were already planning to leave.

I won't be back. Go live your life, and make it a better one. I wish you all the joy in the universe.

Millie

I close the phone and stuff it in my pocket. In case she finds the car before she goes to her notes, which is more than likely, I grab an opened envelope and pen from my purse, and scrawl a handwritten note *"CHECK YOUR PHONE NOTES ASAP — URGENT!!"* and leave it on the dash where she can't avoid seeing it. That way she won't miss my letter and drive home to an ambush.

Now I've done all I can for her, and it's time to fix me. Or, at least, go onto the next version of me — whatever that is.

I lock up the Honda, put the keys in my other pocket, and walk up to the Masons' gate. I step up onto the flat rock by the pillar to see if I can gauge who's home. Bonnie's car is there, as it was when I left last night, along with the Masons' cars and another gray one I don't recognize. Probably another guest — maybe Ben. It looks like something Ben might drive.

The flutter of laughter on the breeze drifts towards me. Sounds like there's a small party on the deck — which makes sense, given it's such a hot day.

If I'm gonna be stuck in a three-day time loop, cycling through multiverses, thank goodness it's nice weather. Unless there's a universe where I've managed to affect the weather through some kind of butterfly effect, but I doubt it.

I'm almost chuckling to myself as I key in 0214 into the gate, and wince as it opens with a metallic clang. Hopefully nobody heard. I also need to be careful not to crunch loudly on this gravel drive.

I step across quietly and slowly, jumping the last bit onto the side lawn. As I descend the slope, the voices on the deck are much clearer. Angela and Frank, laughing. Bonnie, excitedly exclaiming about something, her voice high. A low voice, then — Ben's.

I stop at the door, listening to him. There's a laughter in his voice, too — I can't quite make out what he's saying, but I can tell it's his storytelling voice. He's on a roll with some kind of tale, and Bonnie is chiming in.

It takes all I have not to abandon my multiverse-seeking strategy, and simply go join them on the deck. I could stay in this world, and leave Rufus myself, divorce him myself. Live this life, where things aren't so bad, and the Masons are alive, and Bonnie and Ben are my friends.

I let the low rumble of Ben's voice wash over me. I always feel safe when Ben's around.

It would be so easy, it's so tempting, to just go up via the deck steps.

Then another voice. Female, higher-pitched, a little more nasal.

Amber.

Shit. I forgot that Ben's married to Amber in this version of reality.

Suddenly, the prospect of joining the Masons on the deck is a lot less appealing.

Back to the plan. Anyways, I can't lose my chance to find that perfect life I've been looking for, right? The one I've wished for, for so many years. A life with Stephen.

I tug hard on the basement door, and it comes towards me with its multiverse-portal-opening whoosh.

I step inside.

OCTOBER, EIGHT YEARS AGO

I kicked through a pile of red leaves littering the path through the quad. My hand in Chris's felt a little clammy on this warm fall day. Weren't we past the hand-holding stage, at this point? We'd been dating for a year. Surely there was no need to be so physically . . . *clingy*, anymore?

"We still good for dinner when my folks visit this weekend?" Chris asked, his tone uncharacteristically tentative. "They can hardly believe we've been dating all this time and they still haven't met you. They're beginning to think I'm making you up."

My defensive hackles rose. "And I'm sorry about that, you know I am. But they're all the way in Nevada, so it's not like there's much opportunity to see them."

Chris sighed. He seemed a little pissed, which was unlike him. "You had plenty of time in the summer after I got back from Canada. I was with them in Nevada for *six weeks*. I thought you might be interested in visiting, maybe seeing Vegas for the first time. But for some reason, I couldn't tear you away from Chicago."

He stopped walking and turned to me. "Millie, I'm honestly wondering—" He paused, his attention caught by someone walking towards us. Chris lifted his hand in greeting. I followed his glance to where Ben, all six foot three of him, was strolling through the quad with a guitar case. My mood lifted considerably, and I let go of Chris's hand.

"Ben! What are you doing here? I thought you and Amber were moving into your new place this weekend."

Ben stopped, giving each of us a quick side-hug. "We are. I just swung by to pick up the guitar that one of the theater group sold me." He grinned at me. "I can't believe you and Bonnie are in your senior year now. Soon I won't be able to keep hanging out here, like some kind of loser who can't let go of school."

I chuckled. "Like Rob Lowe in *St Elmo's Fire*." We'd watched it together, once, with Bonnie, in an eighties movie marathon night.

Ben laughed, his hazel eyes twinkling. "Exactly. I'll have to get a real job."

"Anything happening with that?" Chris asked. "A new play in the works?"

Ben turned to him with a friendly smile. "Yeah, I'm writing one now — a play with music, hence the need for a new guitar. Not a musical, though — more like a play that has songs. Kinda like *Once*? But Amber and I are renting an apartment in the city as of this weekend, so I've taken a stage manager job at a small theater to pay the bills. Hopefully I can get them to put on one of my plays." He shrugged his broad shoulders. "When I've paid my dues, of course."

"That sounds awesome, man. Good luck with that." Chris's gaze was caught by a group of his friends standing in the arched doorway to his dorms. "Hold up, I gotta catch someone to get their Chem notes." He turned to give me a perfunctory kiss on the temple, out of sheer habit. "Back in a minute."

Ben set his guitar case on the ground. He looked intently at me, slightly narrowing his eyes, seeming to search for the right words. "You and Chris are still seeing each other, huh? I was wondering if you would be, given the long summer break."

I frowned. "No reason why not. He's a great guy. We didn't break up over summer — it was just that he was away in Canada with friends, then spent the rest of the time in Nevada with his folks."

Ben nodded, and pressed his lips together. "I dunno, Mill. I just . . . get the feeling that maybe you're not as into the relationship as he is. Bonnie told me you said no when he asked you to join him on vacation, and that you also didn't go to Nevada to meet his family. It doesn't seem like you're really making any plans with him. And like you said, he's a great guy. It would be a shame if it turned out to be . . . one-sided."

Christ.

How did Ben manage to cut into my emotions like that, every time? He could always pick up on what was really happening, often even better than Bonnie could. Sometimes even better than I could myself.

I jabbed my toe at a large maple leaf that was stuck to the paving, aware that I probably looked like a sulky teenager. "Whatever, Ben," I replied, childishly. "I just didn't feel like going on a road trip with him and his friends, is all. And Nevada in summer? With my complexion? I mean." I forced an unconvincing laugh.

The truth was, I hadn't wanted to go away with Chris and his best friends Andy and Bella, *or* visit his family, as doing so would cement the two of us as a real, established couple. And something about that thought always made my stomach knot up.

I'd preferred instead to spend the summer with Bonnie at the Lake Bluff house. And with Ben, even when Amber — who was, let's face it, kind of annoying — was around.

Ben screwed up his face — his telltale sign of irritation. "Okay, Mill. Whatever you say. I just like the guy, I think he's cool, and I wouldn't want you to hurt him." He looked away, and waved at someone. "Gotta go say hi to a friend. See you later." He didn't glance at me again.

As Ben sauntered off, I blew out a long breath.

Ben was right — of course he was. I had known, deep down, that I was lying to myself about my feelings for Chris. But he was such a devoted boyfriend, I hadn't wanted to admit it to myself.

Still, none of this was fair on Chris. After a year of dating, I simply hadn't fallen in love with the guy.

I'd have to end it.

Dammit. Another relationship over.

JUNE, THIS YEAR

I'm in the basement, in the dim light creeping in from the doors below the deck. But . . . it's weird.

Electronic green spots flash before me, dazzling my left eye.

I turn my head away from them, but they follow me.

I shake my head, but they mimic my every move.

I blink, trying to refocus.

The lights crystallize, form into type. Words, floating in front of me, slightly to the left, but not so far that I can't read them.

FRIDAY JUNE 16, 6:03PM
1274 CELESTINE DRIVE, LAKE BLUFF, IL
60044
[MORE INFO]
[GO TO MAPS]
[GO TO EMAIL]
[GO TO CONTEXTS]

What the fuck is *that?*

I blink again, several times rapidly, and the words change.

FRIDAY JUNE 16, 6:03PM
CONTEXTS — MOST RECENT:
EVAN CONTACT [TODAY 3:15PM]:
HONEY, PLEASE CONTEXT ME, WORRIED
ABOUT YOU. YOU LEFT IN SUCH A
WEIRD MOOD EARLIER, AND NOW YOUR
CONTACT SAYS YOU FLEW TO O'HARE
AND YOU'RE IN ILLINOIS??! DID YOU GO
VISIT YOUR OLD FRIEND BONNIE? SHE'S
THE ONLY PERSON I CAN THINK OF WHO
LIVES AROUND THERE. PLS CONTXT
ME AND LMK WHAT'S GOING ON. GALA
IS TOMORROW NIGHT AND I NEED YOU
BACK IN CALI. LOVE YOU.

What?

These words in my vision are totally disorienting, and a wave of dizziness washes over me.

I slump down onto a plastic-covered armchair, unable to stop myself blinking in rapid succession as I adjust to the type embedded in my left eye. The words change again, resuming their original text.

What the hell is *in* my eye that's doing this? When I close my eye and move it around, I can ever-so-slightly feel something there — not uncomfortable, more like what I imagine a contact lens would feel like.

And what on earth does "context me" mean?

What crazy world am I in now?

This is nuts. I need to figure out where I am, whose house this is, and what's going on.

Maybe the weird eye-words can tell me, though. Maybe they'll be useful for something.

I blink twice, hard, and the [MORE INFO] text below the house's address obligingly expands.

*1274 CELESTINE DRIVE, LAKE BLUFF, IL
60044
PROPERTY OWNERSHIP: NUMBERED
COMPANY 394756, SHANGHAI, CHINA
RESIDENCY STATUS: UNOCCUPIED
MOST RECENT PROPERTY TRANSFER:
NOVEMBER 2016
FORMER OWNERS: BEN MASON, BONNIE
MASON [ESTATE TRANSFER]
PREVIOUS OWNERS: FRANK MASON,
ANGELA MASON [DECEASED]*

The information rolls backwards through time, showing the full history of the house, the further I read downward.

I blink twice again, and the text goes back to what seems to be the main menu, which is much less obtrusive.

Okay.

Super freaky, but it *is* useful.

Now I know that Frank and Angela are dead again — still — in this reality. Just like in mine, the house was transferred to Bonnie and Ben in the will after the accident. But instead of Bonnie buying out Ben with her half of their inheritance cash, they apparently sold it to some overseas buyer, and it's now unoccupied.

At least I won't stumble across some poor family having dinner this time.

And that gives me some time to regroup and figure out this eye-text thing before I go out into this brave new world.

I tread upstairs, where no lights are on but the sun is streaming into the kitchen. It's in the same decorative condition as the Masons had it years ago, pre-renovation by Bonnie. Clearly the new owners haven't lived here much, although there are signs of occasional use. A toaster on the counter still has a few crumbs on the top; an electric kettle is a quarter full of water.

But the house is uncharacteristically chilly, despite the warmth of the day, as if it hasn't been heated or seen human activity in a long time. I check the fridge, and it's empty aside from a single can of diet soda, which I grab gratefully.

I mean, it's only a very small theft.

In the large living room, a red tufted formal couch has a plastic sheet over it, and there's a small side table, plus a media cabinet with a TV screen on the far wall. Other than that, the room is empty. I check through the windows at the deck, where there is no patio furniture at all, just bare decking.

I open the soda, take a swig before placing it on the side table, and move the plastic to sit on the hard couch. This place may be a good respite for now, but I won't be comfortable here for long. I need to figure out who I am in this world and what the hell is going on.

One thing is for sure — I'm not in a world that's anything like my home, given the text in my eye like I'm some kind of Robocop. If only I could figure out how to work it, besides rapid blinking, which only seems to be getting me to property information, emails, and something called Contexts, which seem to be this world's version of regular texts.

I need to ask more questions. But how?

I pat down my pockets to see if there's also a phone I can use. I'm in a pair of fashionably wide jeans, a black tank top, and some expensive-looking sneakers. There's also a pair of sunglasses perched on my head.

The jeans yield no phone, but there's two sets of keys, one with a car key bearing a Tesla logo and a car rental-branded keychain, and a set of house keys with a fob of some kind. There's also a lump in the small inner pocket of my jeans. I dig into it with what I note are acrylic-nailed hands, way more manicured than usual, and find a case bearing a flat C-shaped logo, and inside, a pair of sleek earbuds, with an empty circular chamber above them.

Maybe the earbuds, which must have a built-in mic, will help me communicate with this eye-information portal.

I put them in, and they beep.

What to ask?

"Where's home?"

Nothing.

Crap, it's probably like Siri, where you have to say "Siri" first before it's activated, otherwise it would be answering all the time. But what's the trigger word for this tech?

Hmm. The earlier text message from some guy I had read said "*PLS CONTEXT ME*" and the texts seem to be called "Contexts" — so maybe "Context" will work? That would be the most intuitive, anyways.

I try again, speaking slowly and clearly.

"Context, where's home?"

Still nothing. Damn. What now?

Something else from the text from that guy that struck me as weird . . . "*YOUR CONTACT SAYS YOU'RE IN ILLINOIS.*" Maybe "contact" is the right word — after all, this thing is definitely something in my eye.

"Con*tact*, where's home?"

A beep. Okay, great, that worked.

An electronic voice, male-ish.

"Your home location is set to 637 Fletcher Drive, Atherton, California 94027."

California?

Oh, right, that's what that text had said. "*I NEED YOU BACK IN CALI.*"

And I've heard of Atherton — it's a famously expensive suburb of San Francisco where a lot of the tech billionaires live, according to my favorite real-estate reality TV show.

Something else the message had said . . . "*LOVE YOU.*"

From somebody called . . . what was it? I blink my way back to the text.

Someone called Evan. Whoever *that* is.

I'm now in a world, as I had feared, where I'm with somebody I don't know in my real life.

Who is this guy? What's our history?

"Contact, who is Evan?"

It's a long shot, given there are a gazillion Evans, but maybe my eye-tech will know who I mean.

A beep, and the voice again.

"I'm sorry. Could you please be more specific?"

Shit. I wish I could.

Oh . . . hold on. He's in a relationship with *me*. So if I add my own name . . .

"Contact, who is the Evan who is in a relationship with Millie MacKenzie?"

Beep.

"Your identity is set to Millie MacKenzie. You are in a monogamous romantic partnership with Evan Chen, founder and CEO of Contact Technologies PLC, a Fortune 500 company. You and Mr. Chen have co-habited in Atherton, California, since 2016."

Contact is a company?

But hold up, that company name is familiar. Yeah, that's right — I remember it as some promising tech company that failed spectacularly, maybe a year or two after I graduated. I even met someone high up at Contact at a fundraiser that the Notables sang at, at the end of my senior year.

And *his* name had been Evan.

Oh my God, it's *that* guy. The cute Asian-American guy I spoke with for all of thirty seconds before he left to take a call, or something. I'd laughed about it with Bonnie at the bar later. And I'd even thought about Evan once more, a year or so after meeting him, when I read that his company had collapsed.

But, in this world, Contact is a highly successful Fortune 500 company. It *didn't* fail. And I must've gotten another chance to see Evan that night of the fundraiser, or later, because now we're evidently together.

"Contact, what does the company Contact Technologies do?"

"Contact Technologies, founded by inventor and CEO Evan Chen, is a publicly traded company under Nasdaq:CNTC that develops, manufactures, and sells augmented reality and telecommunication technology that operates through an artificial-intelligence-powered contact lens worn by the user, along with compatible earbuds. Contact is the fastest-growing company in the US by revenue for the past six successive years, and is currently ranked eighth on the Fortune 500 list of the US's biggest companies, reporting $221BN revenue in the last fiscal year. Contact's core products have been rapidly and widely adopted among consumers in North America and Europe, and in 2022 outsold smartphones in those markets for the first time. In 2021 and 2023, Contact won Tech For Global Good awards for its work on digital vision augmentation for blind and partially sighted users."

Holy fuck.

That tech is what I'm wearing in my eye, right now, and what's telling me all this information. It's telling me about itself.

Talk about meta.

Okay, so I'm wearing the AI-powered contact lens-slash-comms device that never took off in my world, but somehow did in this one. And I'm *living* with the guy who invented it. Presumably someone who is now a majorly famous tech billionaire, in a home in San Francisco's mecca for tech billionaires.

This is *wild*.

My pulse is racing. The caffeine in my diet soda is probably not helping, but I gulp it down anyways.

What about Bonnie, and Ben? This house doesn't belong to them, but are we still friends? The text from Evan had mentioned Bonnie being "an old friend." So I guess we're still in touch, but now that I'm living with a tech billionaire in California, our friendship is probably not what it was.

"Contact, please look up Bonnie Mason social media profiles in Illinois."

A beep, and a list of "Bonnie Mason" profiles — LinkedIn, TikTok, a few Facebook and Instagram, and lots on something called Connect, presumably related to Contact — appear before me. Some are other Bonnie Masons in the state of Illinois, but all have thumbnail headshots, so I can quickly find my Bonnie with her blonde curls. Her LinkedIn profile is like the one where I'm married to Chris — working at Chicago City Hall, not at her store. Her profile on Connect, which seems to be a combination of LinkedIn and Facebook and has a very smooth interface in my eye, shows her career profile as well as some personal entries — vacation photos, and some of the interior of a house I don't recognize.

Her with Ben, him looking tanned, his arm slung round his sister's shoulder. They're both beaming, on a beach somewhere.

And one of the two of them with two other people I don't recognize — a Hispanic-looking guy next to Bonnie, his hand in hers, and a beautiful, tall woman with brown hair, who is clinging to Ben's arm.

They look so happy. Both in loving relationships, without me.

I nod, slowly.

Okay. Bonnie and Ben seem to be doing fine, and they don't need me. And, honestly, I'm wildly jealous of these new people and I don't feel any desire to meet them.

Stephen, then?

"Contact, give me Stephen Powell social media profiles in Illinois."

A list of profiles pops up again, and I pull up Stephen's Facebook page, since there's no Connect profile. He was always a big Facebook user, and this world is clearly no different. Maybe he hasn't moved over to the Contact ecosystem yet.

Tons of photos of him with his wife Eve and his kids — even some from today, on their camping trip. Exactly like in my world.

That's no good to me.

I throw my head back against the tufted couch. What to do?

It doesn't seem like this version of me is in any kind of trouble for me to help with. This is clearly not my original world, nor a world where I'm with Stephen. Plus it's a weird, futuristic, sci-fi alt-reality with insane technology that will take a lot of getting used to. And I don't even have a home in Chicago, but instead one all the way in California, with a guy I barely remember.

Maybe I should just head out of the front door, come back in through the basement, and reset. Throw this life out entirely, and try again.

But something is giving me pause. I mean . . . this *is* a life where I live in presumed fabulous luxury with a tech billionaire. Who, as far as I remember, was a total hottie.

And the technology is incredible — I'm dying to find out what else it can do, now that I'm starting to get used to it.

So, my only alternative to resetting is . . . to go to California, and check out my new life? Even if only for a little while. Just for the weekend, maybe. It's still only Friday evening.

I've got some time.

And presumably, a shitload of money to spend.

My guts churning with excitement and fear, I ask aloud, "Contact, when is the next flight from Chicago to San Francisco?"

"The next flight from Chicago O'Hare International Airport to San Francisco International Airport is at 23:15, arriving in San Francisco at 01:50 local time on Saturday, June 17. There are three business-class seats available. Would you like me to book a ticket with your Executive Traveler loyalty points?"

Oh, crap. I guess I'm deciding right now.

"Erm, yes, please book one window seat in business class."

"Booking flight. One moment."

A beep. The occasional intermittent beep, for maybe a minute.

"Your business-class seat on American Airlines flight 634 from Chicago to San Francisco, departing 23:15 today, has been confirmed. Your assigned seat is 3A. Check-in begins at 21:15. Your boarding pass has been downloaded to your Contact documents. Please scan your Contact at the departure gate B16."

Sure enough, on the main menu text in my left eye, a new line has popped up, bearing the number and time of my flight. I blink twice, and it zooms open, showing me a boarding pass with a QR code, just like on a cellphone in my reality.

I've got nearly three hours before check-in, which is plenty of time to get to the airport and drop off the rental car, which I presumably got from O'Hare anyways.

Okay, then. Let's do this. I'm clearly wealthy enough to just get another plane ticket back to Chicago as soon as I'm ready to leave San Francisco. *If* I want to leave.

I go to the bathroom off the foyer before my journey, checking myself in the mirror. Aside from being too skinny in Rufus's world, this is the most different I've looked. I'm wearing a *lot* more make-up than usual, I have long eyelashes, and my usually straight, plain bob is now a dramatic bob that's much higher at the back, with a graded cut into the nape, and a longer angular line down to my jaw at the front. Very chic.

Some Gucci sunglasses are on top of my head, tucked behind my ears, and I'm wearing what appear to be diamond stud earrings.

Fancy.

I also have a small tattoo on the inside of my wrist, of a slim crescent moon and two stars. I've never been a tattoo person, but it's pretty. What could it symbolize? Then it strikes me — the skinny crescent moon looks a lot like the flat C-shaped logo for Contact, which was on the earbud case. Maybe it's related to the company.

It also confirms something I've been gradually becoming conscious of. That each time I step through that basement door, I'm quantum-leaping into the *body* of the Millie in the new life, rather than bringing my own body with me.

This theory started to coalesce when I saw how thin my wrists were in the world where I was married to Rufus — clearly *not* my own body — and it seems consistent with the discovery of this new tattoo. I carry my own memories and thoughts, but I have each new world's physical form. And everything else that comes with it.

Leaning in closer to the mirror, I can just make out a gray-bluish circle around my left iris — the Contact — and minuscule bright green dots on the side.

With a nervous laugh about this futuristic, glamorous version of myself, I let myself out of the front door and release the driveway gate. The Tesla rental car is right out front, and there's a small Coach overnight bag in the passenger seat, which holds some clothes, toiletries in a wash bag, a water bottle, and some tampons. No sign of a wallet or credit cards anywhere, but if my Contact can be scanned for a boarding pass, I can probably pay for goods by looking into a scanner, too.

Kinda scary, as well as deeply convenient.

A great way for a government to keep tabs on people, that's for sure.

I pull off and, despite the slightly distracting text in my left eye — which I could turn into a GPS to give me directions, if I didn't know where I was going — I can't help but enjoy the quiet, smooth, drive to the airport. It's only a half-hour drive, being conveniently located between Lake Bluff and the city. It gives me tons of time to drop off the car, take the monorail transit to the terminal, and get a leisurely grain-bowl dinner at Terminal 3.

As I come to pay the check, the server asks me, "Cash, credit, or C-debit?"

Time to test my theory.

"C-debit, please."

She holds a scanner up to my left eyeball. Immediately, the check details pop up, including an option for a tip. I blink twice, selecting 20%, and then twice again to confirm.

The server checks her scanner. "Thanks, you're all set. Have a safe flight, Ms. MacKenzie."

"Thanks," I reply, my pulse racing a little from the interchange, and at her reading my name off the scanner.

This tech is unbelievable. And more than a little bit Big Brother-ish. It's kind of incredible so many people across the

Western world have adopted it so easily, given how intrusive it is to their privacy.

What's that quote? "Give me convenience or give me death," is that it?

I can't remember where I heard it, maybe an old song, but it's hitting home for me right now. Everyone has given up their personal privacy for the convenience of this new technology. Including me, evidently. Still, I'm in a relationship with its inventor, so I probably don't have much of a choice.

He had sent me another Context while I was eating, asking where I was and if I was coming home. I reply to it as I sit at the departure gate, after having had my eye scanned once more at the gate desk for identification and to check my boarding pass.

> *I'M FINE. SORRY TO WORRY YOU. I WENT TO VISIT BONNIE, YES — IT WAS URGENT AND SHE NEEDED ME. SHE'S OKAY NOW, AND I'M ALREADY AT O'HARE WAITING FOR A FLIGHT BACK TO SF. IT LANDS JUST BEFORE 2AM, SO I'LL BE HOME BY 3AM. I'LL TRY NOT TO WAKE YOU WHEN I GET IN. SEE YOU IN THE MORNING.*

He replies immediately.

> *THANK GOD! I WAS SO SCARED, MILLIE, YOU WERE ACTING SO WEIRD THIS MORNING, LIKE A ZOMBIE. I HAVE NO CLUE WHAT HAPPENED BUT YOU CAN FILL ME IN. HOPE YOU HAVE A GOOD FLIGHT HOME. MISS YOU.*

Like a zombie, huh? That's bizarre.

I've been wondering how the versions of me in each of these lives found themselves at Lake Bluff. After all, each time I've emerged from the house into a new reality, there's been a car parked outside, and I've had its keys in my pocket. The car didn't drive itself to the Masons' house — some cross-universal instinct must have compelled that life's version of me, each time, to get themselves to Lake Bluff on that Friday evening. Then I slipped through the door and into their lives, and bodies — if only for a little while.

We'll see how long I last in this one.

I board my flight, settle into the luxury of my business-class seat, and get Contact to download a fun, beach-read audiobook to play in my earbuds while it's in airplane mode.

I gotta admit, this Contact stuff is really, really fun to play with. Even if I never get any privacy again. Maybe I can take the lens out? Surely I don't sleep with it in at night — that can't be healthy for the eye.

After landing in the small hours in San Francisco — nearly two a.m. local time, and four a.m. for my body clock — I get Contact to book me an Uber to the house in Atherton. I'm increasingly nervous as it pulls through the quiet, wide streets of this chichi suburb and onto Fletcher Drive. What am I going to find there?

The Uber stops outside a closed, modern, rusted-metal solid gate set between two high, pale-stone walls. The number 637 is cut out of the metal. This is the place.

"C-debit?" asks the driver, who has barely said a word to me. He doesn't even offer me the option of a credit card. Maybe he knows who I am, or who I live here with, so it's pretty obvious how I'll pay.

He turns in his seat and zaps my eye with his scanner, making me start a little. I give him a tip that's more generous than he deserves, and he nods at his scanner approvingly.

"Have a good night, Ms. MacKenzie."

"Thanks."

I drag myself and my overnight bag out of the car, and it pulls away, leaving me in the dark street in a strange city I've never been to before.

Thousands of miles and many universes from home.

I dig in my pocket for the set of keys and fob I found earlier. Now that I know what Contact is capable of, I'm a little surprised that I even have these keys — surely a scan would let me in through the gate and into the house? But maybe the tech is not so ubiquitous that it's fully replaced regular house keys.

I scan the fob on a black panel at the side of the gate, and it beeps, but the gate doesn't open. Instead, part of the matt black panel becomes shiny, and semi-transparent. I peer to look closer in the dark, and it emits a red flash into my left eye.

The gate starts to slide open.

Ah, I get it. A two-step security process, with the eye scan as the second stage. What my Irish father would call a "belt-and-braces" approach.

Instead of a driveway, the gate reveals a wide, shallow set of smooth stone steps leading to a large, ultra-modern, elongated, two-story house at the top of a terraced rise. Subtle lights in the paving guide me up to a huge front door, which has a long handle and a keyhole plate, and another black panel on the wall next to it. I'm holding what looks very much like a house key for this door, so I give it a try in the lock, but I can't fit it in. I give the black panel a pointed stare, it gives me another red flash, and there's a clunk from the door. I tug the handle, but it's still locked. Maybe the scan released the keyhole? I try the key again, and this time, it fits and turns effortlessly.

I guess Evan Chen, being who he is, has to be careful about security. He just didn't bargain on an imposter version of his girlfriend, inhabiting her body and holding her house keys.

I'm almost chuckling at the ridiculousness of it all as I enter a double-height foyer, lit low by a small table lamp on a console. Next to me, through an open door, is a walk-in closet full of jackets and shoes, with an inner door that leads to a powder room. Handy.

I go to the restroom and wash my hands with its fancy soap. Now would be a good time to figure out if I can take this lens out — I don't want to be fumbling about with it upstairs, if Evan is asleep. I really don't want to wake him and face his questions yet, if I can avoid it.

Staring in the mirror, I pull my left eyelid wide open. The outer ring of the lens is clearly visible, slightly past the edge of my gray-blue iris.

I've never worn contacts, so I'm not used to this, but I've seen Bonnie take hers out a million times. I mimic what I've seen her doing — look all the way to the left, then brace myself as I put my finger on the lens and pull it to the right. Instantly, the text that's been at the side of my vision disappears. I pinch my finger and thumb over the curve of the lens, squeezing slightly, and it lifts away with ease.

Close up, it looks like a clear contact lens, but with almost microscopic metal lines joined by tiny dots in a curve around one side. Amazing.

But what to do with it? I can't just leave it on the washstand. Oh, hold up — the earbud case in my pocket. Within it, a central, circular cavity has a clear liquid beyond a membrane at its base, while a dry section below offers two slots for the earbuds. My lens and both the earbuds fit perfectly.

I tuck the capsule back into my jeans pocket and step out into the mudroom. Leaving my sneakers under a bench, I walk silently out through the foyer, getting a glimpse of a huge, modern living area that's in near-darkness, with a glass wall revealing a low-lit terrace and turquoise pool beyond.

This place is pretty amazing. I turn and tread quietly up the floating staircase to my left. On the generous upper landing, there is a series of possible doors to choose from. Which is the right bedroom? Given Evan's loving texts, it seems very likely that we have a healthy relationship and share a room. It would be really weird to wake him by banging my way through the wrong bedroom doors.

I turn to the far left, and there's a set of double doors, grander than the rest. Chances are that's the primary bedroom.

I open one of the doors as slowly and silently as possible. Moonlight is streaming through a huge window that must overlook the pool terrace. It illuminates a massive bed with a plush headboard that reaches the tall ceiling, and a sleeping form under the sheet on one side.

Guess this is my bedroom, and under the covers is tech billionaire Evan Chen. My boyfriend.

I undress quickly, pulling a silky pajama set out of my overnight bag, and climb into bed without even taking off my make-up or brushing my teeth. I don't want to wake him.

Plus, for me it's five in the morning, and I'm dog-tired from all this universe-hopping.

I can make out a crop of black hair on the white pillow as I pull the sheets over me, but that's all.

He stirs, and rolls over.

"Honey. You're back." It's barely more than a mumble.

"Yes. Shhh. Go back to sleep."

"Mm-hmm." That's it. He's silent again.

I lie down, facing away from him. Despite the unbelievable bizarreness of the situation I find myself in, I don't feel unsafe with this man next to me.

On the flight here, I was recalling my brief encounter with him at a charity fundraiser. How in those few moments we'd had an intense connection. How warm and friendly he had been, and how I'd had to hide my disappointment at his departure, over cocktails and laughter with Bonnie.

No, I feel pretty safe in this bed, especially given how concerned he had seemed about my wellbeing in his texts. In fact, right now, despite everything, I have a sense of calm. And deep exhaustion.

I slip quickly into a dream-filled sleep, in which I'm walking into that basement again and again. Ben is always there, as he was that first time, strumming his guitar. But every time I try to get his attention, get him to look up at me by stepping toward him, he disappears and I have to run upstairs, through the front door, back down the side of the house, and into the basement again. I can never get Ben to acknowledge me. It's a never-ending cycle.

* * *

I wake much later, sun pouring through the big window, the blinds fully open. The bed next to me is empty, but there's the sound of running water coming from behind a single door, which I guess is the bathroom.

The door opens, and Evan Chen steps through. Shirtless, in just a pair of Calvin Klein boxer briefs, his relatively slight frame enhanced by an undeniably ripped six-pack of abs. He's even more handsome than when I met him years ago.

He ruffles his mussed-up black hair and smiles at me, although there's a frown line between his brows.

"Hey, beautiful. You slept like the dead. It's nearly noon." He raises his eyebrows. "Good thing it's Saturday. All we have is the gala tonight."

I sit upright, pushing a pillow behind my head. My heart is racing a little, and my stomach performing somersaults, but hopefully my nervousness doesn't show.

"Wow. I guess I was pretty late getting in. I'm sorry about going AWOL yesterday."

Evan climbs back into bed beside me, the ecru skin on his chest gleaming in a sunbeam. He smells amazing. Like spearmint and eucalyptus.

"That's okay, honey. I just wish you would have communicated with me more." He runs a fingertip down my bare arm. "I get that Bonnie needed you urgently, but what was *with* you yesterday morning? You left, like, in a weird trance, just ordered your Uber to the airport, grabbed some clothes, and walked out. Why wouldn't you answer me when I asked where you were going?"

I shake my head. "I'm sorry," I repeat. "I was just super preoccupied with getting to Bonnie, I guess. I probably didn't even hear you. I was worried about her."

I hate lying to this kind man, but what else can I say? I can hardly tell him the truth. I barely understand what the truth is, especially in terms of what specifically compelled San Francisco Millie to suddenly fly to Chicago.

He nods slowly. "Okay. You said Bonnie is fine now? Were you able to help with her . . . issue?"

"Uh, yeah. I was. She was having a relationship crisis, but I talked her off the ledge. They'll be okay, I think."

"Good," Evan replies. "I like Gus, he seems like a good dude. Seems to make her happy, most of the time, right?"

Gus? I guess that's the guy with Bonnie in the photo. I'm happy to hear Evan has met them — that must mean we're still good friends in this life, even if we don't see each other much.

"Yeah." I smile back at him. "I won't worry you again, promise."

I'm making a promise his real girlfriend will have to keep after I leave, but I figure that's her problem. Assuming her mind, her consciousness, her *essence* will return to this body once I'm gone.

After all, as much as my curiosity got the best of me about this life, I won't stay here. I just want a weekend glimpse into what it's like to be a tech billionaire's girlfriend. I'm only trying on this life before I move on. And, lying in this soft bed with this beautiful man, it doesn't suck so far.

"I hope not," he replies. "Come here."

Come here. That's what Rufus said to me, twenty-four hours and one universe ago. But this time it's said with warmth and affection. Desire too, yes, but a desire born of love, rather than control.

Still, even though he's super cute, I barely know this guy. And this *body* might be in a monogamous sexual relationship with Evan, but *I* had sex with someone else yesterday. It just doesn't feel right.

Evan smiles gently at me, reading my hesitant body language. "Still too sleepy, huh? Okay, how about you nap here a while longer, while I hop in the shower and then fix us brunch? I'll give you a ping when it's ready."

Ping. He probably means a text through my Contact lens.

I take him at his word, drifting in and out of a light doze for another half-hour, before reaching down to yesterday's jeans for the capsule in my pocket. I take it into the bathroom and spend nearly five minutes struggling to put the lens back in my eye. Eventually, after much blinking and redness, I get it into place, and then jump in the shower. As I'm drying off, after I've readjusted to the green type in my vision, a new Context from Evan appears.

YOUR BRUNCH AWAITS YOU, MADAME. XX

He seems very thoughtful and indulgent. I can definitely see why I fell for this guy.

I pull on a fresh set of clothes from a huge walk-in closet full of designer gear that I'll totally have to examine more thoroughly later. Downstairs, Evan has whipped up mushroom and cheese omelets, a side of brioche toast, and fresh orange juice and coffee.

Once again, I'm impressed.

We spend the entire afternoon chatting easily, Evan not seeming to notice as I carefully get him to reveal things about our life together.

"Remember the night we met?" I ask him, over a glass of ice tea around four p.m., my feet on his lap as we lounge on the patio couch by the pool. He nods, rubbing my soles with his thumbs.

"I'll never be more glad to have been covered in a tray full of champagne." He laughs. "If it hadn't been for that clumsy server . . ."

A clumsy server? Oh yeah, I vaguely remember that. But in my world, Evan managed to dodge him, and kept going.

Maybe *that* was the difference.

"What do you suppose *would've* happened instead?" I ask, one eyebrow raised. "If, as you say, it hadn't been for that clumsy server."

He grins, looking out over the shimmering flat surface of the infinity-edge pool. "Well, I wouldn't have had all that champagne tipped over me, right? My phone call with Sanjeet *wouldn't* have been interrupted, so I guess I would have continued out to the lobby to take it, and you and I might never have spoken again. You *wouldn't* have seen the whole thing and come to my rescue, even though all you could do was dab at my suit with a napkin. My custom Tom Ford, ruined." He shakes his head. "But it was totally worth it to keep talking to you." He pats my legs, and pushes them off his lap. "Speaking of fancy galas, we need to get ready. We have to leave at ten after five if we're going to make it there for six. Cynthia hung your dress in its bag on the closet door."

I can't ask who Cynthia is, since I'm evidently supposed to know, but I assume she's some kind of housekeeper or assistant who deals with our dry cleaning and probably a bunch of other stuff. I mean, Evan doesn't strike me as a guy who needs to do his own chores.

"Okay, I'll be up in a few," I tell his back as he disappears through the sliding-glass wall into the living room.

Well, this is not a bad life at all. Super weird, given the sci-fi technology, and also just foreign to me, being in California. But undeniably fabulous and luxurious.

Upstairs, I dress in an angular, one-shouldered, violet-colored midi dress and black Jimmy Choos. With this haircut, I barely need to do anything but brush my bob into place and give it a light spray. I add a black choker, and put my lipstick and pale-powder compact into a Dior clutch, along with my house keys and lens case.

Evan drives us in his red Tesla to the Ritz-Carlton in downtown San Fran, tossing the keys to the valet waiting ahead of the grand, pillared entrance. We are swept along a red carpet under the porte cochere, where several photographers are waiting. They shout out when they see Evan.

"Evan! Millie! Over here!"

We pause a moment, smiling, Evan's arm around my waist. He's careful to look at each photographer in turn, giving them their shot, while I mostly smile at him.

He murmurs in my ear. "That should be enough." We turn and join the sweep of other guests entering the opulent lobby, and are guided to the elaborate ballroom with its many chandeliers. The event is some kind of technology industry foundation launch, looking for donors, and Evan — as a previous Tech For Global Good award winner — is evidently the guest of honor. We're seated at the top table for a dinner of sea scallops and halibut, and Evan is called on to stand up for a round of applause during the after-dinner speeches.

As Evan schmoozes with tech types, I'm temporarily standing alone by our table, sipping on pink champagne. A tall man approaches me — middle-aged, with black hair graying at the temples, and a well-trimmed goatee beard.

"Ah, the luminous Millie MacKenzie," he says, reaching out an immaculately manicured hand. "I've been hoping to meet you. I'm a big fan of your partner's work, of course, and I know you have played a large role in that. Amir Habib." He has an unidentifiable accent, maybe Saudi or Israeli.

I shake his hand with a smile. "Thank you. But I don't know how much of a role I've played in Evan's achievements. That's all him."

Amir lets go of my hand, and tilts his head graciously. "Oh, my dear, you are too modest. Your influence on Contact and its success is legend. Even your Mr. Chen himself has proclaimed, in every interview I've read, that the company's breakthrough would never have happened without you."

What?

That can't be true, surely. I know precisely squat about technology — I *can't* have influenced it that much.

"He gives me too much credit," I reply, with a smile that I hope hides my sudden fluster.

"Not at all," Amir says, determinedly. "I'm a big follower of Mr. Chen and Contact Technologies, and his story is consistent. He was about to give up on the company, which was floundering without a true purpose. Then he met you, and you convinced him that, quite aside from the main purposes it is used for by consumers today, his technology could do so much to augment the vision of partially sighted people, as well as helping deaf communities and others with disabilities. He reapplied his work with renewed vigor and a fresh mission, all because of you." Amir smiles, revealing perfect white teeth. "Of course, nobody ever expected adoption to be so widespread among the general public, did they? Or that it would prove to become the pervasive communication medium of our generation, stuck in every eyeball in the Western World."

I stare at him, my glass poised halfway to my lips.

I influenced all that? Without meeting me, Evan's company would've failed, and people would still be using regular smartphones like in my world?

But I *didn't* get together with Evan in my world. And his company *did* fail.

It's the butterfly effect.

That server, back in Chicago at an event very like this one, spilling a tray of champagne, eventually resulted in one of the most revolutionary technologies this world has ever seen. Via my relationship with one man.

I nod at Amir, slowly. A word he used has stuck with me. "Pervasive?" I raise an eyebrow. "That doesn't sound like a compliment."

He takes a sip of a dark brown drink over ice. "It is not meant to be, my dear." He gives his head a tiny shake. "Something that was invented with the best of intentions, now being used by your government to monitor and control *not only* its own citizens — the sheeple, as they say — but any and all humans using this technology."

Amir leans in, lowering his voice. "Rest assured, you will never find *my* compatriots using Contact. Cellphones and social media are dangerous enough for monitoring behavior — we won't be placing insidious tracker implants in our eyes that can pass information on *my* people's habits and whereabouts to *your* government. Not to mention, potentially sending us subliminal messages that we can barely perceive, in order to do their bidding." He grins again, too close.

My pulse races and I take a step back, with a slight scoffing laugh. "Mr. Habib, I'm sure you're exaggerating. But of course, what technology you and your compatriots use is entirely up to you." I take a swig to finish the rest of my drink. "If you'll excuse me, I need to find Evan and a fresh glass of champagne."

I turn and stride away, slightly shaken, wobbling a little in my heels on the carpet.

I had scoffed, but the truth is, I *don't* know that Contact isn't selling data to the government to monitor US or other citizens. And I don't believe Contact would ever send subliminal messages to users, but I *do* know any technology can be hacked, and that rules can change in times of crisis or war. I'd be naïve to think that wasn't ever a possibility.

This tech, built for convenience, communication, and to help those in need — technology that *I* was instrumental in advancing — might at some point be used for evil.

Evan being celebrated tonight for winning the Tech For Global Good award is beginning to have a sour taste in my mouth.

My billionaire boyfriend finds me at the bar, reaching for another drink. He slips an arm around my waist. "Don't let me deny you another champagne, but I'm about ready to get outta here. I've got to drive us home, and I have an early flight in the morning."

I turn to him in surprise. It's the first I've heard of his flight tomorrow.

He squints at me. "Don't tell me you forgot about my trip to DC. My flight leaves at eight a.m. so I can be there in time for the senator's meet and greet."

I smile at him, feigning dumbness. "Sorry. Totally forgot," I lie. I put the glass back down. "Let's head out."

We make our way out of the ballroom, although it takes some time as people come up to Evan on the way, wanting to chat or say goodbye. Evan is the perfect statesman, greeting them all warmly, and deftly moving on without making them feel slighted. We eventually make it out to the porte-cochere, where the valet rushes to retrieve our car.

"Who was that mysterious guy you were talking to so closely?" he asks me, as we wait.

I blow out a breath. "Random dude. Said his name was . . . Amir Habib." I pause. "Speaking of DC and senators, he was pretty shady with me about Contact. Talking about how it had been corrupted from something to help the partially sighted and deaf communities into a tool for the government to monitor the 'sheeple,' as he put it." I screw up my nose. "He was a bit intense. I had to extricate myself."

Evan nods slowly, scanning the drive for his Tesla. "Sorry you had to deal with that. I hate that the position I'm in with the feds is trickling down to you. It's hard for me, you know that — but it shouldn't be tough on you, too."

What's hard for him?

What's the trip to DC about, meeting with politicians? What "position" is he in? What are the feds asking of him?

But I can't ask him that. Clearly, I'm supposed to already know. Maybe this version of me knows stuff she shouldn't.

Maybe it's not such a charmed life, after all.

Maybe it's time to get out. Back to Lake Bluff to reset.

And Evan is going away tomorrow, for several days. That gives me the perfect opportunity to get back to Chicago without him noticing I've disappeared for another twenty-four hours. The other Millie will be back in San Francisco by Monday, and Evan will never know the difference. Unless, of course, he checks her Contact geolocation.

I'll leave her a note to tell her why she's finding herself in Chicago, and make sure she talks to Evan about the dangers of Contact. I'll even book her a flight home. But more than that, I cannot do.

Back at the house, upstairs in bed, Evan and I crash out. He's a good man, but I can't be with him. I don't love him, he's not my partner — and he's not my problem.

In the morning, after he's gone, I'll be gone too.

EARLY JUNE, SEVEN YEARS AGO

"Congratulations again, both of you! We couldn't be more proud."

Frank lifted his flute of champagne high, and we clinked glasses across the long table.

"Yeah, congrats. Welcome to adulthood," Ben added, giving Bonnie a wink and me a warm grin.

My mother, sitting regally in a flowing tie-dye dress at the other end of the table, took a silent sip of her champagne, bangles jingling.

Ange added, "That arena is something else, huh? I bet you've seen a lot of games there." The School of Communication undergraduate convocation ceremony had been held at the university's arena, where the Northwestern Wildcats basketball team ruled.

"Sure," I replied. "I mean, we're not really team sports people, but the basketball games are fun." I glanced at my mother, who was looking away, clearly not listening. "Go Wildcats," I added, weakly.

Around us, the buzz of the packed Ten-Mile House restaurant was loud with other families also celebrating graduation day, many of us still in our robes. Mom would be finding the noise hard — she was never good at dealing with busy places and high levels of ambient sound. She'd clearly been deeply uncomfortable in the arena during the ceremony, and the experience had left her irritable and distracted.

I made eye contact and gave her a small smile, which she returned, wordlessly and with little enthusiasm.

If only she would make more of an effort in front of the Masons. But social situations like this were tough for her, I got that. Deep down, I knew she was proud of me for graduating from a top-tier university, even if she wasn't especially vocal about it.

She was here, after all. She hadn't made an excuse not to come to Chicago for the ceremony, which I had half-expected. She'd even put up the money for the two of us to stay in a downtown hotel this weekend, before she headed back to Indianapolis on Monday. That was very generous of her, considering her paltry income. And considering she was quite obviously offended that I'd chosen to move in with the Masons until I found a job, instead of moving back to Indy with her after school ended.

So, yeah, her effort wasn't much, but it wasn't nothing. I'd take it.

"What's the plan now, Millie?" Ange asked, warm affection coating her voice. "Where's our girl taking her life next?"

At the foot of the table, Mom twisted her mouth into a tiny smirk at the phrase "our girl."

I ignored her, and turned to Ange.

"Get a job, I guess, so I can get out of your hair." I laughed. "I'm sure you don't want me living with you the entire summer." Ange lifted her hand to protest, but I placed mine over her arm. "No, really. I'm so grateful for your generosity, but I can't stay with you forever."

After dorms closed two weeks ago, I'd moved my meager possessions into the Masons' guest room, as Bonnie moved back into her childhood bedroom. It was a fun time, and Ben was often at the house — usually when Amber was busy doing something else. But I did need to find a way to stop depending on the Masons for everything.

Getting a job was the top priority. Anything to give me some semblance of independence. While still being able to spend time with the Masons on a regular basis, of course.

"You're not thinking about doing the IMC Masters at Medill?" Ben asked. "I thought you wanted to do that."

I swallowed a sip of my drink and sighed. The Masters of Integrated Marketing Communications at Northwestern's Medill School would've been a great next step for me, and a lot of the Comms graduates in my class were going on to do it. But it was expensive.

"I was hoping to," I admitted, with a wry smile. "But the Bank of Dad has dried up, so I can't fund it. His construction company in Ireland isn't doing all that well right now, so he can't pay for any more studies for me. I'm on my own." I shrugged. "Medill offers a part-time masters for professionals so, if I need to, I can pay for it myself later, while I'm working. We'll see. I'll have to get a job first."

My mother cleared her throat. "I'm sure you'll find something, honey. And at the rate your dad is drinking himself into an early grave over there in Dublin, you'll probably get your inheritance from that huge McMansion of his sooner than later." She emitted a slightly bitter laugh. "You'll be fine."

Seriously, Mom?

Despite the chatter around us, a thick silence descended into the airspace above our table, and Bonnie shuffled nervously in her seat beside me. I glanced over at Ben, who gave me a soft, sympathetic smile, and then at Frank, who looked gravely at his hands.

Did Mom really just wish my father dead so I'd get some inheritance? Right in front of everyone who mattered to me?

I opened my mouth to form a response, but nothing came out.

Ange, bless her, piped up, breaking the awkward silence. "Well, I'm sure Millie will be just great forging her own path. But she'll always have our support, and she can stay with us just as long as she wants to — no matter what she says." She turned to me. "We were talking about it, and we hope you *will* consider staying the whole summer, and taking some time to have some fun after working so hard at school. You can always get a job in September, right? Summer's a horrible time for job hunting, anyways."

I smiled. Angela always made me feel so much better about myself. So safe and cared for.

Beside me, Bonnie issued a little yip of excitement. "Yay! You've got to stay the whole summer, Mill. You know my classes don't start until the fall, and I need you to keep me company."

She'd already gotten into an interior design program at the art school in the city, and would commute from Lake Bluff for the five months it would take to complete. I was thrilled that she'd chosen to pursue a creative career, given that she'd been wavering about maybe going into public policy. She'd definitely chosen the path that would make her happiest, I was sure of that.

"Plus, you're coming to the beach house in Oregon with us in August," Bonnie added, pointedly. "No point in you starting a new job in July, only to be away for three weeks in August. You may as well wait until we get back."

We'd been planning this vacation with Bonnie's parents for months. Ever since Bonnie's grandmother had passed last year, leaving her Oregon beachfront home to Frank, the house had been undergoing massive renovations for use as a vacation home. As of this summer, it was finally ready — and I couldn't wait. I hadn't been back to the West Coast since the summer I met Bonnie.

I glanced over at my mother, whose over-plucked eyebrows were arched. I could almost physically feel the waves of disdain coming off her, vibrating over the table, stacked as it was with unfinished champagne glasses and generous family-style food platters.

To Mom, summers spent having nothing but a good time, family-owned beach houses in Oregon, and generational wealth — even celebratory meals like this — were a level of privilege she had never known. Her disdain was part envy, part lack of respect for anyone with money. She always assumed that anybody wealthy had had their lives handed to them on a platter, just like the smoked meat on the table.

The Masons were privileged, yes. But they were also good, kind, generous, hardworking, career-driven people who didn't deserve the thinly disguised sneer coming from my mother's end of the table.

I turned back to Frank and Ange with a smile. "Thanks, that's so kind of you. If you're sure, I'd love to stay. But I'll be applying for jobs while we're in Oregon, so that I have interviews lined up in September. I don't want to be a burden on you after Bonnie has started classes."

Across the table, I caught Ben's eye and he gave me a silent nod, and a grin.

Maybe he would join us on our Oregon vacation, too — at least for some of the time. That would be fun. But then again, I wasn't sure I wanted Amber and her perfectly tanned bikini body there with us. Less fun.

Bonnie gave my shoulder a friendly nudge. "It'll be great. We'll have the best time."

Our harassed-looking server came to clear away our plates, and Frank quietly paid what must've been an exorbitant check — no doubt with a giant tip, judging from the server's smile. Mom, I noticed, barely mustered more than a quiet "thanks" to Frank as we stood and gathered our belongings.

Such a *chip* on her shoulder.

But then, it was probably hard for her to see her daughter being lavishly taken care of in a way that she could never have afforded. That had to hurt.

We said our goodbyes, and Mom and I walked to Evanston train station, my heavy graduation robe draped over my arm as I carried my cap. The day was warm, and I was glad of the light sundress I'd worn beneath the robe. Mom's brightly colored dress flowed out behind her, the thin straps exposing her tanned, leathery arms. She'd never believed in using sunscreen. "Too many chemicals, Millie," she'd tell me. "It's not natural."

Yeah, Mom. Skin cancer was much more natural. But still definitely worth avoiding.

We settled into our seats in the two-level train to Chicago, Mom insisting on sitting on the lower level to avoid the tiny, steep steps to the mezzanine seats. The train was packed, and we shared our four-seater spot with a gray-haired couple who were also carrying a convocation ceremony program. I smiled at them and they grinned back, nodding at the purple graduation robe and four-cornered tasseled cap resting in my lap, a silent congratulations between strangers.

The train pulled away from the station, and Mom looked out of the window, twisting the jeweled rings on her fingers.

"You're going to stay with the Masons the entire summer, then, and get a job in the fall?" she asked, not looking at me, her eyes flicking at the passing townscape. "Are you sure that's wise?"

I shrugged, immediately on the defensive. "You heard Bonnie and Angela. It's hardly worth applying now, to start a job in mid- to late July at the earliest, only to be away for three weeks in August. I'll make sure I get something in September, and move out then. Even if it's only an interim job to pay the rent until I get something permanent. I'll be fine."

Mom huffed, and finally made eye contact. "Well, you'd also be *fine* if you came and stayed with me, and started applying for jobs right now, and spent the summer going on *interviews* instead of living it up on the beaches of Oregon." The bitter edge to her voice had returned. "I mean, you might miss out on a job that starts in early September, if you wait to start applying. Sure, Bonnie wants to spend the summer with you, but she's already got her next phase locked down. She's already *fine*. People like us have to work harder, and make sacrifices in life, you know? Not everybody has it all figured out like the Masons."

Beside us, the sweet couple who had smiled at me shifted uncomfortably in their seats, the woman pretending to read her ceremony program rather than unwittingly eavesdrop on our conversation. The man cleared his throat nervously.

I sighed. "I get it, Mom. But Ange is right — there's hardly any recruitment in July and August. *Everybody* is on vacation. And those graduate programs that start in early September — they're already filled, and I'm not going for something like that anyways. I'll find an entry-level job at a marketing agency, or something. September will be fine for that. I promise."

Mom furrowed her brow, evidently unconvinced. "If you say so. I've said my piece."

I leaned forward, trying to engage her in a smile. "And I appreciate the offer of staying with you in Indy, I really do, Mom. But as I told you before, it's not good for me there. I can't see my friends in Chicago, and even if I did spend the summer applying for jobs from your place, it's a nightmare to get the train four hours each way to go for interviews in Chicago — I'd have to stay overnight with Bonnie anyways. It just makes sense for me to stay nearer Chicago." I reach over and put my hand on her tanned arm, above the bangles. "I do love you, Mom, but my life is here now. I'll come visit for a few days before Oregon, okay? You can show me your new rose-gold product line."

Mom nodded, somewhat placated, then squinted a little. "Are you sure there isn't anything else keeping you in Chicago? You've been real quiet about your love life recently. Have you met a boy?" She gave me a twisted grin, and I laughed, relieved at the break in tension. Even if it meant touching on a topic that was another sore spot for me.

"No, Mom, I'm not seeing anybody. It's not that."

Mom pursed her lips. "That brother of Bonnie's is pretty cute, though, isn't he? I saw him looking at you over lunch — don't think I didn't notice."

My stomach did a little flutter, which I ignored. "Ben? No, no. He's got a long-term girlfriend. He's not *remotely* available. And even if he was, you know, he's Bonnie's *brother*. I'm sure that would be weird. So, you know. Not an option. *Definitely* not."

Mom's thin left eyebrow had gradually risen to its highest possible point throughout my protestations. "If you say so," she repeated, this time with a tiny smile. "And no other prospects on the horizon? I haven't heard you speak of anybody since you broke up with Chris. You're such a beautiful and smart girl, I can't understand why you're not beating them off with a stick. I'm sure you meet nice boys all the time."

Wow. I couldn't remember Mom ever calling me "beautiful and smart." Not in the same breath, that's for sure.

"Thanks, Mom. But . . . no. There's nobody."

My mind flitted back to my final singing gig with the Notables a week ago — a fundraising gala in which I'd briefly met a really cute guy, Evan, the founder of some skyrocketing tech company. We'd spoken for only a few minutes, but there had definitely been some chemistry. Then he'd suddenly rushed off — narrowly missing a server with a tray full of champagne, I recall — to take an urgent phone call. I didn't see him again for the rest of the evening. The next day, I'd pondered trying to connect with him on LinkedIn, since I knew his name and company, and we'd arguably met at a work event. But in our brief exchange, Evan had told me his company was on a hiring freeze, so there was no chance of a marketing job. Plus he was based in San Francisco, so he wasn't a good romantic prospect. I'd decided to let it go.

Mom was watching the passing townscape again, which was getting increasingly vertical as we approached the city. "You haven't had much luck with men, have you?" This was said quietly, almost more to herself than to me, and for a second I wondered if she actually meant her own love life. But she turned her face to me, as if expecting me to respond.

I pulled in a long breath. I wasn't going to get into all that with her right now — not on a public train, with two polite strangers next to us trying desperately not to listen to our conversation.

Instead, I looked out of the window myself. The highrise towers of Chicago were now in view, and I felt my heartbeat slowing. This was where I belonged.

"Like mother, like daughter, I guess," I replied.

We sat in silence for the rest of the journey.

JUNE, THIS YEAR

With nobody occupying the Lake Bluff house in this reality, I'm able to jump the front gate pretty easily, and walk across the gravel drive with no fear of being caught. Down the side lawn, in front of the basement door, I remove my Contact lens and place it in the capsule in my pocket. I take a deep, cleansing breath.

Here I go again.

I pull hard, and the now-familiar rush of air and released suction washes over me. A moment ago, it had looked all dark behind this door.

But as I step into the vestibule, all the lights are on. People are actually down here, in the basement recreation room, chatting, laughing. Teenagers, watching a movie.

I can't escape back the way I came. God knows what would happen if I did that. Back to Evan's world, maybe? Into a new world where everything is backwards? I really don't want to find out.

No — as the saying goes, the only way out is through. And in this case, up the stairs. And out the front door.

I'm gonna have to make a break for it.

I suck in some air through my nose, brace my shoulders as if for impact, and march into the recreation room.

Five or six late-teens, some of them distinctly bigger than me, stare up at me in shock, their movie forgotten. A bowl of popcorn spills.

To start with, nobody says anything, and I avoid all eye contact as I stride my way quickly across the room, stepping with a half-leap over a pair of gangly legs belonging to a bewildered guy on the floor. Then one of the girls screams, and I break into a run up the stairs.

"Who the *fuck* is that?"

"What the hell?"

"Moooommm!!! Daaaddd!!"

At the top, I don't wait to look around the kitchen, as footsteps are starting to follow me. I glimpse a pair of adults in my peripheral vision, somewhere near the kitchen counter, but I'm already running into the foyer. I push out through the front door, sprint across the gravel, and bash the gate release button as hard as I can. They're already at the front door, shouting at me.

The gate starts to swing open and I squeeze through, sprinting down the street. I have no idea where my car might be, assuming I even have a car stashed nearby, but I just need to get away. I run for several minutes towards the wooded ravine, around several bends, until I'm sure I'm safe.

My heart is beating so hard that it feels like it'll come out of my mouth, and I lean over, head at my knees, gagging and panting.

Fuck.

That was a bad one. Even worse than that first family I came across.

I straighten up and pat down my clothes for keys and a phone.

That's *really* weird.

I'm wearing a rough wool coat, even though it's a hot summer evening. Below that are stained gray sweatpants with ragged edges, and a Cubs sweatshirt with a peeling logo. My sneakers are ill-fitting and caked with dirt.

No keys.

No phone.

No wallet, or ID.

Nothing in my coat pockets but two scrunched-up dollar bills, a single quarter, a couple of folded-up documents, and a UP-N train ticket.

My scalp is itching, and I run my nails — short and bitten though they are — through my hair.

It's long. Like, really long, four inches past my shoulders. And slightly tangled, in places.

What the *fuck*?

What kind of condition am I in, in this world? Stained clothes, unkempt hair? Almost no money, and no house or car keys?

Jesus . . . Am I *homeless*?

I stand on the grass verge, bewildered. Across the street, a woman inside a fancy house is twitching her net curtains, watching me. Probably worried that I'm a criminal about to break into her home.

Given that I just broke into a house up the street and terrified a bunch of kids, she has every right to be nervous.

I move on, further along the tree-lined street, towards the ravine. What to do? I can't go back to the house right away and reset my reality — I won't even make it to the basement door if I go back right now. The family has probably called the cops. I need to wait this one out a while before I can reset. Maybe find a café where I can get something for two bucks.

Does *anything* only cost two bucks, these days? Maybe a soda.

Plus, there's the small matter of how I told myself I would try to help the versions of me who are in trouble. I can't run out on this one without at least seeing if I can do *something*. Can I? After all, I did tell myself that I'd try to leave each Millie's life better than I found it, if there was anything I could do. Like with the Millie who is married to Rufus — I have to hope that she returned to her body, and got out of her awful marriage.

149

I *have* to see if I can help. This Millie is still me, and I'd want help, if it could be given.

It's a few miles to the commercial center of Lake Forest, and these sneakers are crappy, but at least they're comfortable to walk in. I can check to see if Bonnie's store exists in this reality. Probably not, given that I helped push the store into existence, and it's hard to imagine this is a reality where Bonnie and I are friends.

She never would have let this happen to me.

How had *I* let this happen to me?

As I walk through the suburbs, there aren't many people around and I can stay pretty inconspicuous. But when I get to Lake Forest's small shopping district beside the train tracks, where it's humming with activity, that's when I notice it.

People avoiding me. Giving me a wide berth. Throwing side-eyes my way. Treating me like I have a contagious disease. The more I search strangers' faces for some kindness, even a little sympathy, the more they blank me.

When I reach what would have been Bonnie's store, I'm shaking, choking back tears.

And Bonnie's store, as I feared, is not her store — it's the bagel place.

At a loss for what else to do or where else to go, I step inside. At least there's hardly anybody in here. I walk up to the counter, trying to take measured breaths to control my panic.

A mirror behind the counter reveals what everybody else has been seeing. My hair is long and frizzy, and my oversized, stained clothes look like they were grabbed out of a lost and found. My skin has a sickly gray pallor, and my make-up-free eyes are wide and fearful.

I probably would have side-stepped me, too, if I'd seen me on the street like this. But . . . I'm just a person, and not a bad one. I'm not *contagious*.

A sweet-looking woman comes out from the kitchen. Her eyebrows lift as she sees me, but she recovers quickly, and gives me a warm smile. The first I've gotten since I got to this world.

"What can I get you, ma'am?"

I hold up my two dollar bills. "What can I get for two bucks?" I ask, my voice small and wobbly. "It's all I have." Moisture is brimming on my lower eyelids.

She smiles again, even more kindly, and I just can't take it. I break down into a torrent of tears on her counter. My whole body is wracked with sobs, and I can barely remain standing.

"Oh, hush, you poor thing," she says, hurriedly coming round the counter to support me, laying a hand across my back. "You just go ahead and sit here, honey, and I'll get you something. You put that money away." She guides me to a table. "You want some tea? I'll bet you could use some tea. And something to eat?"

She doesn't wait for me to answer, although I am hungry — I haven't eaten since my Executive Club Lounge brunch before my flight at San Francisco airport, which was nine hours and one universe ago. "I'll bring you a pastrami bagel. Sound good?"

I nod, wiping my wet face with a paper napkin. It comes away with a gray smear. "Thank you," I manage, a fresh tear dripping down my nose. I blow it loudly on the napkin as she moves deftly into the open kitchen.

So. Much. Mucus.

The sweet lady gives me regular reassuring smiles as she bustles about the kitchen, and I begin to calm down. At least there are kind people in the world who will help someone down on their luck.

It's warm in the café, with the evening sun streaming through the plate glass frontage. As I sip my tea and wait for my food to arrive, I tug off the wool coat, remembering the letters and documents I'd found in the pockets earlier. They should provide some clues as to my current situation.

I pull them out, unfolding the larger items, and lay them side by side on the table.

A typed document, seemingly an official letter of some kind, with a Chicago Women's Shelter logo, the text circling a crude graphic of female forms holding hands. Addressed to me, confirming that my application was successful and I have a confirmed place at the shelter assigned to me, in Dorm 5, from June 12 until June 30, after which my status will be reassessed.

Not *completely* homeless, then. A spot in a shelter isn't nothing. It's somewhere to go, at least.

What else? A return train ticket, dated today at 4:43 p.m., from the Ogilvie Transportation Center in downtown Chicago, to Lake Bluff Station.

I can get back to the city. I can get myself to the women's shelter, if I decide to do so, without any money. If I need to stay in this world overnight, or longer, at least there's a bed for me.

What else? A hand-scrawled, torn-open envelope, addressed to me, at what looks like it could be some kind of rehab clinic, outside the city — Reseda Refuge Center in Pontiac.

In handwriting I haven't seen in many years.

My mother's.

My stomach lurches as I take in her looped scrawl on the envelope. In my world, I'm in very little contact with Mom these days. The occasional text, and annual birthday phone call, in which we make small talk about my job and why I'm not dating anyone, and about her (failing) online jewelry business.

Every couple of years around the holidays, usually when all the Masons were away visiting other relatives — pre-accident — I would go visit Mom for a few days. Less so since Bonnie moved into the big house after her folks died, I think only twice since then. The last time I visited Mom was probably three years ago now, back home in Indianapolis. But the return address on the back of this envelope is Baltimore, a city I've never been to.

Maybe it's not only *my* life that's different in this universe.

I pull out the letter, which is on several pages of thin, ruled paper. My bagel arrives, with another generous smile from the café owner, and I eat while reading.

Baltimore, June 1

My darling girl,

Wow, I don't know how many years it's been since I wrote a physical letter on paper! But I hear there are no phones or computers in your rehab place. So here I am, writing with a real pen like I'm Emily Dickinson. Although I guess she didn't have a Bic. Ha!

First, I'm writing to say that I'm so proud of you for committing to this process, sweetheart, and letting your Dad pay for your treatment. Finally, he's good for something!

I know things have been hard for you ever since your time with me here in Baltimore, after losing the Masons like that. I understand they were like second parents for you, and I'm sorry I wasn't able to be a better mom after you lost them. And even before you lost them, for that matter.

I feel terrible that it turned out so badly when you were here, and I wasn't able to protect you better from what happened. I really miss you, but I truly admire the strength it took for you to move back to Chicago and try to start again. I know it hasn't been easy there either, especially because of that horrible landlord. But now you're taking the steps you need to move forward with your life, and I'm so happy for you. It might be hard, but I believe in you.

I think for you to heal fully, you need to stop blaming yourself for what happened with the Masons. Even if Bonnie still does, you know it was her grief that made her say what she did, and it doesn't mean that the fault lies with you. Most importantly, you have to forgive yourself for that night. When you do that, you'll be able to feel brighter about your future.

You still have so much promise and talent, and despite how rough things are for you, you know that I'm still so proud of you.

The clinic said you'll be at a shelter in the city after you're discharged, but I know that's only a temporary solution, and you don't have any funds to rent a new place in Chicago. I hope you know you can always come stay with me until you're on your feet. I get that you wouldn't want to come back to Baltimore, but I'm moving away in two weeks anyways.

My friend Crystal has invited me to set up a jewelry concession at her fashion boutique in Cleveland, OH, and she has a two-bedroom, what she calls a "garden-level suite" in her big house that she's willing to rent to me real cheap. I hope you'll consider coming to stay with me there after your treatment. It would be a safe place for you, you could get back into some creative writing, if you wanted to.

Think about it, anyways. After I'm settled and you're out of rehab, I could come see you in Chicago and we can talk about it more. Give me a call when you can — I assume the shelter you're going to has a landline you can use, since I'm guessing you haven't been able to get a new phone yet. My cell number is still 555-387-4847. Call any time.

Love and hugs,
Mom

Wow.

I sit back in my chair, brushing the crumbs from my mouth with a grimy thumb.

So much to take in.

Bonnie *blamed* me in some way for what happened with her folks? We fell out, and I went to stay with Mom in Baltimore — a city I've never been to — and something happened there that led into . . . what? Alcohol addiction? Cocaine? Meth? *Crack*?

At least I'm not a crack addict on the street.

That's how I had comforted myself, a few universes ago.

And now — maybe — that's *exactly* what I am.

I don't *feel* like an addict. Aside from my horrible clothing and hair, and my wrists being too thin again — even thinner than in Rufus World — I *feel* relatively fit and healthy.

Well, I guess I have just done a stint in a rehab center, so whatever toxins must be out of my system.

I read somewhere once that, once a physical addiction is gone, the rest is psychological. Learned behaviors, mapped neural pathways. A trap the brain can't get out of.

But although those neural pathways may still be there, I've brought *my* mind, *my* memories, *my* healthier psychology, into this body — at least for now. So, for the time I occupy it, maybe this body is no longer that of an addict. Maybe that will help.

One thing I can't grasp, though, is how my life could've fallen apart so quickly, and so badly, after the Masons' deaths. What can Bonnie possibly have blamed me for? It hadn't been my fault. It wasn't anybody's fault. It was just a terrible accident. Bonnie knew that — in my world, at least.

I suppose it's possible that just one tiny thing was different that night, in this world, that put the idea in her head that I was to blame. One minuscule deviation that meant we fell out irreparably, and ultimately snowballed into me becoming a homeless addict.

It's terrifying, when you think about it. How close we all are, at any time, to life being so incredibly different than it otherwise might. One wrong move, one misspoken word, could be all it takes.

Still, though, there's surely hope for this version of me. I've just completed a recovery treatment. I have a shelter spot to stay in for now. And Mom has offered a more permanent — or at least semi-permanent — solution, and really sounds like she means it.

Maybe Mom's a little less flaky than she used to be? Can the me in this life trust her, after whatever shitshow happened in Baltimore?

Maybe I should. This could be the other me's chance for a fresh start. Maybe I need to help her take the offered olive branch, in case this world's Millie is reluctant to do so herself.

This could be how I help her, before I move on to the next world.

Okay, then. Time to formulate a plan.

Get the train back to the city, and find the shelter. I know the street it's on, from the address on the printed letter, and I know it's walkable from OTC station, so I can get there on this train ticket alone. Call Mom, get her to come meet me in the city, as she offered — preferably tomorrow. Talk it through, and agree to go stay with her in Cleveland. That way, when I'm gone, the me in this life will have it all set up for her. It might help her make a good decision.

I pack up my documents into my coat pocket, and thank the kind woman behind the counter for the food. She gives me another sweet smile. "You take care of yourself, now, you hear?" she replies, as I walk toward the glass front door. I nod back at her.

That's exactly what I intend to do over the next day or so. Take care of myself.

And then get the hell outta here.

* * *

It's nine a.m. on Saturday, and I'm meeting Mom off her overnight train at Chicago's Union Station.

I'd called her last night, when I'd arrived at the women's shelter downtown, and she'd immediately, excitedly, booked her train ticket to arrive the next morning. Which was generous of her — although, of course, it still meant me staying the night at the shelter.

The place was rough around the edges — more than just the edges — as were the women living there. But they had been kind, and the women in my four-bunk mini-dorm had called me by my name and said they were glad to have me back. They asked where I had wandered off to earlier that day.

"We were in the middle of a conversation, and you just got up, grabbed your coat, and walked out the front exit," a woman called Trixie with peroxide hair had told me. "We were worried you'd gone off to score."

I shook my head. "Just went to see a friend."

The shelter manager, Susan, had welcomed me back with fewer questions, and gave me a clean set of less-stained clothes to change into after a hot shower.

I'm wearing the blue hoodie and gray leggings now, as I wait on a long wooden bench in the lofty, opulent Union Station concourse for Mom's overnight train to arrive. She couldn't afford a sleeper berth, but she's a champion at dozing anywhere, so I'm sure she would've found a stranger's shoulder to sleep on at her seat. A handsome older man who she's now given her number to, most likely.

She's here now, pushing through the Saturday tourist crowd, her dye job a vivid scarlet with graying roots. She sees me as I stand to greet her, waving her arm violently, the many metal bangles sliding around her thin, tanned wrist.

She hugs me with excessive enthusiasm, then pulls back to look at me. "My sweet girl. You poor thing. Let's get some breakfast inside you."

I haven't even said anything to her when she pulls me away towards the escalator leading to the station's mezzanine cafés. We choose a nondescript sports bar that offers a breakfast menu, and sit at a table overlooking the food court.

Mom suddenly drops the menu, her face an exaggerated picture of concern. "Oh, is this okay — eating somewhere that serves booze? I mean, I know that wasn't your vice of choice, but I'm assuming you can't drink either, now?"

Not alcohol, then.

"It's fine," I tell her. "I'm not drinking, but I can be around alcohol. Don't worry."

"Well, I won't have a mimosa," she says, resuming her perusal of the menu.

Like *that* would help.

"Thanks, I appreciate it," I reply instead.

I'm not entirely sure how my mother is paying for all this — not to mention the not-cheap train ticket to Chicago and back — but on the phone she had assured me it was all on her. So, I order my favorite breakfast of eggs benedict, along with coffee and orange juice, and listen as she tells me all about her new place in Cleveland, where she moved last week.

"It's such a sweet little apartment, Millie. It's in the basement of Crystal's house, but the back French doors open up to the yard so it doesn't feel like a basement — lots of light!" She beams. "Two little bedrooms and a living-kitchen area, as well as a kind of den that I'm using as a studio for my jewelry. Crystal and Keith live in the house above, but they're hardly ever home — he's always taking her off on cruises and whatever. She said I can work at her store to cover her any time she's away, which is a *lot*. And she's given me this whole beautiful French oak cabinet near the checkout to sell my jewelry!" She claps her hands together. "It's a pretty cool gig, this one, Millie."

I nod at her through a big mouthful. It really does sound like Mom is finally getting it together. I don't know how her life in Baltimore was, but the Mom I know, who still lives in Indianapolis, hasn't been doing so great. A string of disappointing men, and never a truly permanent home. Also a jewelry designer, but with a crappy online store that she has no idea how to market.

Maybe now that this version of Mom has a space in a fashion boutique, her business will take off a little more. The Millie in this life could surely help make that happen. Although, given that this Millie is a drug addict who has never worked at Magnolia, maybe she's not as hot on Instagram marketing as I am.

"What do you think, hun?" she asks. "Want to give Cleveland a try with me?"

I wipe my lips, nodding slowly. "I think it would be good for me. A fresh start, until I can get a job and figure out my future." I laugh, a little humorlessly. "I clearly don't have much in Chicago to stay for."

She raises an eyebrow. "No boyfriend, or anything? Not been seeing anybody?"

Honestly, I have no idea if there's a man in this life. No cellphone to check messages, no home to figure out if I'm living with someone. But, given the desperate state of my life in this world and my recent rehab stint, I sincerely doubt it.

My mind jumps to Ben. Does he blame me for what happened to his parents as much as Bonnie apparently does? I can't imagine he's in my life at all, these days.

And I sure as hell don't want to look him up and have him see me like this.

I take a sip of my coffee. "No, Mom," I reply. "No boyfriend here. No money, no possessions. I'm a blank slate."

Mom screws up her nose. "I could kill that asshole landlord you had. Breaking in and selling all your stuff just because you got behind on rent, and then kicking you out anyways? Who *does* that? What an asshole."

Jesus. So that's why I've got nothing.

I can't even imagine what must've happened to me after that, out on the street with a drug problem and no money or possessions. Thankfully, I have a father in Ireland who may be useless and unreliable but, having turned his construction business around, has deep pockets again. Not to mention, a guilty conscience about leaving me and moving back to Dublin.

Mom is still talking. "Maybe you'll meet somebody nice in Cleveland. Somebody steady, who can help get you back on your feet. You've always had such trouble with relationships — even before everything went downhill."

I bristle a little at that. It's not like I was set a great example.

"Well, that's not much of a surprise, is it, Mom?" I reply. "*You* always ran from men. Dad included. Yeah, he left for Ireland, but only after you'd pushed him away with your affair. No *wonder* I'm scared of commitment. I know you didn't mean to, Mom, but it was your behavior that taught me to be afraid of relationships." I shake my head. "I've always either chosen the wrong men, so that they'd never get close enough to be an issue, or men that worshiped me, and then *I'd* be the one to run, just like you always did."

I'm talking about Rufus and Chris, in my own world, of course. But I'm pretty sure the same applies to this drug-addict version of Millie. I'd be willing to bet that, when I was at my most vulnerable, it was some sexy, dangerous guy in Baltimore who first got me into . . . whatever it was.

Mom places an overly bejeweled hand on mine. "I'm truly sorry we didn't show you a better model, sweetheart. But I've been working hard on myself, and realizing I need to figure out life on my own terms before I can have a healthy relationship. Maybe that's true for you, too. Maybe we can figure it out together, and then move on."

She pats my hand, and pulls back. "Okay, sweetie, let's get the check. I couldn't afford a hotel, so I'm on an afternoon train back to Cleveland, and I wanna see the Bean before I go home. Let's do some tourist stuff and figure out when you'll be able to come live with me."

We walk the mile or so to Millennial Park to admire the Bean sculpture, and spend the rest of the morning exploring the waterfront parks and Field Museum. Over an exorbitantly priced salad at an outside café at lunch, we agree that Mom will buy me a train ticket and I — or, as far as I'm concerned, the other Millie — will join her in Cleveland when my stay at the shelter runs out at the end of the month.

I walk Mom the two miles back to Union Station, and see her off on the train with a warm hug. Today has been about the best my relationship with my mother has felt in more than a decade, and I'll take it.

Back at the shelter, I ask Susan for a pad of paper and a Bic, and — like my mother did to me — write the other me a physical letter. I tell her that she might not remember this twenty-four hours, but that she connected with her mother, and it was pretty good. I tell her about the new chance she has to start fresh, and hopefully stay clean, in Cleveland. It's not a perfect situation, and will require a lot of patience to live with Mom again, but it's the best option right now.

I just hope she'll take it.

I fold the paper into the pocket of the hoodie where she'll find it when she is back in her body, outside the Masons' old house in Lake Bluff. Which is where I need to go now, to reset.

Hopefully to find a life better than this one.

FEBRUARY, SIX YEARS AGO

Frank Mason switched off the office lights and held open the glass door to the twenty-second-floor elevator lobby while I grabbed my coat and bag. He looked at me with fatherly affection in his twinkling eyes.

"Great work today, Millie. Alain says your copywriting skills are excellent, and he's looking at giving you first crack at the sports center ad campaign. You're enjoying it, right?" He locked the office door behind them.

"It's a lot of fun," I replied, pulling on my winter coat. "I'm so grateful to you for creating this opportunity for me. Really, it's amazing. Thank you — again."

We stepped into the elevator, and Frank gave me a light punch on my arm. "You don't have to keep thanking me, kiddo. I'm proud of you — Ange and I both are. We're just happy to be able to give one of you kids a leg up into the working world. God knows I haven't been able to do that for either of my offspring. Obviously, Ben was a lost cause, being so into theater and music." He laughed. "You'd think maybe Bonnie would've wanted some work experience with me, given she's looking at interior design, and here I am running an architectural firm. But apparently sports centers and hospitals are not good enough."

I nodded as we stepped into the building's foyer. Outside, in the dark evening, downtown Chicago was deep in snow. I tugged my thick wool scarf around me, silently thanking myself for the grippy boots I'd changed into, leaving my impractical office pumps under my desk.

"Yeah, I think Bonnie's interior design ambitions definitely run more towards dressing homes in gorgeous, shabby-chic decor than programming healthcare spaces."

We walked out into the street, the cold hitting us like a wall of ice.

"You need a ride to your place? My car's right there." Frank gestured to where his Lincoln was parked down the street, covered in a dusting of snow. "I'm meeting Ange for our date-night dinner in about fifteen, but your place isn't far, so I can take you."

I shook my head with a smile and a shiver, despite my thick coat. "No, I'm good. I'm meeting both your 'offspring' at our favorite diner, just around the corner. I haven't seen Bonnie in a week, and Ben's play has the night off."

Frank put a hand on my shoulder. "Good. We still worry about all you kids, even though you're all now adults. God knows we'll worry about you till the day we die." He crossed the street with a little chuckle.

I called after him, "Drive safe! And say hi to Ange from me!"

Frank gave me an affirmative wave, and I pulled my coat tighter around me. I scurried in the snow to the end of the block, and Frank gave me a friendly farewell beep as he cruised past. The beautiful, teal-green car didn't look like it was built for this kind of weather.

I hurried into the retro-style Va-Va-Voom Diner, kicking gray-brown slush off my chunky boots onto the large entrance mat. The place was a beacon of joy and sunshine on this dark night, decked out in creamy vanilla and pale turquoise fixtures, classic 1950s style, with dozens of framed photos of convertible Cadillacs on the wall. The long, stainless-steel trimmed counter had rounded corners and padded cream-leather stools, and the booth tables matched perfectly. I'd been in the diner often enough to wave hello to the owner, Greta. She waved back and pointed to the booth where Bonnie was already studying the menu.

"What looks good tonight?" I slid into the banquette, pulling off my coat and scarf.

"Oh, hey girl." Bonnie flashed her teeth at me through bright red lips. "Everything. I need comfort food, and I'm going to eat it all. How was work?"

"Amazing, honestly. I love it. And I thought it'd be weird working at your dad's firm, kind of like working with my own parent, but it's really not. I mean, he doesn't get involved in the marketing or media buys — he lets Alain have free rein on that — and he's way too busy designing buildings to worry about me. I don't even have any meetings with him. So it just feels like a regular job that I got on my own merit."

Bonnie shrugged, turning back to the menu. "Well, you did. I mean, Dad introduced you to Alain, and passed on your resume, but Alain wouldn't have given you the job if he didn't think you could do it."

"I guess. But having the boss encourage him to hire his daughter's best friend definitely helped." I frowned at my friend. "What's up with you? You seem a little . . . I dunno. Grumpy." I reached across the table and put my hand on Bonnie's. "Where's my cheery Bonnie?"

Bonnie sighed, squeezing my hand and pulling away. "I dunno. Winter, I guess. I hate this weather, and it's so goddam dark all the time. Plus, you know . . . my course is finished, and I'm still stuck at home, trying to get my folks' rich friends to pity-hire me to decorate their houses, and failing to do even that, while you and Ben are both doing so well in your careers. Feels kinda rough right now."

I gave her a sympathetic smile. "I get it. And I know this time of year can be hard on you. But soon it'll be spring, and people will start up with their renovations. You're super talented, and I'm sure you'll be able to make a design business work. I keep telling you, you just need to get better at promoting yourself on social media. People need visual proof of your aesthetic, otherwise they won't hire you, when compared with some designer with a gorgeous photo feed."

Bonnie gave me a small smile. "I guess. I'll be fine. I probably just need to get laid."

I laughed. "There's my girl." I turned back to the menu. "Hmm . . . gotta do the bacon-cheddar burger and fries again."

A tinkle of the bell on the diner door and a fresh blast of cool air made me look up. Ben was stamping his feet on the mat, pulling a gray woolen beanie off his thick, dark-blonde crop. He was wearing a long, snow-dusted dark coat that suited him perfectly, giving him that artsy, theater director vibe. As he scanned the room, his gaze met mine and he gave me his easy, wide smile.

Ben always had that talent of lighting up a room, somehow. Well, Bonnie did too, of course.

Ben hung his coat on a peg near the entrance, and stopped at the counter on his way to our table. He chatted for a moment with Greta, who giggled like a teenager at something he said, despite Greta being at least sixty-five years old, before coming to sit at our booth.

"Flirting with Greta, as usual, I see," Bonnie said to her brother, digging him in his ribs with her elbow as he sat next to her, opposite me.

"You know it," he replied, grinning at me. "I can't resist a woman who can cook like that."

I raised an eyebrow at him. "Is that right? What about Amber — is she a dab hand in the kitchen? Somehow I don't see her as a cook."

Ben's expression faltered. "Erm . . . well. Amber has many talents. But no, she's maybe not so into cooking."

Beside him, Bonnie curled her lip into a fleeting sneer that Ben didn't see. "Also not into theater, or music, or movies, or reading . . . or *anything* you like," she muttered.

I'd witness Bonnie doing her absolute best with Amber over the past three years, but it had been an uphill battle to find any common ground — except for the occasional conversation about new clothes or cosmetics. As for me, I'd barely managed to get to know Amber at all. She didn't seem interested in me. On the rare occasions we'd all been together in Lake Bluff, or at the drama parties back at Northwestern, or even during those three weeks last summer at the Oregon beach house, Amber had all but ignored me.

Ben turned to his sister, his brow furrowed. "Oh-*kay*, mean girl. I know you're not that crazy about Amber. But she's a very entrepreneurial, and very skilled, cosmetologist. I respect her passion for her business, and you should too. I admire her . . . single-mindedness."

Bonnie scoffed slightly, but said nothing more as Greta came over to take our order. We gorged ourselves on giant cheeseburgers and cones of skinny fries as I quizzed Ben about his new three-person play, which had opened a week ago in the small but achingly hip Den Theater, not far from Ben and Amber's chic loft. The play was about two male best friends in love with the same woman, and the deterioration of their friendship over the escalating rivalry. It was riveting, and disturbing, and surprisingly sad. Bonnie, the Masons, and I had, of course, been in attendance on opening night and had cheered and whooped in a full-audience standing ovation as the curtain fell. Amber was conspicuous by her absence, as she was away in Arizona at some retreat for female direct-to-consumer small-business owners. When we'd taken Ben for celebratory drinks after the show, Ben looked lighter and freer than he had in months. And I was sure it wasn't just because opening night had gone well.

I was slurping up the last of a highly unnecessary choco-late milkshake when Ben brought up Amber again.

"It's Amber's twenty-sixth birthday next week — plus, you know, Valentine's Day — just after the play closes, and she's back from Scottsdale. I was thinking of taking her to Grand Rapids for a long weekend as a surprise. They have this winter festival, plus it's beautiful countryside for snowy hikes. I thought it'd be really cool. What do you think? A good idea?" He looked across the table at me, his eyebrows quizzical.

A pang tugged somewhere deep inside, between my heart and stomach. Why didn't *I* have a lovely guy to take me for long weekends to winter festivals? I hadn't had a boyfriend since I broke up with Chris, and that was nearly eighteen months ago. And that had barely even been a real relationship.

I shrugged one shoulder.

"Well, I mean . . . *I* would love something like that, sure. A great idea in theory. But in practice, for Amber . . . do you think *she'd* definitely be up for an outdoor winter festival? I mean, it would be very pretty, and look great on Instagram, but also very cold and snowy, and she'd need to have the right kind of warm gear. And you'd have to stay somewhere . . . you know. Really nice. Fancy."

Bonnie was nodding into her ice cream sundae, crunching on a triangular wafer. "Millie's right. Plus, Amber's not really the kind of woman who likes surprises, is she? Didn't you surprise her with a night at the Ritz-Carlton, and spend a frickin' fortune on the room, and she insisted on switching to a better one because there were, like, ten things wrong with the room you booked?"

Ben turned abruptly towards his sister. "What the hell is this? Rag on Amber night? She's my *partner*, Bon, we live together. I know you're never going to be best buds, but you could be a bit kinder."

Bonnie stuck the rest of her wafer defiantly into her melting scoop of vanilla. "Partner? Gimme a break," she replied, with no small amount of scorn. "You may live with her, but she's no partner to you, Ben. A partner would be someone who *cares* for you, and supports your dreams. Someone you can actually do stuff with that you *both* enjoy. The two of you have zero in common, she doesn't give a crap about your theater career, and she's proven herself pretty controlling on more than one occasion." Bonnie paused, seeming to make a decision. "She even suggested to me that you should work at her uncle's shipping company — like you're seriously gonna give up the theater to push around paper for a bigger paycheck. I guarantee, Ben, that if you didn't have a steal on rent on that awesome apartment, she wouldn't even be living with you — not unless you joined the corporate rat race." She spread her hands. "I'm sorry — I just say it how I see it."

"Well, *fuck*, Bonnie." Ben stared into his empty coffee mug. "That's about the meanest thing you've ever said to me. Like *you've* always made the greatest decisions about guys."

I reached my hand across the table. "I think we just both want you to be with someone who deserves you, and appreciates the things that you care about."

Ben's gaze lifted to meet mine, a fire glittering in them that I hadn't seen since the night he saw the texts from Rufus. "You're just as bad, Mill," he said, almost under his breath. "Talking about being with people who deserve you? The only guys you've ever wanted have been assholes, and any good guys who *do* get close to you, you push away. Seriously, you're one to talk. Both of you."

He suddenly slid out of the booth and grabbed his wallet from his back pocket, pulling out two twenties, way more than his share of the check, and dropping them on the table. "I can't listen to this. I gotta go home — I'm out. See you both soon, I guess."

I reached out for him again, but he shrugged me off. "Ben, don't. You don't have to leave like this. We are honestly just looking out for you. And you're right, we haven't made great choices, ourselves, either of us."

Bonnie was sliding out of the booth too, trying to hug her brother. "Yeah, I'm sorry. Please don't run off. Besides, I'm crashing at your place tonight, remember?"

Ben sighed. "Honestly, Bonnie, I just wanna be alone tonight. You know we'll keep going over this if you come back to the loft. Let me just head home by myself — you stay at Millie's, or go home. Mom and Dad are in the city tonight, so they can take you."

With that, he was gone, pausing only to grab his coat and scarf from the hooks, not even getting them fully on by the time he was out of the door.

Bonnie sat back down. "Well, damn. That was a shit-show." She widened her eyes at me. "Sorry you got dragged into the middle of that. We're both really suffering this winter, I think."

I twisted my mouth, and leaned sideways to see through the plate glass window if Ben was gone. Below the glare of the neon sign hanging in the window, his long coat and jeans were visible. He was pulling on his beanie hat against the cold.

"I feel awful. I'm gonna go after him." I started to shuffle out of the booth, but Bonnie stopped me with a hand on my arm.

"Let him go, Mill. He wants to be alone, and there's nothing more we can say. We've both apologized already. Plus he only got mad because he knows we're right — Amber isn't the woman for him, and he hasn't ever really been happy with her. Let him go mull over what we've said. Maybe he'll finally start coming to those conclusions himself."

Ben had moved away, and was now out of sight. There was nothing but a neon glow in the slush on the street outside.

I resumed my place at the table. "I guess you're right. Okay, so are you staying at my place tonight, then? Both my roommates are home, so I can only offer the couch."

Bonnie pulled her mouth down in an exaggerated grimace. "That lumpy-ass couch? Christ, no. The last time I slept on that thing I had a backache for a week. No, I can get a ride home with my folks."

I put up my hands. "Well, don't say I didn't offer my hospitality. Where are your folks having dinner tonight? Can they come pick you up from here?"

Bonnie was already pulling out her cellphone. "Yeah, they're eating at Doc B's tonight. So that's, what, only ten minutes from here? It's in the opposite direction to home, but they won't mind." She pressed a button and held the phone to her ear. "To be honest, they'll probably prefer to

take me home themselves, with the weather being like this."
Her gaze flicked away. "Hey, Dad. Are you having a nice
dinner? . . . Good . . . No, no, I'm fine. I'm with Mill at the
Va-Va-Voom Diner, near your office. I was gonna crash at
Ben's, but he's gone home and honestly, I was hoping to get
a ride home with you. I know it's a bit out of your way . . .
Oh, sure, he's fine. Just . . . you know. Being Ben. So is that
okay? . . . Thanks, Dad. You're the best. See you soon — love
you." She ended the call. "All set. They've paid the check, so
they can come now — they'll be here in ten."

"Cool. I'll wait until they get here." I grinned at my
friend and sat back in my seat. "So, tell me more about this
need of yours to, and I quote, 'get laid.'" I used finger quotes
theatrically. "What are you planning on doing about that?"

Bonnie laughed as we fell into conversation about our
respective dating prospects — zero currently for me, a couple of possibilities for the more open-minded Bonnie, who'd
recently installed a new dating app. It was nearly ten p.m.
when we realized it had been almost forty minutes since
Bonnie's call to her folks.

"Okay, where the hell are they?" Bonnie pulled out her
phone again. "Dad will be driving, so I'm calling Mom."

She tried her mom's cellphone, and then hung up.
"Going to voicemail. Guess I'll try Dad again. Maybe they
took their sweet-ass time leaving the restaurant, and the journey's just taking longer because of the snow."

I nodded. "Absolutely. They'll be here any minute."

Bonnie tried making a call to her dad, holding eye contact with me as she waited. It was getting quiet in the restaurant, and I could hear the ring on the other end. It kicked
into a muffled, low-toned voicemail message. Bonnie shook
her head at me. "Hi Dad, erm, it's been a while and you're
still not here, so give me a call if you've got delayed or something, okay? See you soon. I hope." She put the phone on the
table. "That's so weird. It's weird, right?"

I gave her arm a reassuring pat. "They probably got talking to someone on their way out of the restaurant, and your

dad is now driving, so he's not answering. And maybe your mom's phone has been on silent all evening. Let's give them another twenty minutes before we start wondering."

Bonnie pursed her lips. "You're right. It's just not like them, that's all."

I tried to distract Bonnie over the next little while, with talk of my new sports center campaign at work, but it was tough not to talk about the office without making Bonnie think of her dad. By the time the clock above the diner counter displayed 10:25, and it had been over an hour since Bonnie had called for the ride home, I began to allow myself to get worried. Bonnie tried both her parents' cells again, and neither picked up.

Bonnie was right — this was not at all like Frank and Ange Mason.

"Try Ben's cell? Maybe he'll know something, or be able to help?"

Bonnie shook her head. "He's home tucked up in bed by now — his phone will be off. And even if I could call him, I don't want to worry him unnecessarily. What's he gonna do? It's not like they'd've called him to let *him* know what's going on, and not me." She bit her lip. "Shit. And the diner closes at eleven, so we'll have to get out of here either way."

I nodded. "Well, we'll stay here until eleven, then. And if they still haven't shown up, and we haven't gotten through to them, we'll go to my place and leave messages telling them to come pick you up from my place. It's only a few extra minutes' drive."

Bonnie frowned. "Sure. Yeah . . . okay. It's a plan." She stared at the phone on the table in front of her, as if willing it to buzz.

Her telepathy didn't go unanswered. The phone started buzzing and singing a tinkly tune, and Bonnie snatched it up, her gaze fixed on mine. "Dad?"

Her eyes widened. I was able to make out a deep voice on the other end, but none of the words. Bonnie's face was unreadable — she was staring at me, but not seeing me. Seeing something else. And she wasn't saying a word.

After what seemed like several minutes, but might only have been thirty seconds, Bonnie eventually spoke. "Thank you. Yes, I will." Her voice was quiet and strangely thick. She ended the call and put the phone down, slowly, on the table.

"That was the hospital. Mom and Dad got into a crash on their way here."

JUNE, THIS YEAR

I'm in the basement at Lake Bluff. It's dark, aside from the light coming in from the doors under the upper deck, and totally silent. No furniture at all. Hopefully this is another unoccupied version. Which means that the Masons are still dead, but at least I won't get run out of the house by another family.

I'd caught an evening train back to Lake Bluff — another return ticket, bought with cash given to me by Mom, so that drug-addict me can get back to the city and hopefully make better choices. I managed to creep over the gate without being seen, it being a warm Saturday night, and the family with the teenagers seeming to all be out.

And now it's Friday evening all over again. This time, the first thing I do is check my clothes. The hoodie and leggings given to me at the shelter have been replaced by shorts, a sleeveless summer blouse, and a light cardigan. I've never been a cardigan person, but whatever.

I check the shorts pockets. A phone — thank Christ — in a pink case, as well as a lip balm and a set of keys. Good. This already looks like a more regular life.

I take the stairs up into the kitchen, which is also void of any sign of occupation, and scan the living room. No furniture, appliances, or even fixtures — definitely an empty house. Definitely no Masons.

I lean against the kitchen counter and check the smartphone, which opens at the touch of my fingertip. I go straight to the texts.

And my heart all but stops.

Stephen.

Dozens of texts . . . God, more like hundreds, going back and back forever.

All from Stephen.

Mundane stuff, mostly. Groceries. Chores. Where he'll be, and when. A bunch about work client accounts, even though this is clearly my personal phone.

But always with love and affection. Sometimes a sign-off like, "See you then, love you." Or, "Thanks, honey. xoxo"

"Love you."

Is this *it*?

Have I landed in the life where Stephen and I are together? So soon? I mean, I figured it would take a lot more multiverse-traversing attempts than this — I'm only on version . . . what? Five? Six?

My stomach is somersaulting as I scroll through the texts. Then . . . Instagram, of course! That should confirm to me what our relationship is like — at least in the public eye.

I flip to Instagram, where my feed has dozens of photos of me with Stephen. On vacation, on a boat, at some work event. A smattering of me with Bonnie, but not as many as usual. Several of me with a couple of women I don't recognize, seemingly on some kind of spa retreat. Me with Stephen again, and his parents, last Christmas, in front of a huge, decorated tree. "Holidays with the in-laws!" reads the caption. It's geotagged Grand Rapids, MI.

That's right . . . Grand Rapids is where he once told me his parents live. Back when we were first getting to know each other over our desks at Magnolia.

And, in several of the photos, clearly visible . . . both of us wearing wedding rings.

I look down at my left hand. I hadn't noticed it before, but I'm wearing it now, along with a slender engagement ring with a small, round stone. Subtle, tasteful. Maybe a bit simple. But pretty enough.

I take a series of deep breaths.

Okay, then. This has to be it. I'm married to Stephen; we spend Christmases with his family. This was what I've been looking for. This was endgame.

Time to go live my best life, right?

I step through the echoey house and let myself out of the front door. The keys in my pocket are for a Toyota, which is blue and parked right outside the gate. I set the phone's GPS to home, and it points me to Aurora, a smaller city to the east of Chicago.

Aurora. I went there once, I think, when I was small, with my parents. Back when they were together, and we were living in Illinois, before Dad's job had taken us to Indianapolis when I was ten. Mom had grown up somewhere near Aurora and had friends there. I vaguely remember a pub with a terrace overlooking a river that flowed through downtown, and my parents and Mom's hippy friends were all drunk, and I played with a cat all afternoon and got sunburned.

Mostly, though, the word Aurora makes me think of aurora borealis, the Northern Lights — a phenomenon I know Stephen is passionate about. He was always into space, and stars, and galaxies, and had so much to say about them. I think that was why I fell for him.

Maybe we chose to live in Aurora because of its name.

As I drive the hour or so from Lake Bluff — stopping to get gas, which is weird in someone else's car, using the credit card in their purse — I'm clammy with nerves. Finally, my life with Stephen is ahead of me.

How did it happen? Did he leave his first wife for me? Or did we simply meet first, at Northwestern? Maybe we met somewhere else, under totally different circumstances. I'll need to uncover all these answers if I'm going to live here in this life with him. Assuming that's what I get to do, if I choose never to go through the basement door again.

Of course, I won't have any memories of our life together, which will likely cause a whole bunch of problems. I've been able to get away with it before now, when trying on these alternate lives with Chris and Rufus and Evan — mostly because I didn't stick around long enough for it to be an issue. But if I'm planning on staying with Stephen, I'll need to figure out at least the majority of what happened.

Maybe Bonnie can help. A girls' night with her, fueled by wine, with a bit of nostalgic gossip should reveal some history. Bonnie loves to rehash memories. Although, from the relative lack of photos together, I'm not sure Bonnie and I are as close in this life as we usually are. Something else to figure out.

Right now, though, I'm just itching to get to Stephen, in whatever home we share. Because if I'm married to him, if he's mine at last, that means I finally get to kiss him. And more . . . much more.

I mean, I've wanted to be with this man for *years*.

In Aurora, I'm right by the river in the city center when I find the address. The building is not at all what I'd expected. It's a tall, red-brick-and-stone building, about fourteen or fifteen stories, close to the water by a bridge. It's a lot taller than the surrounding buildings, and looks more like an Art Deco hotel than an apartment block.

Plus, I guess I had Stephen down as a detached house kind of guy. A family man, I suppose. But then again, it doesn't look like we have any kids yet, so maybe we're enjoying apartment living while we still can.

Kids. Now *that* would be weird, to quantum-leap into a life where I have kids. It's not like, at thirty, I'm not old enough.

Still, now that I've found the Stephen life — hopefully my forever life — it doesn't look like that's a risk I'll have to take.

My phone's GPS has taken me to the building where we live, and a fob on my keys lets me into an underground parking garage, but it takes a bit more email research to figure out which parking spot to take, and which unit I live in. Twelfth floor . . . not bad. Views should be good, although Aurora isn't a particularly spectacular skyline.

But maybe the view of the night sky is good from our place.

I take the elevator and find the apartment on the twelfth floor, pausing at the door. Will Stephen be home? It's past seven-thirty on a Friday evening, and there was no text from him about having plans tonight, so I should assume he's here.

And I need to act like this is my home, and that I know exactly what's going on.

Here goes.

Welcome, Millie, to your new life.

I unlock the door and push it open. I'm in a narrow entryway that opens to a small apartment beyond.

"Hello?" My voice is way too timid. I try again, more confidently. "Honey? You here?"

A metal clang, and then footsteps from around the corner. Stephen.

Right in front of me, seeming even taller than usual, especially in this small space. Brown hair a little mussed, shirt sleeves rolled up.

He raises his eyebrows and pushes his black-rimmed glasses further up his nose. "Wow. You're late. Did the Gellermans keep you talking all this time? You must be starving." He steps forward, puts a hand on my shoulder, and kisses me lightly on my sweat-moistened temple. "I just put an eggplant and potato bake in the oven, but it'll be forty minutes. I can fix you a snack, if you're hungry." He disappears around the corner again, leaving me standing foolishly in the foyer.

I'm really here.

We're really married. We're a regular couple.

Beside me is a small console table with a set of keys, some mail, and a phone charger. I act like this is my home and drop my own keys and phone on it, then remove the sandals I'm wearing and place them next to the other shoes by the door.

Around the corner, Stephen is clearing up the counter of a wall of kitchen units that faces out into the modest dining-living room. A dining table with four chairs divides the kitchen from the lounge area, which has a couch, armchair, TV cabinet, and river views from two windows.

It's . . . sweet. Cozy. An ideal love nest for newlyweds, if that's what we are.

How long *have* we been married? How did we even get together?

"You want a snack?" Stephen asks, turning from his task to me. "Something to keep you from getting hangry? We still have some of that goat cheese."

My last meal was lunch with my mother in a park in Chicago, about five hours and one universe ago, plus it's dinnertime in this world and this body is probably hungry.

But I don't *feel* hungry. I'm in an apartment, alone with Stephen, and we're married. My stomach is flipping non-stop.

He lifts an eyebrow at me, and smiles, waiting.

Oh. I haven't responded to him.

"Sorry. No, I'll wait for dinner. Thanks."

He nods. "A drink, then? Let's open a Friday night red."

He moves toward a cabinet, and I move toward him. I put a hand on his bare forearm as he reaches for the door handle. His arm is skinny, but soft, with thick hair.

"Maybe with dinner," I reply. "Come here."

Come here.

I'm repeating the words Rufus had said to me — also in the kitchen of an apartment we shared in another life. *Come here.* God, what those words had done to me. That tug between my legs.

I reach my hand up to Stephen's neck, and pull down gently. Finally, a moment like this with the right person. A good man *and* the man I wanted. Finally, I get to break the pattern I've been in for so long.

He raises his eyebrows, and chuckles lightly. "Not as tired and cranky as I thought, huh? I guess we've got some time."

Stephen lets me pull his face to mine, and our lips meet. Softly at first, at least on his part. Maybe lacking a little passion, but then, for him, it's not the first time we've kissed. Far from it.

I'll just have to reignite that passion. Remind him who he's married to.

I kiss him harder, deeper. I slip the other hand under his loose cotton shirt, grazing my fingertips around his ribcage, tucking my hand below his beltline at the back and pulling his pelvis towards mine. I kiss his neck as I take a hand from his face and use it to unbuckle his jeans belt and undo his fly. His rapidly growing hardness is pushing out his white boxer briefs, and he's beginning to respond to my kisses with more fervor, his long fingers on my blouse buttons.

"I don't know what's gotten into you, but I like it," he murmurs into my mouth. "Let's take this into the bedroom."

With his jeans halfway down his butt, he shuffles us through a door off the dining area, which opens to a small bedroom with a river-view window, a queen bed in green linens, and a pair of matching nightstands. He pulls off his pants and socks, leaving him in nothing but his half-buttoned shirt, white underpants, and black glasses.

Adorable.

I reach for him again, unbuttoning and removing his shirt, draping it on a chair next to a closet. I've never seen Stephen shirtless, not once in all the years we've worked together, which has included a lot of summer company events at the lakefront. He's one of those guys who always keeps a T-shirt on. And sure, he's pale and skinny, with some uneven dark chest hair, which might make a guy self-conscious around the buff, tan guys at the beach. But he's always been beautiful to me.

I kiss him again, running my fingers over his chest, and pause to let him take off my top and jeans. My underwear is a sweet, slightly chaste-looking set in white cotton with a tiny floral print.

Stephen guides me slowly, respectfully down onto the bed, before taking off his glasses and setting them down on the nightstand. He kneels forward onto the bed beside me — and once again seems surprised when I grab him and pull his pelvis hard towards mine. Seemingly emboldened, his kisses down my neck become more passionate, and he tugs my bra off with enthusiasm. His tongue lightly flicks my nipples, left then right, and I become desperate for him.

I pull off my own panties, and he takes the cue to down the same with his own briefs. I glimpse his penis for a moment, slender and long, before he rises up the bed and pushes directly into my wetness with a groan. I'm so hungry for him, my legs wrapped around his back, and he glides easily in and out of me, faster and faster. It's probably only a minute or so when he throws his head back, groans again, more gutturally, and the tendons on his neck strain. He collapses on my shoulder, chest heaving, as I stroke his long back.

"Wow," he mumbles into my neck. "I feel like I needed that and didn't even know it." He raises his head to me. "But you didn't get there. You want me to . . . ?" His question trails off as he lifts a finger suggestively to me. I'm still grinding against him, unsatisfied, so I give him a slightly embarrassed nod.

Stephen reaches down and slides a long finger between my legs, nuzzling my neck. "You're *so* wet," he says. "I can't remember the last time you were this turned on." He rubs in small circles, slowly gaining speed and pressure, taking his time, moving his mouth down once more to my nipple. His tongue matches the movement of his finger, until I'm starting to moan — then his finger movement gets even firmer and much more rapid as he sucks on my nipple, his teeth and tongue squeezing. I give a small cry as I gently come, and he slows, then stops.

He kisses my shoulder, pleased with me, and resumes his previous position against my neck. He wipes his hand on the sheet beneath us. "Guess we need to change the bedlinens," he says, a smile in his voice. "It was time anyways. Your turn for laundry this weekend."

I chuckle a little, although my laugh feels slightly performative. Something Stephen's real wife might find amusing, that he would say that to her right after an orgasm, but me? Maybe not so much.

It's weird, though, given that Stephen's sense of humor was one of the things that attracted me to him. As well as lots of other things. His passion for the stars. His work ethic, his commitment, and how considerate he is.

And maybe — just maybe — that he couldn't ever be mine.

Still, now he *is* mine, which is great. Sure, maybe the sex wasn't quite as spectacular as I had imagined, but that's doubtless because we're a married couple who have been doing it for a while. I just need to learn how to be with Stephen as his wife.

Assuming that I get to stay here with him on a permanent basis, that is, which would mean replacing the Millie that was here. And never going back to my original world again.

Then again, I'm increasingly convinced it's not possible to ever go home. So what choice do I have? This *has* to be the best option. My only option.

Stephen rolls off to lie beside me, and I snuggle into his slightly bony shoulder. The possibility of alternate realities was always a favorite topic of conversation between us, so maybe he has a theory on this.

"Do you still believe in the multiverse?" I ask him softly. "All the infinite different possibilities of our lives playing out?"

A light huff of a chuckle lifts his chest. "Wow. We haven't talked about that in years. Not since Astrophysics Society. Uh . . . sure, I guess so. Theoretically, at least." He pauses. "What makes you ask?"

Oh, no reason, just the fact that I literally just arrived here from another world, via a bunch of other realities, and I'm trying to figure all this out. No biggie.

I trace a finger across his bare chest. "I still think about it, that's all. Like, if you *could* travel across the multiverse, and try out alternate versions, whether you could find yourself in a reality that *looked* a lot like your own but wasn't. Maybe only something tiny and unnoticeable was different — a grain of sand in a different position. How would you know what's truly your home universe? And how would you know which you is really *you*?"

He shakes his head. "You never could. And arguably, there *is* no 'home' universe, and there is no real you. All those possible versions of reality, some with infinitesimally tiny variations, are . . . well, infinite, after all. And who's to say that, at every moment, an infinite number of brand-new worlds aren't spinning off — and all the worlds where we already existed now have new Stephens and Millies? And all those versions of ourselves . . . they're *all* us. And we are all of them."

"I guess so." I pause. "So, you don't think if you somehow found yourself living in an alternate reality, that you would've . . . I dunno . . . *displaced* the version of yourself who was previously there? That you'd be an imposter?"

He shrugs lightly, lifting my cheek with his shoulder. "No, I don't think it'd work like that. Even if all those versions of ourselves exist and are multiplying constantly, we're all one being — and we're each all of those infinite versions of ourselves. Changed by circumstance and decisions, but still ultimately *us*. In the end, I think home is where you make it — where it feels right to lay roots and commit." He laughs. "But I don't think we need to figure this out now. It's not like it's something you or I will ever have to worry about experiencing."

Yeah . . . I wouldn't be so sure of that.

Still, I can't help but feel Stephen has helped justify my search for a new life with him. If the multiverse is truly infinite, it has to be virtually impossible to get back to my home reality. Which, in turn, means I have every reason — and every right — to stay in this new life. The life I've been looking for.

Stephen extricates himself from my arms and swings out of bed. His naked body is pale and flushed in the evening light, even skinnier than I had realized when he was clothed, and his butt is cute and toned.

Something he had murmured to me during sex pops back into my head.

I can't remember the last time you were this turned on.

Isn't that what he said?

Is it a rare thing that I'm fully turned on by my husband? I sure hope not.

But if that's true — well, that was before *I* showed up. This new and improved Millie is hot for Stephen, and he's gonna love it. And, despite being a new version of myself . . . I'm still Millie. I may not remember our lives together, but I'm still his wife. I'm sure of that.

It just might take a moment for this world to feel like home, is all.

"Well, thanks for the impromptu quickie," Stephen says with a chuckle, pulling on his underpants and jeans. "Maybe this time it'll take. You should lift your legs up, keep it in. I'll go check on dinner."

Lift my legs? *Keep it in?*

Wait . . . are we trying for a *baby*?

APRIL, FIVE YEARS AGO

The cherry blossom tree in the yard beyond the pool was in glorious bloom, the pale blush of pink offset against the deep teal of the lake. The Masons had planted it when they moved in, back when Ben was six and Bonnie only three. Cherry blossoms were Angela's favorite, inspired by the time she'd spent in Osaka as a student.

Or, they had been.

More than a year from the accident, and it was still hard to think of Angela and Frank Mason in the past tense. They seemed so present, in the house and garden and lake view, even now.

And their presence in my life had meant so much. A support system like one I'd never known, not even when my own parents were together. Frank and Ange were so encouraging, to all three of us. It had been like I was one of their own kids, and they were just as enthusiastic about my marketing career, and my writing hobby, as they were about Ben and Bonnie's ambitions. Without them, I felt somewhat adrift. I was still working at Frank's architectural firm, but it was weird without him there, and the work was a little dry at times.

Plus, I hadn't jotted down a word of creative writing in over a year. Not since that night.

I stood upright from my position leaning against the deck railing, rolled my shoulders and shook out my arms to bring myself out of the nostalgia, and went back into the shade of the house. In the kitchen, Bonnie was laying out fixings for lunch for the three of us.

Through the archway into the living room came the strains of Ben picking out a tune on the guitar his father used to own, which Ben still kept in the family home. He had several guitars at his and Amber's loft, but he was spending a lot of time at the Lake Bluff house these days. It felt like ever since Bonnie had used some of her generous inheritance to buy out Ben's half of the house, he'd been spending even more time there — despite having bought that gorgeous loft in the city for himself. As though he needed a way to hold on to his parents.

It had been a rough year, for both of them. For all three of us.

I'd tried to be strong for them, and help out where I could, or just to be there to listen. But sometimes it had been hard to be the strong one when I almost felt like I'd lost my parents, too, in a way. Of course, I knew it wasn't the same as losing the mom and dad who had raised you. But I had loved Frank and Angela — very much. Sometimes I'd wished it could be me sobbing on Bonnie's shoulder, or grieving while wrapped up in a warm Ben hug, rather than the other way around. But their pain had been worse than mine.

"Come get it," Bonnie yelled, unnecessarily, given both Ben and I were close by. The strumming stopped, and Ben lumbered through the archway. His dark-blond hair was disheveled and over-long, his beard needed a trim, and his posture seemed a little stooped — his whole countenance somehow lower than his tall frame usually offered.

He glanced up as he gathered a plate of ham, cheese, and bread. "Oh, hey, Mill. I didn't realize you'd gotten here."

I smiled at him, but he had already turned to the fridge to grab a soda.

"Hey, Ben. Yeah, just about ten minutes ago." I paused. Asking him how he was doing was probably fruitless, given that the answer was apparent in the set of his shoulders.

I glanced at Bonnie, who gave me a twisted half-smile and a tiny shake of her head. Clearly Bonnie was fully aware of Ben's low mood.

She clapped her hands. "Let's sit out on the deck," she exclaimed, with a forced sing-song brightness.

"Great idea! It's gorgeous outside," I replied cheerily, then cringed a little at my over-enthusiasm. Ben would see right through both of us.

Ben silently followed us out into the sunshine and we settled ourselves around the large glass table. The umbrella was not yet set up for the warmer weather, and the light was a little dazzling, but none of us could be bothered to lug the huge umbrella out of the storage box. We dug into makeshift ham, cheese, and salad subs, uncharacteristically lacking in conversation. It was mostly Ben's grumpiness that was bringing us all down, though.

Bonnie, in contrast, had mostly emerged from her hole of grief at this point. Her cure had been using a chunk of the inheritance to lease a tiny storefront in nearby Lake Forest and set up a beautiful little store full of shabby-chic tableware and decor items, with an interior design consultancy on the side. Since deciding to take that step six months ago, she'd been incredibly busy finding the right location, arranging the lease, sourcing suppliers and setting up relationships, working with local artists and ceramicists to showcase their work, then decorating the empty store in time for its launch, just two weeks ago. I'd helped as much as possible, on evenings and weekends, with social media marketing and a bit of local promotion and advertising.

And it was working, at least so far. The store wasn't packed, but there was definite interest from the wealthy locals, with a steady stream of customers. The "A Bonnie Home" social media account had amassed nearly a thousand followers already, all ooh-ing and ahh-ing over Bonnie's styling of rustic candelabras over locally hand-woven table runners.

Bonnie was a hit, as I'd always known she would be.

I took a sip of my lemonade, and gave Bonnie a grin. She responded with a smile of her own, and raised her eyebrows.

"Hey, Mill," she said, breaking the silence, "did I tell you about the woman with the house by the golf course?" She didn't wait for an answer. "So this woman, like, *dripping* with diamond rings, came into the store Thursday, and was in for maybe ten minutes examining everything — and you know there's not even that much to examine — and then was like, 'So you do interior design consultancy too, right? My daughter saw your TikTok,' and she wants me to come to her house next week, and maybe style her dining room, because she's got a big dinner coming up."

I put down my glass. "Bonnie! Wow, that's awesome. Good for you! I *knew* the Real Housewives of Lake Michigan would start hiring you before long — it was only a matter of time. And it's only been, what, two weeks?"

Bonnie giggled. It was so good to see her truly joyful again.

"Well, it's all thanks to you, Mill. If you hadn't made me do those dumb video clips, she might never have heard about me."

I chuckled. "Not so dumb now, are they?" I turned to Ben, who was sitting next to me, staring out over the water. "You must be feeling very proud of your sister."

Ben glanced my way. "Huh? Oh . . . yeah. Super proud of her. She's doing amazing." He turned to his sister. "You know I'm impressed with you, right? Way to make a silver lining out of what happened."

Bonnie's expression darkened a little. "What's *that* supposed to mean?" She tilted her head at her brother. "You think I'm *glad* it happened, and we got the inheritance?"

I reached across the table to touch Bonnie's arm. "I'm sure he didn't mean that."

Ben sighed audibly, and returned his gaze to the lake. "No . . . of course not. I just mean . . . I don't know. That you seem to have been thriving recently, I guess, and totally turned yourself around from a year ago, while I'm . . ." He didn't bother to finish his thought.

I sat back in my chair. I couldn't hold it in any longer — I had to ask. I pulled in a long breath.

"What's really going on with you, Ben? I mean, I know it's been a rough time, of course it has, but . . . is that *all* it is? It feels almost like you're sadder than you were even six months ago."

Ben nodded slowly. "Yeah. I guess I don't feel much better. Plus, things are always tough for me between plays, when I don't know where the next production is coming from. And I haven't done much new writing in the past year." He shrugged, with a nonchalance that was unconvincing. "It's just a whole bunch of stuff at once." He clearly wanted this conversation to be over.

"Okay," I replied. I cast a glance over to Bonnie, who gave a quick nod of encouragement to keep pushing. I knew what Bonnie wanted me to ask. "And . . . how's Amber? I was kind of expecting to see her here this weekend."

Ben's sandy eyebrows furrowed. "She's at a spa getaway. And . . . I guess I didn't tell her I was coming over here. I needed a bit of time apart, and away from our place."

"Everything okay between you?" I asked, as Bonnie quietly stood and collected dishes to take into the kitchen. That was Bonnie's way of bowing out of the conversation, knowing Ben would probably be more open with me on our own. Ben always seemed to struggle with admitting hard stuff to his sister, especially since their parents had been gone. Like he had to be the strong one — even though he didn't have to, at all.

Ben passed Bonnie his plate, and waited until she'd gone inside before responding. "Honestly, I'm not sure. I guess we're at a crossroads. She's made it clear she wants to get married and move out of the loft, buy a big house together, and start having kids in the next two years." He screwed up his face and ran a hand through his thick mop of hair. "And we've been together four years — we just had an anniversary, and she obviously totally thought I was going to propose at dinner, and she was basically furious that I didn't. We had a big fight about it when we got home. And I get why she's mad. It's been four years, all of our mid- to late twenties, and that's the time you find your life partner, right?" He shook his head, and turned his body to face me. "But I just don't know."

His eyes looked sadder than I'd ever seen them — except at the funeral.

I spoke quietly. "So, what do you think is holding you back? I mean, Amber's not *wrong* — you've been together all this time, and it's reasonable for her to expect the next step."

Ben grimaced. "If I'm being really honest — and this is just between you and me — she's . . . well. She's very ambitious, as you know, and entrepreneurial, and driven. I've always admired that. But her cosmetics line isn't doing well, and she comes from a stay-at-home-mom kind of family. Her mom was an Avon rep, supplying the local housewives with products while raising kids in the suburbs, total *Edward Scissorhands* kind of deal." He paused. "I can't help feel like Amber's just been waiting all this time to see if I'll be able to support her in the way she wants to live. Like, a fancy house in the suburbs — kinda like this one, but, you know, with more bling — and she can stay home with the kids." He sighed. "And I guess she's been waiting to see if I would become successful enough as a playwright, because God knows we weren't expecting any inheritance for another thirty years, right? But since we came into the money, she's suddenly all about buying the big house and having her fairy-tale wedding. She even told me in our fight that it doesn't matter if I don't write any more plays — I can afford not to." He shook his head. "I'm starting to wonder if she really loves me for *me*, or the life I can offer. But I don't want *that* life. Just because I also want a family one day doesn't mean I want that life in the suburbs. With her."

Ben turned back to face the lake, his cheeks flushing. "Man, she'd be furious if she knew I was talking to you about this."

I raised an eyebrow. "Yeah, she probably would. She's never liked me."

Ben chuckled quietly. "She doesn't get how I could be close with my sister's best friend. That's weird for her. She doesn't have any male friends herself, not one. Or even that many friends at all. She's become kind of reliant on me." His smile faded. "So . . . what do I do? Marry her, knowing we've been a pretty good cohabiting team over the past four years, and we could both do worse, and just find a compromise for our lifestyle and dreams? Or break up, which means I've wasted the best years of her life and she'll have to start from scratch? We both will."

I placed my hand on Ben's bare arm, my heart aching for him. I couldn't stand to see him in pain. "I'm so sorry you're going through this. It's gotta be tough. But I remember a piece of advice you had to give me, years ago, when I was in a relationship with Chris and I wasn't feeling it. You've got to do what's truly right for both of you, no matter how hard."

Ben nodded, and gave me a sad half-smile. "Yeah. I'm so wise." He placed a hand over mine, just for a moment, then stood. "Thanks, Mill. You're the best."

JUNE, THIS YEAR

"Morning, honey."

Stephen is in bed beside me, in our little apartment in Aurora.

Not a dream, then. I really made it to this life, with Stephen. The life I've been looking for.

He grins at me. "Sleep well? I made some coffee — I'll get you some."

I smile back at him, sleepily, pushing my hair out of my eyes. "Thanks."

He bounds out of bed with enthusiasm, his bare butt pale and skinny and cute, and pulls on a pair of boxer briefs.

Oh God. Is he a *morning* person?

This could be a problem. But, I mean, not an insurmountable one.

I sit up in bed, propping myself up with pillows, and check the phone on the nightstand beside me. Not yet a quarter after seven on a Saturday morning. I'm usually asleep until around ten, having been out late with Bonnie, and sometimes Ben, on a Friday night.

I guess I live a more wholesome life with Stephen. He's a clean-living Catholic guy, after all.

The coffee had better be good, otherwise I'm gonna have to make some changes around here.

Stephen returns with a disappointingly small mug, which he hands to me proudly, and then reaches into the closet for some clothes.

"I'm heading out for a run along the river — my usual route." He pulls on track pants and a T-shirt. "You have your lazy Saturday snooze, and I'll see you for breakfast. I'll grab some of those muffins on the way back." He kisses me on the forehead.

"Thanks. I feel like a bagel, though — could you pick up a couple of sesame ones, please?" I take a sip of coffee. "Have a nice run."

Ugh, no, the coffee is definitely sub-par. I'll have to do something about that. And since when did I stop taking sugar?

Stephen pauses by the bedroom door, pushing his heels into a pair of sneakers. "Bagels? You know I can't eat those. I don't even want gluten crumbs in our toaster, honey. I thought we agreed, no gluten in the house at all?"

Shit, that's right — Stephen is strictly gluten-free. I've noticed this at work and when we're out for client dinners, but it's never affected me before, of course. Now I'll have to be more careful, since I'm living with the guy.

I shake my head. "Sorry, wasn't thinking. Gluten-free muffins are fine."

He gives me a quizzical look, one eyebrow raised. "You okay? You haven't seemed like yourself ever since you got back from the meeting with the Gellermans. I'll have to catch up with you about that."

"Sure. I'm fine. Don't worry about me. You go enjoy your run."

Crap. Not only has he noticed I'm "not myself" — although, like Chris in a former life, he has no idea how literally that is true — but he also wants me to get him up to speed on some client meeting. One that I have absolutely no idea about.

I'm also still hazy on how it works when I'm entering a new universe — how the new world's version of me somehow knows I'm coming, so their body is ready for me to somehow jump into. I'm not even sure that Stephen's real Millie would have *been* at that client meeting yesterday. After all, her car was there for me at the Lake Bluff house. Her body, with its cardigan and shorts outfit, was there for me to quantum-leap into.

In my weird, futuristic San Francisco life, Evan had told me that I — or *his* Millie, anyways — had left in some kind of trance-like state, as if compelled to go. The women at the housing shelter had said something similar, too. I have to assume that's what happens each time I switch universes. That the Millie in that world always manages to get to Lake Bluff that Friday evening, no matter where she was previously, so that I'm able to try on her life for a while.

Or, in this case, in my new reality with Stephen, to live this new life on a permanent basis.

Well, if I'm here indefinitely, I'd better figure out how to be Stephen's wife and what I'm supposed to know. With Stephen now out of the house, it's a good time to poke around and see what I can learn.

I abandon the mug of bitter coffee, pull on a robe from the closet, and examine the other clothes. Nice enough . . . definitely a little more conservative and cutesy than my usual wardrobe. Lots of cotton tops with floral prints, several cardigans and cute little sweaters, some capri pants and cotton shorts. A distinct lack of the faded jeans and well-worn graphic T-shirts that I usually favor.

I step into the little foyer and through the door behind the kitchen wall, which last night I discovered led to a small interior bathroom. There's a light above a mirrored cabinet, which contains many mysterious prescription pill bottles with "*STEPHEN POWELL — TWO PER DAY*" printed on them. Probably more digestive health stuff. Various, but limited, cosmetics for me, and other standard fare of toothpaste and dental floss.

Below the sink is a larger cabinet full of rolled-up, clean bath towels — a stack of yellow on the left, blue on the right — and spare toilet paper. I pull a thick yellow towel out to use for my shower, since I have no idea which of the two currently hanging towels belongs to me. As I pull it out, a large, floral make-up bag falls forward — it must've been tucked down behind the towels. I unzip the bag, then realize why it might've been there — it's full of sanitary pads and tampons. Maybe there isn't room for all those in the tiny cabinet above the sink. Or maybe the Millie in this life doesn't want Stephen looking at tampons every time he takes his morning prescription.

A bit prim, but whatever.

I dig through the make-up bag, and my fingertip catches on the edge of a blister packet of pills.

Contraceptive pills, with the blisters marked for the day of the week.

The next one to be taken is marked as a Saturday — today. That makes sense. Okay, so this Millie is on the pill. That's fine — I've been on the pill myself, in the past, although I gave up a couple years ago as it was giving me breakouts and I wasn't sleeping with anyone anyways.

I open the Saturday blister, swallow the pill down with a splash of water, then examine my face in the mirror. My dark hair is much the same as it usually is, a just-below-chin-length bob, cut maybe a little squarer at the back. My weight is about the same as in my regular life, my skin clear and blemish-free.

Hold up.

Last night after sex, Stephen had said, "Maybe it'll work this time. Lift your legs up. Keep it in."

We're trying for a baby.

So why is this Millie *on the pill*?

Plus, Stephen is a devout Catholic. I'm pretty sure he doesn't believe in using contraception.

Is that why the bag is tucked down the back of the cabinet, behind the yellow towels? Is Millie hiding her contraception from Stephen?

Is she *lying* to him about wanting a child? Letting him believe they're trying, while secretly taking the pill to prevent it?

I tuck the pills back into the bottom of the make-up bag, and hide the bag back behind the towels. I turn on the shower, hang the robe up on a hook, and step under the hot water, my mind racing.

Crap. This isn't good. There are potentially some serious cracks in this marriage, and I've only been here twelve hours. Who knows what else I'll find? There may be a host of other secrets I don't know about, and may not find any physical evidence of, so I'll never be any the wiser.

Although, maybe that's a good thing? Maybe it's a fresh start for them, with me being innocent of any and all of this Millie's secrets. Maybe I can be an honest, true wife to him going forward.

But then, that would surely involve throwing away that pill packet, and genuinely trying for a baby.

I shudder slightly, despite the warmth of the water running over my body. Absolutely no way. I'm not ready for a child. I may be thirty, but I'm just not there yet. It's not that I'd never want children, it's just that I haven't really had any long-term relationships, and it's so hard to imagine raising a child with someone, when I don't even know how to live with a partner yet.

And, now that I'm here and really thinking about it, it's kinda tough to imagine co-parenting with Stephen. He's a wonderful guy — warm, and kind, and thoughtful, and incredibly smart. But he's also a *lot* more traditional than I am. I've noticed in my regular life, with Stephen as a colleague, that he's very much the breadwinner while his wife Eve stays home with the kids. That's not what I'd want. I have a career that's important to me, and I don't subscribe to such traditional gender roles.

Maybe I can talk to Stephen about not wanting a child yet. Needing to spend more time being married, just us, before we go down that road. But then again, that would mean me taking contraception, which I'm almost certain he would *not* be on board with.

How did Stephen and I find our way to marriage, with such different viewpoints? It's a wonder we worked out at all.

I rinse off, step out of the shower, and head into the bedroom to get dressed. I pick out a sleeveless button-down with a yellow stripe, and put on the same white cotton shorts as yesterday. I haven't looked out of the window yet, but I already know this Saturday is a hot day. I've lived it several times at this point.

Although, not that many. It's a bit strange how relatively few lives I had to live, to find the one I was looking for with Stephen. Given that there are infinite possibilities. Infinite chances.

It's almost *too* easy.

After dressing, and throwing yesterday's clothes into a laundry bin inside the closet — no sign of a washing machine anywhere, though, and *please* don't tell me it's a shared laundry room — I poke around some more. The nightstand drawers yield no further secrets — no sex toys or lube, no well-thumbed erotic fiction — and the kitchen cabinets are equally anti-climactic. Very few spices or seasonings — I remember now that Stephen doesn't like spicy foods — and a fairly dull selection of canned soups, tuna, chickpeas, and lentils. The fridge bears the rest of last night's dinner in its oven dish, a lot of salad ingredients, a carton of eggs, margarine, several cans of seltzer, a block of mild cheddar, and a large carton of lactose-free milk.

Pretty pedestrian ingredients, compared with my usual love of spicy and interesting cuisine — instilled in me through the years by both Bonnie and Ben. I recall one Friday evening, maybe six months after graduation, at the Lake Bluff house when Bonnie was on her way back from her course in the city, the Masons still alive then but away for the weekend, Amber busy doing something else, and Ben and I were cooking dinner for the three of us. He had taught me that night to be adventurous with the chicken stir-fry we were making, liberally adding chili flakes and cumin without measurement, tasting along the way, him feeding huge spoonfuls of it into my mouth, me laughing through giant, hot mouthfuls.

A pang of nostalgia ripples through me, making my shoulders heave. I miss those nights. The ones with just me, Ben, and Bonnie. My favorite people.

I haven't Googled them yet in this world. I need to figure out what they're doing, who they're with, if we're still close. I won't like this Stephen reality as much if I'm not spending quality time with my people.

I make a green tea in the kitchen, given the poor coffee situation, and take my phone over to the couch. Out of the window, the sun is glittering on the river, twelve stories below me. Aurora is spread far and wide — a low-rise, low-density city with some greenery punctuating the buildings.

I turn to LinkedIn on the cellphone, and type in "Bonnie Mason." Okay, so she has her design store and consultancy in this life — that's great news. That *should* mean that we're still good friends, given that my encouragement seems to have been a significant factor in her opening the business. I check Instagram, and her page looks much as it does in my life, including some very similar posts to the ones I have recently helped her with. Despite the relative shortage of photos of us together, it looks like we're still friends, at least, and I'm still helping with marketing her business.

I blow out a breath of relief that I hadn't realized I was holding in.

Now, Ben.

Like Bonnie, Ben's online presence is largely as I remember. Playwright-director, living in downtown Chicago. Successful, celebrated. Seems to be single, although he doesn't have much of a personal social media presence, so it's hard to tell. There's the same article on him in a local arts magazine that he had in my original life, with the same beautiful black-and-white side-profile shot of his face filling the entire first page of the digital edition. His blond beard is a little longer than usual in that photo, and he's wearing a black turtleneck — every inch the hot young theater director.

I'd teased him about it at the time. "You'll be in one of those Chicago's Sexiest Bachelors lists next," I'd said, giving him back the thick print edition they'd sent him. He had raised an eyebrow at me, saying nothing. Just looking at me. I had wondered, in that moment, what he was thinking — before Bonnie burst in and started exclaiming about the article.

So, Bonnie and Ben both seem normal in this life, and I'm still hanging out with Bonnie, at least sometimes. That's good, right?

Why, then, do I feel weirdly disappointed?

Had I been looking for a reason for something to be badly wrong in this world? Am I subconsciously looking for an out?

There's no doubt I'm rattled over the whole trying-for-a-baby-but-taking-the-pill thing.

And, yes, by the encroaching suspicion that the *fantasy* of being Stephen's wife may be more romantic than the *reality* of being married to a conservative, religious man with digestive problems.

No time to dwell on that right now. He'll be back in fifteen, and I still haven't figured out any of the work stuff that I know he wants to catch up on over breakfast. I guess we're still colleagues at Magnolia? Maybe we work from home some days, given that the commute would be kinda long each day. In my reality, Magnolia has been giving us the option of hybrid work since the pandemic, so that's probably true here, too.

I check my own LinkedIn career profile . . . and the difference is *shocking*. No work at Magnolia, at all. After graduation from Northwestern, there's a couple of two-year stints at advertising agencies I recognize the names of. But, for the past four years, my profile reads, "Co-founder and COO, Powell MacKenzie LLC — a digital marketing agency."

My own agency, with Stephen. We have our own marketing business together.

I click through to the company's website, which has a slick, professional home page with an interactive grid of images and client logos. Mostly company names I don't recognize, lots that look like Aurora-based restaurants or local sports clubs. A couple of business names that ring a faint bell, like Gellerman's, a family-run construction company outside Chicago that I've seen on housing development signs. A solid portfolio — definitely enough for a small, successful marketing agency.

I click through to "Our Team" where the page has a grid of four headshots — Stephen's first, as CEO, then mine, as the slightly inferior COO, which rankles slightly. Below us are two faces I don't recognize. Someone called Emma Robson, digital marketing specialist, and an older guy called Randy Jones, CFO and office manager. Looks like we're a small and scrappy team. The company's address is listed as in Aurora, although not this home address, so I look it up in Google maps. It's in a low-rise business park about three miles away — presumably we rent a workspace there. Kind of dull looking, but practical, and probably affordable for such a small business.

Okay, then. This is my life. Living here and working with Stephen — probably a lot of driving around to visit with locally based clients, with the Aurora office as a practical base. Occasional visits and girls' nights with Bonnie; holidays with Stephen's family.

A solid, well-defined, stable life.

Maybe a little dull?

Aside from the secret contraception, of course. That adds a frisson of excitement. It could be that Stephen's Millie is feeling a little bored, or trapped, or something, and needs to keep hold of some semblance of freedom in the only way she knows how.

But, let's not forget, this *is* the life I was looking for. Right? The one I was dreaming of, where Stephen and I are together, unencumbered? No life could ever be perfect, and this is the life I said I wanted.

All I have to do is . . . live it.

* * *

A week gone.

A week as Stephen's wife. Living with him in our little apartment. Going to work with him in our little agency in a mediocre business-park office. Having to figure out, without being able to ask any questions, what's going on with our client accounts and marketing campaigns. Fortunately, I already know very well how Stephen works, and both he and I are meticulous in record keeping and calendar planning, so that adjustment has been easier than expected.

Much less easy, in terms of adjustment, has been living such a quiet life, with pretty much only Stephen for company, in this small city. Eating simple meals together at the dining table. No alcohol on weeknights — a rule I unwittingly broke when I poured us both wine on Monday evening after we'd spent the Juneteenth day off with his sister and her family. Nice, wholesome people. *Very* religious.

And a week — well, three instances — of okay, but kinda disappointing sex.

It's only been seven days in this life and already, if I'm *really* honest with myself, I'm kind of bored.

Maybe I can text Bonnie and see if she is free to hang out tonight. Maybe even Ben, too.

Would that be weird?

The click of the front door opening, and Stephen's light footsteps in the foyer after his Saturday morning run. Like clockwork, every day without fail — leaving at seven fifteen sharp, back on the dot of eight am.

I smile at him from my seat on the small living room loveseat, where I've been scrolling through Instagram. "Good run?"

"Great," he replies, kicking off his shoes. "It's getting hotter out there. You eaten breakfast yet?"

It's just turned eight a.m. on a Saturday morning — I'm barely awake, and it's a miracle that I'm dressed.

"Not yet," I reply. "I was waiting for you. You want me to scramble some eggs?"

"That'd be great — I'm starving. I'm really sweaty, but do you mind if I don't shower until after breakfast? I'll make us some coffee."

I wince at the thought of Stephen's terrible coffee. "You go ahead and make some for you. I'm fine. I'll do the eggs."

I make us both scrambled eggs and toast some sorry-looking breakfast muffins, thankful there is at least cheese to grate over the top. Stephen, who is lactose-intolerant, doesn't take any cheese, and eyes my generous grating with an eyebrow-raise that looks like judgment. We sit down at the table and I dig in as Stephen clears this throat, somewhat performatively.

"Millie, I need to talk to you about the meeting with the Gellermans last week," he says, his tone surprisingly serious.

Oh crap, right. The meeting I was supposed to report back to Stephen about, which took place last Friday, just before I arrived. I've been avoiding the topic, as I have no idea what happened at that meeting. Fortunately, I haven't had to explain until this moment, as we were so busy with other accounts all week. I'd been hoping Stephen would forget to follow up entirely.

"I had a pretty surprising email from Mike Gellerman late yesterday," Stephen continues. "He asked if you were feeling better this week, and whether we could reschedule. So, while I was out just now, I called him to ask what he was talking about. He said that about ten minutes into last Friday's meeting, when Bunny was explaining about the new lot parcels, you just got up without a word, walked out of their boardroom, and never came back. Without saying that something had come up, or that you had to leave, or anything. And you didn't answer when they called your cell." He shakes his head and picks up his coffee, his eggs getting cold in front of him. "What in the world *happened*, Mill? And why didn't you tell me?"

My stomach drops. Yep, that about tracks. This world's version of me, in a fugue state, compelled to get to Lake Bluff on a Friday afternoon for no apparent reason.

Not exactly something I can explain to Stephen.

"Right, I was going to tell you about that — I totally forgot to mention it," I lie, flustered. "Uh, yeah, I sat down with them but I was . . . suddenly feeling really ill. I had to get up real quick and find the bathroom — I couldn't even talk without risking vomiting across the boardroom table. I was, uh, really sick. Then I was too embarrassed to return, I just got in the car and drove away." I shake my head, feigning remorse. "I feel awful about it. I should've emailed this week to apologize to them, and told you about it, but we were so busy, I totally forgot. But I'll apologize. I'll send them some wine, or something."

Stephen sighs, heavily. "Well, okay. Don't send wine, though — remember Bunny is a recovering alcoholic?" His expression softens. "I'm sorry you were feeling so bad, though. Were you really sick in their bathroom? I wonder if it was a sketchy sandwich from that new café we tried that day." He reaches to pick up his fork, but then stops, his hand hovering mid-air. "Wait. Do you think . . . ?" He looks at me expectantly. "Could you be . . . pregnant?"

Shit, I didn't think this lie through.

"Oh, no, I don't think so," I reply hurriedly. "I'd know. Probably the sandwich."

He nods, disappointed, and finally digs into his slightly congealed eggs. "I figured that sandwich shop wasn't great. I'm sorry."

God, I can't stand lying to this man, and now he's the one apologizing to me. "No, *I'm* sorry. It was still very unprofessional of me, and I should have told the Gellermans before I left."

"They'll be fine — they were just worried about you," he replies, giving me a forgiving smile, which gradually slips as his brow creases. "But then . . . how come you were late home that night, if you left the meeting so early? I had assumed they had kept you late."

Jeez, this guy doesn't miss a thing.

"Oh, right. Yeah, I, uh, was still feeling ill while driving, so I pulled over and spent a while sitting in a park, until I felt better. It took some time for the nausea to pass. And it was such a warm afternoon, I just chilled there for a while.

I'd turned my phone off for the meeting, so I guess I never heard Mike's calls."

Ugh. These lies upon lies are making me feel genuinely nauseated. I push my plate away, my breakfast only half eaten.

Stephen nods, sympathetically, and then surprises me by chuckling. "I'm surprised you were so energetic when you got in that evening, after that experience."

Yeah, my story really isn't adding up. I'd all but ripped his clothes off when I got to the apartment for the first time.

"Me, too," I reply, laughing to cover up the moment. "I guess you just do it for me, no matter what. You always did."

He finishes a mouthful of food with a slight head shake. "Oh, I don't know about that. You gotta admit it took a while at Northwestern, after you joined the Astrophysics Society, before you liked me in a romantic way. You were too obsessed with that sleazy theater professor for anyone else to get a look in your freshman year."

I grimace. That sounds about right. And it's useful information — so, Stephen and I got together in my second year, after an affair with Rufus that sounds like it ended earlier than in my version. And before Stephen would've met Eve, his wife in my reality.

I met him first, as I've wished so many times that I had. But it's not feeling like I thought it would.

I tilt my head at him. "Yeah, but I saw sense in the end, didn't I?"

Stephen gets up to clear our plates. "Thank goodness you did. Okay, I'm taking a shower."

I clean up the kitchen while Stephen showers, my stomach tumbling with discomfort. And, if I'm honest, disappointment. In this life, and in myself, for lying so much to Stephen, and for not being able to enjoy being with him as much as I should.

The truth is, in the week that's passed, my attraction to Stephen has taken something of a nosedive. Sure, I've had a massive crush on him all the years we've been working together in my regular life, at Magnolia — but the truth is, he wasn't available to me in that life. It's very easy to romanticize the idea of a relationship you tell yourself you want, but know will never happen. It's a whole different ballgame to actually live the banal day-to-day of life with that person.

Be careful what you wish for, I guess.

Stephen emerges with a puff of steam from the bathroom behind the wall of kitchen cabinets, where I'm stacking dishes into the dishwasher. He's dressed in nothing but a blue towel around his waist, his chest pale but flushed red in patches from the hot water, his hair wet. And his face a strange, sickly white.

He holds something up.

"Do you want to tell me what the hell this is?" His voice is dark and low, his normally blue eyes stormy.

In his hand, the packet of contraceptive pills I found last weekend, and have been taking daily ever since.

Shit.

"Stephen," I reply, my stomach churning. "I wanted to talk to you about this."

He throws them down onto the counter. "What the fuck, Millie? You're taking the *pill* and not telling me? I think we're trying for a baby, while you're *deliberately* perverting the natural course of our bodies, not to mention *God's will*, to prevent it from happening? What possible excuse can you have?"

He's furious. I've never seen him like this, nor ever heard him curse before — not even when he lost it once at Magnolia, after a client pulled their account and he had to scrap months of work.

I hold my hands up, then reach for him. "Stephen, I'm sor—"

"No," he interjects, backing away. His towel is about to drop, and he grabs onto it. "I don't want to hear some . . . some *bull* right now, Millie. I honestly can't even look at you." He shakes his head, his brow deeply furrowed. "I need to think for a second, okay?"

"Okay, I totally get it," I reply hurriedly, holding up my hands in defense once more. "We can talk later. I'll go out for a walk, give you some space. We'll talk later, okay?"

He says nothing in reply, just gives me a single nod, and turns to march into the bedroom, slamming the door behind him.

My pulse racing, I grab my phone from the table and my purse from the foyer, and slip on my sandals. I pick up the keys from the console, and quietly let myself out of the door.

Where to go? I still don't know Aurora very well. But I had spotted a café a few blocks away, when I was out grocery shopping earlier this week, and it looked okay.

I find the café on my phone's map, and walk the three blocks to it. Inside, it's buzzing with friends and couples having Saturday morning brunch, and seems like a fun community space. Probably the nicest place I've seen since I arrived in this town. I order a double-shot latte and a blueberry scone, with lots of gluten to spite Stephen, and take it to a small metal table in the sunshine outside.

This is not good.

This is not how my new, perfect life with Stephen was supposed to go.

The two of us at opposite ends of the religious spectrum, disagreeing over whether to have children, me lying to him about using contraception, us working together on small-fry accounts in a mediocre business park. Living in Aurora, which has nowhere near the buzz or culture of Chicago, which I've been craving all week.

Maybe the Millie in this life is okay with a quieter life, and has grown into it, having been with Stephen since university. But I'm not that girl. I'm a different Millie now, and I don't think I can change myself enough to fit into this world. Not even for a much-longed-for relationship with Stephen.

Oh, God.

I know what that means.

I *knew* finding this life had been too easy.

EARLY MARCH, FOUR YEARS AGO

I examined my reflection critically, attempting to smooth down the lapels of my new green Zara blazer, which had gotten a little bunched up in delivery. Damn. I wished I'd thought to press it before my first day, and now it was too late. Hopefully nobody would notice the creases.

The blazer wasn't the only thing looking less than perfect. Sure, I'd washed and blow-dried my hair, so that was pretty sleek — especially given I'd had my trademark bob re-trimmed just a week ago. But all the make-up in the world wasn't hiding my tired, puffy eyes.

It had been a mistake to go out with Bonnie on a Sunday night, right before the first day of a new job. Now, after maybe four hours' sleep with several interruptions due to acidic indigestion from the wine we had drunk, I had to make a good impression with my new boss and colleagues at Magnolia Marketing + Advertising.

I shrugged on my wool coat, as it was still cold this early in March, slid my office shoes into my tote bag, and shoved my feet into sneakers for the walk to the office. It was only twenty minutes away, and I still didn't own a car. It was hardly worth it, living so centrally in Chicago.

At the sleek, high-rise building, I paused to switch into my pumps before entering the triple-height lobby. This place was even nicer than the offices of Mason, Saunders, & Rose, where I'd spent the last two years working in the Marketing department. I'd only been working at the architectural firm for three weeks when Frank and Ange Mason died, and I'd felt an obligation to his memory to stay there, even though the work wasn't exactly what I was looking for. When the remaining partners had finally changed the firm's name to Saunders, Rose, & Associates, it seemed like a sign that I could move on.

After three months of applying to agencies, I'd landed the role of Digital Strategist at Magnolia, which had a roster of exciting clients — fashion and sportswear brands among them. I'd be writing digital advertising copy, blog content, and marketing emails, and working with a colleague on online ad campaigns. It was the perfect step to developing a great marketing career, and being able to write every day, work with interesting people, and earn enough to rent a studio alone in downtown Chicago.

I would finally be fully self-sufficient, with a good life I had earned on my own merit, despite the hand I'd been dealt with my crappy family background.

I'd be a *real* person.

I emerged from the elevator on the forty-sixth floor. Through many layers of glass doors, I could already tell that the views were going to be spectacular from up here. I pushed through the first set of doors into reception. "Hi, I'm Millie MacKenzie," I told the cute young woman at the desk — a redhead, a few years younger than me. "It's my first day here. I was told to report to reception and Erin would come meet me."

The receptionist beamed. "Millie! We've been looking forward to you joining us. I'll let Erin know you're here." She picked up the phone. "I'm Shira, by the way."

"Thanks, Shira. It's nice to meet you." I stepped away from the glass counter and sat on a white leather chair in a chrome frame. I'd been here only twice before, for the interviews with my new boss, Erin, who had been joined for the second round by two more senior people whose names I'd already forgotten. There would be a lot of new names and faces to remember.

Erin emerged into reception, her blonde hair in a tight ponytail, hand outstretched in greeting. "Millie. Welcome to MMA. Come, let's get you settled."

The next two hours were a whirlwind of office information, a tour of MMA's half of the forty-sixth floor, a meeting with Human Resources, and countless introductions. Eventually, I settled at my desk, which was in an open-plan area close to another person's spot. That person wasn't at their seat, but the desk, in contrast to my blank canvas, was a mess of documentation, sticky notes, and several pinned-up photos of a wedding.

"That's Stephen's desk," Erin said, noticing my gaze. "He's our Senior Campaign Strategist, so you'll be working together on a lot of digital marketing projects. But he also gets pulled into a lot of the sportswear advertising campaigns, so he'll have other stuff going on too. He's a great guy — I'm sure you'll hit it off. He's with a client this morning, but he'll be in soon. Here, let me show you the login, and then I gotta get to a Zoom meeting. I'll take you for lunch later."

I was pretty quick to get oriented with my laptop and shared document system — thank goodness for those two years at Frank's firm, which had given me the grounding I needed. It was 12:30 already, and I was considering putting my head round Erin's internal office door to see if she was ready for lunch, when a tall, slim guy with dark-framed glasses marched into the desk pod and slung a shoulder bag onto the desk chair next to mine.

"Oh, hey," he said, not looking at me, leaning over to switch on his computer. "You must be the new digital strategist. It's . . . Mel, right?" He turned to me, shrugging off his coat. When his eyes met mine, he gave me a wide smile.

Cute. Kind of nerdy, but in a geek-chic kind of way.

I smiled back at him. "Millie. Hi. Nice to meet you. Stephen?"

"Sorry . . . Millie. And yeah, I'm Stephen." He pulled some documents out of his canvas bag, dropped the bag on the floor, and sat, swiveling his chair to face mine. "I'm the . . ."

He trailed off, an unreadable expression on his face.

"Wait a minute," he added, his tone a notch higher. "Don't I *know* you?"

Now that I was really looking at the guy, he seemed incredibly familiar too. Where *did* I know him from? Hold on . . . it was coming . . .

Stephen held up a finger, then pointed it at me. "You were at Northwestern, right? You were, like, a year or two behind me in the Comms program?"

That was it! Yes, I'd seen Stephen around campus, and maybe even been to a couple of the same lectures. And I'd met him during Orientation Week, hadn't I?

Oh yeah. It was all coming back.

I'd thought he was attractive then, too.

"Right!" I exclaimed. "Yeah, that's me. I spoke to you once, as well, at Student Club Week. Didn't you . . . run some kind of astronomy club, or something?"

Stephen chuckled, rubbing his brown hair. "Astrophysics. Yeah, I was president of the astrophysics club in my sophomore and junior years. I'd been really torn about whether to study sciences or comms, so I compromised by doing the comms program, but hanging out with science geeks in my spare time."

I laughed. "I *remember* now. You were trying to get me to join the club, and you got me talking about parallel universes and such, but your club night clashed with the a cappella group, so I didn't."

Stephen slapped his forehead. "Yes! I took my girlfriend to see one of the shows your group sang in, and I remembered you at the time. A production of *West Side Story*. It was awesome. That was only our second date." His bright blue eyes flickered to the pinned photos on his side of the half-wall dividing our desk pods.

"Yeah, the theater group never had enough singers for their musicals, so our vocal group was usually brought in to help the chorus," I replied, following his gaze. The photos were of Stephen and a pretty young Asian woman — him in a sharp suit, her in a strapless wedding gown, its train cascading around her feet and down the steps of some formal building. In another, they were kissing on a manicured lawn.

I glanced down at Stephen's left hand. On his ring finger sat a very shiny gold wedding band, slightly too big.

Dammit.

The good ones were *always* already taken.

I forced the brightness back into my face, and nodded towards the photos. "Is that the same girlfriend?"

Stephen nodded. "Eve. Yeah, we met senior year at Northwestern, been together ever since. We just got married this last Christmas."

"Congratulations."

"Thanks. She's the best."

Erin came up behind us, pulling on an expensive-looking cream wool coat. "I'm glad you two are getting to know each other. Ready for lunch, Millie?" I nodded. "Stephen, you're welcome to join."

Stephen was already typing away at his keyboard. "Thanks, but you two go ahead. I gotta catch up after this morning."

Erin led me out into the elevator lobby. "There's a great place around the corner we always take clients to. Think of it as a welcome-to-MMA treat."

"Awesome," I replied. "I'm starving."

I stepped into the elevator, holding the doors back for Erin. Honestly, it was probably a good thing Stephen was already married. It wouldn't be a good look to get involved with my closest colleague — the guy I had to sit right next to, for God's sake, and work with on multiple projects. What a disaster if a relationship like that didn't work out. And either way, as a new staff member, I wouldn't want to be the subject of office gossip, which getting involved with a coworker would definitely prompt. It was much more important that I did well at my new job and was respected, so I could develop in my career.

No, it was absolutely for the best that Stephen was not an option, romance-wise.

Now I would just have to find a way to *not* develop a massive crush on him.

JUNE, THIS YEAR

I may have made a mistake with this latest reset.

I've just been chased out of the Lake Bluff house by a burly guy with tattoos and a bushy beard, who had been making toast in the kitchen as I crept upstairs. I sprinted out of the front door in record time, despite being in impractical shoes. I practically vaulted over the gate in the driveway, not even waiting for the gate to release, before running at least three blocks to ensure he didn't catch me. Fortunately, the guy wasn't in great shape and had given up halfway down the first street.

Panting heavily, I squat on the grass verge several blocks away, wondering what kind of world I've landed myself in this time.

The life with Stephen had been a disappointment, undeniably. And, after he got so furious with me for being on the pill, I couldn't face him. I never even went back to our apartment. I just finished my coffee and scone, got into my car in the apartment building's garage, and drove all the way to Lake Bluff to reset.

I had written other Millie a quick note to let her know what had happened, but I couldn't do any more than that. Let Stephen's Millie deal with the fallout of her contraceptive-taking deception — I was outta there.

Now, it's been a full half-hour of recovering my breath and waiting it out, before I dare creep back towards the house to try to find the car matching the keys in my pocket, with a brand logo I don't recognize. I aim it at every car in the street, and around the corner, and several other streets, but there is no telltale unlocking beep. These keys do not belong to any of these cars.

Research on my strange, small cellphone gives me a clue as to why. I don't live in the Chicago area, in this new life. I don't even live in the States.

I live in *Paris*.

Apparently with some guy named Grégoire, who is impossibly handsome and appears to be a highly successful photographer. There's a link on his Instagram page to a gallery website, which is full of black-and-white photos, three times larger-than-life nude studies. An arched back, a pert nipple in profile, a bent leg with the curve of a thigh, a lower back with seated buttocks and matching dimples like a cello.

All of *me*.

Jesus.

How did Paris Me even get to Lake Bluff, or know to do so? I have to assume that — like San Francisco Millie — she got on a plane in her fugue state, flew all the way from Paris to Chicago, then got an Uber to Lake Bluff, since there's no car matching this set of keys.

What to do?

Okay, regroup, *think*.

That bagel place in Lake Forest where Bonnie's store should be, where the lady was kind to me when I was homeless, is a good place to hang out until I figure out this life. Unless Bonnie's store is there, in this life. Presumably not, given I'm a Millie who lives in Paris and there's no evidence of me and Bonnie being friends.

I walk the few miles to Lake Forest's commercial center, my feet blistering painfully in the expensive-looking, pointed-toe ankle boots I'm wearing. It's hot, as usual — is it going to be hot every day for the rest of my lives? — and I slip off my inappropriate navy designer blazer and fling it over my shoulder. I'm also in tailored pants and a white collared shirt, and carrying a Chanel purse.

The compact cellphone inside it is pinging constantly, but I ignore it until I can sit down. I reach the bagel place, which is again the bagel place. The sweet lady behind the counter doesn't recognize me, and I order a smoked salmon bagel and a Diet Coke, leaving her a massive tip to thank her for her help in another universe. I have no idea when this body last ate, but I know it's dinnertime in this world, and this time I'm hungry.

I sit at the same table as when I was homeless, now dressed so very differently, and pull out the phone. There is a stream of texts from Grégoire, all in French, going backwards until forever, but with dozens in the past twenty-four hours alone. Presumably because his Millie-muse went into a fugue state and has gone missing.

> *Ma chérie, où es-tu? Tu me manques, et je m'inquiète telle-ment pour toi. Texte-moi, s'il te plaît!*

Shame I don't speak a word of French.

I let my eyes wander through the words, hoping Paris Millie's French-reading ability will somehow kick in, like a muscle memory . . . but nothing. Except the last phrase is "text me, please," I think?

I do my usual search of social profiles. Okay, I'm a moody Paris model, Bonnie works at City Hall, Ben is a stage manager again, and I'm definitely not friends with them at all. We've obviously never met. I didn't even go to Northwestern — I moved to Paris right after high school.

That was brave of me.

It doesn't even look like I made the trip where I met Bonnie in Santa Monica — we've never even met. Nor have I ever met Ben, or Stephen. My life is wildly different — in many ways even more different than sci-fi San Francisco world. At least there, I still knew Bonnie.

213

And that's something new about this reality. I mean, in every other life I've encountered so far, I've *known* Bonnie and Ben, even if I'm no longer close with them. But this Millie doesn't know them at all, never met them, and presumably has never had any reason to go to the Masons' Lake Bluff before. Yet evidently, she still was somehow compelled to get herself here, all the way from Paris, in order for me to be able to jump into this body and try on her life.

Evan, and the women at the shelter, told me about the trance state I left in, which must be when the compulsion to get to Lake Bluff comes over me. But of course, I'll never really know how that happens. Christ, I'll never understand how *any* of this is happening.

So, what to do now? I've always wanted to go to Paris, of course, and it seems I have the money to do so. I could fly to Paris, just like I did to San Francisco, and try on a life with sexy Grégoire for a while.

But then again, I'm clearly expected to be fluent in French, and things could go very badly wrong for me when I can't speak to him or any of my people there.

Not appealing.

I guess I'd better bail on this one right out of the gate. Paris Me doesn't seem to need my help, with her blown-up naked body being celebrated in the Parisian art scene — which I presume she's okay with, given that *I* wouldn't mind — and with her hot French boyfriend. No, Millie-in-Paris — you're on your own.

I'll give it a while, so the coast is clear with the scary tattooed guy at the house, and go back and reset once more.

Au revoir, Grégoire.

* * *

The house is quiet this time around. Lived-in, kinda messy in fact, but empty. Whoever lives here is not home right now. I can take my time as I let myself out of the front, and the driveway is empty of cars. Halfway down the block, a beat-up black Ford responds to the keys I found in a canvas tote bag I'm carrying, which is full of junk. The interior of the car is equally disorganized, with mud in the footwell and candy wrappers between the seats.

I've got an old-model iPhone in the bag, which doesn't seem to have any home address pre-programmed into it. But the calendar app has Friday night blocked off for the Va-Va-Voom Diner, seven to eleven pm, for some reason. It's now nearly six-thirty, so whoever I'm supposed to be meeting, I'll be late for, since it's an hour's drive from here.

At least I know where the Va-Va-Voom Diner is. Bonnie, Ben, and I used to go there all the time — it was right by Frank Mason's office building, where I worked before Magnolia. The same diner where the Masons were supposed to pick us up, the night of their accident. I haven't been back since, as I'll always associate it with that terrible night.

But now, I'm expected there. And I guess I may as well figure out something about this life, and see if it's a good one. Given that there's no evidence that I'll ever get back to my original life.

And who knows who might be waiting for me at that diner?

An image springs to mind of Ben, flirting with Greta behind the counter, his smile wide, his laugh generous.

What are he and Bonnie doing in this life? A quick search, as I sit in the Ford's driver seat, shows me that he's doing well in theater, and Bonnie has her usual store in Lake Forest. Social media reveals that we're friends again, seemingly as much as we ever were. Maybe this is a really great life for me here.

Part of me is tempted to drive right to Bonnie's store and spend the evening with her. But her store will be closed by now, and I don't know where she lives, considering the Lake Bluff house is clearly now occupied by someone who isn't Bonnie.

Plus I'm late to meet someone at Va-Va-Voom, and I don't think I can resist the temptation to see who it is. If they're still waiting for me.

I drive the hour into the city, in the opposite direction to the heaving rush of evening traffic escaping downtown for the long weekend, and park up near the diner. I'm wearing scruffy jeans and a washed-out old T-shirt, which doesn't seem suitable for a date, but I don't have much choice. I check my reflection in the sun-visor mirror, add a slick of slightly garish lipstick from the tote bag, and rake my fingers through my hair. That will have to be good enough. It's not like we're meeting at a fancy restaurant.

I lock up the car, cross the street, and step through the diner's door, which tinkles its little bell. The sound brings back another Ben moment — him on a winter night, pulling a beanie off his head, stamping snow off his boots. That same night.

I scan the room for who I might be meeting, trying to ignore the fact that it's Ben's dark-blond head I'm searching for. But he's not here, and nor is anyone else I recognize. Greta, the owner, comes out of the kitchen to the area behind the counter.

"Millie! For God's sake, there you are." She reaches behind her, grabs a striped apron off a hook, and throws it at me. Hard. I catch it, clutching it against me in surprise. "You're a half-hour late *again*, and we've been slammed since seven." She holds up a hand before I can say anything. "Just get started. And I'm sorry, but I'm docking your pay this time. Table five needs clearing."

I'm not *meeting* someone here. I *work* here.

Shit.

I mean, the diner is great. But *why* do I work here? And what happened to my marketing career?

No time to think about that now. Greta is mad as hell, and I don't want to mess this up for Diner Millie, so I'd better work this shift and figure it out later.

Thankfully, I know the diner well, and I've worked casual café jobs in the past, during summer breaks, so I'm a confident server, and know how to work this kind of cash register.

"Sorry, Greta," I tell her with a sheepish grimace. I tie on the apron and get to clearing table five. Greta and I work together in surprising harmony and, although I stumble a few times with not knowing how the kitchen staff like their order tickets or where the new ketchup is stored, it's a busy shift and she doesn't seem to notice my failings.

As she's closing out the cash register, I apologize to her again for my lateness.

"It's okay, Millie," she replies, softer this time. "I know things have been hard for you since you lost your mom. But try not to let it happen again, okay?"

Lost my mom?

I nod, my tongue suddenly thick in my mouth. I don't even trust my voice to thank Greta as she hands me a week's paycheck, with a tear-off attachment bearing my name and what must be my home address. My fingers trembling, I remove my apron and put it in the laundry bin, and slip out without another word.

In the beat-up Ford, which now makes more sense given the pitiful paycheck I was just given, I pause and take a few deep breaths before I can think about driving.

Lost my mom.

This is a world where I work in a diner, and not only are the Masons still presumably dead, given the state of their house, but my own mother is gone, too. And I've no idea how.

I don't think I'm going to like this new reality very much.

Then again, maybe there will never be a reality that I like very much. I know that life is never going to be perfect, and I'm not looking for perfection. I swear, I'm not. But finding one that I like as much as my original life is surely possible.

Exhausted, I drive to the address on my paycheck, which is a slightly shabby bungalow in Galewood, a half-hour west of downtown. I unlock the front door, expecting to find the place empty, but two young women around my age are in the living room, watching TV.

I have absolutely zero idea who they are.

217

"Hey, Mill. There's still some gelato in the freezer, if you want some," the platinum blonde one says.

"Uh, thanks, I'm good," I reply.

Oh God.

Roommates.

Not only do I have a low-paying job and an apparently deceased mother, but also roommates in a crappy house.

What the hell happened to me? And what happened to *Mom*?

I turn a corner into a cramped corridor with four doors. One of these will presumably be my bedroom, but which? It'd be really weird if I walked into one of my roommates' bedrooms — plus who knows who else might be here?

I open one door to find a shabby bathroom that doesn't look like it's been cleaned in months. Terrific.

Saving me from a potential bedroom faux-pas, the two girls in the living room turn off the TV, and walk past me into two separate rooms.

"Night, Mill," says the redhead, pausing at her bedroom door. "Gimme a shout when you're out of the bathroom."

"Oh. You can have it now — go ahead," I reply, stepping away from the bathroom door. At least I know now which my room is. I'll crash here for a night, then head back up to Lake Bluff in the morning. I'm way too exhausted from my diner shift to make the long drive tonight.

Not to mention, way too tired from all the universe jumping.

I step inside the fourth door, closing it with some trepidation behind me. It's a messier room than I'd normally have, but I soon spot some recognizable stuff among the junk — clothes I've had for a long time, and some shoes, plus the crystal pendant Mom gave me when I turned eighteen is hanging over the mirror. Yes, it's definitely my room. There's a laptop on the desk, which unlocks with my usual password, and reveals a manuscript for a novel that I appear to be writing.

What a cliché I am — working in a diner while I try to write a book.

The manuscript is unfinished, in chunks of disconnected pieces, with no coherent plot outline. It seems semi-autobiographical, about a young woman in Chicago whose mother has just died of skin cancer. The young woman, Mandy, is beating herself up about whether she could have helped her survive if she'd been around early enough to encourage her mom to seek treatment.

Maybe I can help Diner Millie with a few ideas for her story while I'm here. After all, I know a thing or two about what-if scenarios.

I spend the next hour writing out plot ideas for different life paths for Mandy, which Diner Millie will be surprised to find when she's back in her body, and crawl into the unmade bed. Tomorrow, I'll wake up early and drive straight back to Lake Bluff to reset, so that Millie can be back in time for her afternoon shift at the diner.

Thank you, next.

* * *

This is a freaky one. Like, *way* too meta.

Only last night, I was helping Diner Millie out with ideas for alternate scenarios for her novel's character to save her dying mother. And today, I've just stepped into a world where *I* appear to be saving my dying mother.

My phone's home GPS is set to Indianapolis, where Mom lives in my usual life. From what I can figure out, through researching a backlog of emails on this phone, I recently quit my job, which was my regular one at Magnolia, to go live with and care for Mom as she goes through treatment for skin cancer, which seemed to be what she died of in the previous life I found myself in.

Okay, good. At least in this world Mom found the cancer in time to treat it, and I'm helping her through it. Great. I'm sure it's a bonding experience for us, and hopefully it all works out and she'll be okay this time.

Doesn't sound like a ton of fun, though, and I'm not sure there's anything I can help out with in this world, that

Cancer-Care Millie isn't already doing. Probably best to get that version of Millie back to her sick mother, asap.

The Lake Bluff house is unoccupied again, so I can go right back in and reset without even interacting in this world.

Thank you, next.

* * *

This one appears more promising, at least to start with. I'm apparently living in New York, having left Chicago after Northwestern for an advertising job. I even remember applying for that New York job in my real life, right after graduating, while I was on vacation with the Masons in Oregon — but in my world I didn't get the job.

I've always loved New York, so I take the opportunity to try on this seemingly glamorous version of my life, and hop on the first flight from O'Hare to JFK. My social media reveals that I'm still in touch with Bonnie, but barely see her, now that we live in different cities. Instead, I'm living with a slightly older guy, who seems around forty but is really cute — a video game designer called Peter. As soon as I get to his — our — cool Brooklyn apartment, I feel like a ridiculous imposter and wonder what the hell I'm doing there. Who am I trying to kid? This isn't my life.

What's more, over dinner, he keeps mentioning another woman, some ex-girlfriend of his called Josie. He's clearly still totally hung up on her, and not really into me at all.

I sleep in his bed with him that night, but we don't have sex, even though he's really attractive and funny. I write a note on Brooklyn Millie's phone saying "Leave Peter — he's still in love with his ex Josie" and slip out of the apartment when Peter is out getting Saturday morning coffee and pastries. I get an expensive Uber to JFK and wait for the next flight to Chicago.

What the hell am I *doing* with all these lives?

Next, I guess.

* * *

This time, my research tells me I'm living in Dublin, having never even gone to Northwestern, and for some unfathomable reason having agreed to go live with my father in Ireland right after high school. My job appears to be in a Dublin employee management firm doing office admin and a bit of PR, and I have a ruddy-faced boyfriend called Liam. I've never met Bonnie, or Ben.

I really do *not* have the energy to go to Dublin myself, and figure out if that is a worthwhile life. It's too damn far, and it doesn't look that exciting.

I'm exhausted.

There's no car for me outside the Lake Bluff house gates, and I don't even make it halfway down the street before turning around to go back and reset.

Next.

* * *

In this one, things seem really good at first. It could be the one.

Frank and Ange Mason are alive and well in the kitchen as I tread upstairs from the basement, surprising them with my unexpected arrival. Bonnie comes over for dinner, and it turns out we share a house in Lake Forest, which Bonnie has decorated gorgeously. We also work together, as co-founders of a wildly successful TikTok and Twitch lifestyle and home decor brand that has over a million followers. Ben is doing well in the theater, but is married to somebody called Camila, who I see on Instagram is chestnut-haired, gorgeous, tall, possibly Brazilian, and I instantly hate her.

And what's weird is, the Masons and Bonnie are being especially kind to me tonight, constantly asking me how I'm doing and if I'm feeling okay.

It turns out I'm being stalked by an obsessive fan of our Twitch stream, on which I have presented many episodes of our home decor show, and we've had to call the cops several times *and* get a restraining order. Further probing reveals that he now knows where Bonnie and I live, and he was trying to get into my bedroom window last night, and we had to call 911 again.

Nope.

This is theoretically a pretty good version of my life, with the Masons and Bonnie so close to me, and a fun job to do, but it's a hard pass on being Stalker-Victim Millie. Plus I've no idea what I could do to help her.

And the Camila thing is really bugging me.

"Home isn't a place, it's a feeling," the Masons' poster in the basement still reads. But this world doesn't *feel* right.

Next.

* * *

I stand on the deck of the abandoned Lake Bluff house in the next universe, researching my life.

It seems now I'm a novelist, a successful one this time — apparently living in *Rome*, of all places. Another city I've always wanted to visit, and another place I'm just too exhausted to attempt right now. I speak zero Italian, and I have no idea where in the city I live. My emails would probably tell me, if only I could read Italian. From social media, I seem to live alone and have no partner, and I'm not friends with Bonnie or Ben anymore, although I used to be. A hunt around in my emails digs up the last message Bonnie ever sent me, a few years ago, telling me she can never forgive me for using her parent's deadly car accident as inspiration for my bestselling family saga.

Novelist Millie in Rome sounds in some ways like an appealing version of the multiverse, but I can live without it, and I can't live without Bonnie.

I don't even make it out of the driveway this time.

* * *

This one, something bad is happening, and I have no idea what the hell is going on.

The house is occupied by somebody, but not the Masons or Bonnie, and it's empty right now. I pause in the foyer to check myself in the mirror. I have a massive, tender black eye, and a split bottom lip. My hair is shoulder length and uncombed.

I walk out of the house and exit the gate, nervous of what I'm going to find. There's no phone in any of my ripped jeans pockets, just some keys.

And, in my back pocket, a switchblade knife. Like, a *real switchblade* with the super-quick blade-release mechanism.

What the hell would I need *that* for?

I'm trying cars up and down the street with my keys, when a dark-haired guy with a mustache comes into view at the far end of the avenue.

"You fuckin' bitch!" he screams at me, and comes thundering down the pavement.

Holy *shit*.

I've got a decent head start on him, and take off running, back to the house. I fling myself over the gate, drop down onto the gravel drive, and I'm halfway down the side lawn by the time the guy is able to haul himself over the gate.

I waste no time, pulling the basement door to me with a hard whoosh.

In an instant, I'm gone from that world too, leaving the scary guy fifteen feet and a universe behind me.

I really hope Switchblade Millie is super tough and can handle that asshole.

Fuck.

* * *

It was bound to happen, at some point in my lives.

I'm a mother.

To a gorgeous, dimple-cheeked nugget of a baby girl, who looks from Instagram to be no more than five or six months.

Angie.

That's the baby's name, apparently. Same as Bonnie and Ben's late mom.

No sign of the father, whoever he is, being in the picture.

No sign of me still being friends with Bonnie or Ben in this life — no pictures of us together, or messages from either of them. Only my daughter's name is a clue that I once knew the Masons.

No sign of Frank and Angela being alive this time, or the house being occupied.

According to my email research, as I lean against the kitchen counter in the empty house, this world's Millie is on an extended maternity leave, for six months, from an admin job at a logistics company. Unpaid after the first six weeks, the company-issued emails tell me. But it looks like my dad is helping with funds for a while, and I've emailed him photos of the baby. A strange lack of correspondence with Mom, given I've just produced a granddaughter, so maybe something bad has happened there. Maybe she's dead, again.

I seriously contemplate resetting immediately, but a deep tug in my core compels me to go and meet the baby. At least spend some time with her.

I mean, how could I not?

This is my *daughter*.

In an aging white Ford Focus, I find my way "home" from Lake Bluff to a small first-floor apartment in a four-story building in Oak Park, a semi-urban western Chicago neighborhood. My phone, in a battered red case, is buzzing constantly as I drive, but I ignore it. Parking outside the apartment block, I use the largest key to get into the building, and see unit 1A immediately to my left. I push my way through a heavy front door with the smaller key, and step into a small, open-concept apartment.

A dark-haired, middle-aged woman is in the messy living space, holding and jiggling the baby, who is screaming with remarkable fury over the woman's shoulder.

The woman thrusts Angie at me, clearly furious herself, and I'm forced to drop my purse and grab the child.

"You *said* you wouldn't be long." Her voice is icy. "I fed her an hour ago, but she probably needs changing again, and she has terrible gas. Shit, you've been over *three hours*, Millie. What was so urgent that you couldn't call me back? I had to get Andre to cook for his brothers."

The woman yanks open the front door, and turns back to face me as I stand before her, in a foolish stupor, holding the baby awkwardly away from my body. She spits out, "That's the *last time* I watch her for you, Millie, I swear. And you still owe me for when I sat for her last week. You can put the cash under my door. And you *better* pay me the same rate for today, as well."

She slams the door behind her, and I can make out her footsteps stomping across the hallway's linoleum floor, and into the apartment opposite. Another door slam.

I pull the wailing baby close to me and jog her on my shoulder, like I've seen people do. She makes an unpleasant gurgling sound and promptly vomits a surprising amount of milky liquid onto the T-shirt I'm wearing. A Taylor Swift tour shirt, of all things.

The baby is still whimpering, a little less fiercely now, and I hold her up to look at her face. A fat tear has stuck on a cheek below the enormous, wet-lashed blue eyes that are staring at me.

She's beautiful. Even when crying, and with a dribble of milk on her chin.

"Angie," I whisper to her, softly. "Don't worry. It's me. Your mommy."

It's me.

And it's not me.

Can she tell?

We stare at each other for several minutes. Then Angie emits a long, low, wet fart.

"Ugh, baby!" The smell is hitting me. "Okay. That's fine. Totally fine. I've watched people change diapers. How hard can it be? Huh, Angie?"

It's hard.

Not so much the diapers, which come with instructions, but more the *wiping*. Then I think I'm supposed to do something with diaper cream, or powder or something, so I sprinkle a bit of powder on her skin and hope for the best.

At least now she's not crying.

I settle down on the slightly stained couch with her, cradling her head in the crook of my elbow. She's getting tired now. I pick up a baby book, and read a story about a giraffe to her, slowly and quietly. Her wide eyes flicker from time to time, then droop, and she's gone.

I stay up all night with baby Angie, holding her in my arms. Feeding her a couple more times, when she wakes and cries, with pre-prepared bottles from a half-empty fridge. Changing her three more times.

Not sleeping once myself. Just holding, feeding, rocking, staring, feeding, changing, rocking, staring. To be honest, I'm terrified something bad will happen to her on my watch. After all, I'm not used to taking care of a baby. I might do something wrong. If I fall asleep, I won't be able to see if something is wrong, or be able to save her.

After her fourth time waking and falling back asleep, I put her into the crib in the apartment's only bedroom, and lie in the twin bed beside her. But still I don't sleep.

I'm *nearly* dropping off, at around seven in the morning, when she wakes me with her whimpers again.

She's the sweetest, most beautiful thing I've ever seen. And I think I might die if I had to live like this.

In the small hours of the night, I had researched emergency daycares that were open on the weekend. There's one in Lincolnwood, right by highway 94 that leads back to Lake Bluff. It's expensive, but I need somewhere safe to leave the baby in the morning, and I clearly can't ask the neighbor.

Because I can't do it.

I can't live this life.

The baby is gorgeous, but she's not really *mine*, and it already seems incredibly hard to be a single mother with very little support. I'd need Bonnie, and Ben, and the Masons, and even my own mom, and all sorts of other people to help me. Not just some pissed-off neighbor.

At eight am, I get up, put on some clean clothes, feed the baby again, she throws up on me again, I change into new clean clothes, I change the baby's diaper and clothes, and we make it out of the house. It takes me another twenty minutes to figure out how to secure the infant car seat in the back of the car, but I get there. I drive to the daycare in Lincolnwood, and tell the person behind the desk — a woman younger than me with a name badge reading "Shelley" — that I'll be back by the end of the day. I add that she shouldn't get freaked out if I don't remember much, as I have memory issues. Shelley seems indifferent to this — as an emergency, indiscriminate daycare center, I'm sure she's seen much worse.

Before handing Angie over in her carrying cot, I kiss her on the top of her finely haired head, and she looks up at me with those huge eyes.

"Bye, baby girl," I tell her, surprising myself as my voice catches in my throat. "Mommy will be back to pick you up. I love you."

Driving away from her, heading back up to Lake Bluff, is the hardest it's been. Even harder than leaving Stephen. A lot harder. This time, the entire way, my vision is thick with tears and exhaustion.

I park outside the house, leave a long note on Mommy Millie's phone and a shorter paper one on her dash, and jump the gate into the empty driveway, the house shining bright in the midday sun.

I head for the lower side door, and tug it open.

The basement is dark, cold, and lonely.

AUGUST, TWO YEARS AGO

"That's our time for today, Millie. Just remember what we talked about last week, about self-worth. Keep setting aside time for writing, and keep your gratitude journal up. I really think it's helping."

"Thanks. I will."

I rose with a struggle from the too-deep armchair, and slung my jacket over my arm. It was roasting hot in Chicago, and I hadn't been able to wear my blazer at all today.

I paused by the office door. "See you next week," I said.

Nancy, my therapist, looked up from her notes and smiled. "Yes, same time."

I dodged a drawn-looking woman with a toddler in the narrow hallway outside, and pushed my way through the heavy exit door into the tree-lined street. It was now seven p.m., and it hadn't cooled off much in the hour I'd been inside, but at least this street was well shaded. The psychiatrist's office was on the main floor of a brownstone in Lincoln Park, a half-hour bus ride each way from my studio apartment.

I wasn't sure it was worth the travel, let alone the astronomical money I was paying for an hour's therapy each week. Had been for nearly two years now. I almost could've bought a used car with that money.

And the gratitude journal? A good practice, sure, but definitely *not* solving my issues.

I stood in direct sun at the unsheltered bus stop on the busy main street at the end of the avenue. With my pale Irish skin — thanks, Dad — I could burn easily, even at this time of the evening. But there was no shade to be found here.

I pulled my sunglasses out of my purse, and waited. The bus would be sweaty and crowded. Terrific. Maybe I *should* save my therapy money and get a crappy car next year instead.

It had seemed like a good idea when I started seeing Nancy, who was also Bonnie's therapist. Bonnie had been seeing Nancy ever since losing her parents, and Nancy had been an old friend of Angela and Frank Mason's. Nancy had definitely been helping Bonnie come to terms with her grief and self-blame. Bonnie had enthusiastically recommended her when I had admitted, two years ago, that I probably needed help with breaking patterns of behavior that I was repeating again and again.

Namely, falling for unavailable men.

After starting at Magnolia, two-and-a-bit-years ago now, it had taken . . . oh, about a week to develop a crush on Stephen. Within two months, after working closely together on a couple of campaigns, and bantering and laughing on a daily basis, it had become clear.

I had developed very strong feelings for a very attached man.

Again.

Dammit.

I'd confessed this to Bonnie over brunch one summer weekend, and Bonnie had promptly fished out Nancy's creased business card from the depths of her disorganized purse.

"You need to quit going after men who will never be yours, Mill," she'd said, her glare sterner than I'd ever seen, except for maybe that time when she found the texts from Rufus. "You seem to only fall for them when you *know* they won't fall for you. Or if you *do* date someone who is actually available to you, you reject them. But you deserve to fully love someone, and be fully loved back. You know that. For Chrissake, fix it." She'd pressed the card into my hand, and I knew I'd be in trouble if I didn't make an appointment.

Coming from a stoic Irish father who hadn't believed in talking about his feelings — right up to the day he'd walked out, totally blindsiding me — and a flighty, bohemian mother whose head was in the clouds, I hadn't been raised to express myself, or be vulnerable. But now, here I was, sharing my deepest thoughts with a total stranger on a weekly basis. For a lot of money.

"Why do *you* think you gravitate towards men who aren't available to you, or reject those who are, Millie?" This question, numerous times, from well-intentioned Nancy over the past couple of years.

Because I was afraid I would be left, like my mother was, so it was easier to fall in love with men who would never leave because they would never fully be with me. And anyone who *would* devote themselves to me felt clingy, because I'd never known an example of a healthy relationship.

Obviously.

I didn't need to pay anyone nearly two hundred bucks an hour to figure that out.

Mom had had a string of boyfriends after Dad had gone back to Ireland, and she'd rejected any and all who seemed like they might stick around. Instead, she had mooned after the emotionally unavailable ones, or those who had some kind of mental health issue. Sometimes both.

And Dad? I'd only seen him one time since he walked out when I was a teenager — I'd visited him for a few days in Dublin on my gap-year trip to Europe. Since then, I'd only spoken to him a handful of times on birthdays, and it had been more than five years since our last phone call. I'd heard Dad was in a new relationship now, and was acting stepfather to his new partner's twin boys. He clearly didn't need his adult daughter any more.

How was I supposed to be able to form healthy relationships, with those two as my models?

The only couple I'd ever looked up to had been Angela and Frank Mason, and they were gone forever.

I sighed. Still no sign of the bus, and the sun was scorching my bare arms. I slipped on my blazer for protection, even though it was way too hot for another layer.

Thoughts of Mom reminded me that it was probably time for our weekly check-in text. I'd gotten used to texting her on the bus ride home from therapy, when our relationship — even with all its flaws — was on the surface of my thoughts.

I fired off a text.

> *Hi Mom. Hope you're having a good week and your knee is feeling better. I'm doing fine and work is good. Planning a road trip to the Carolinas with Bon in September, so we'll try to swing by and see you for a night. I'll let you know. Take care, M xo*

Slipping my phone into my purse, I glanced up to see the Number 22 bus approaching. As I stepped on and tapped my pass against the reader, my phone dinged. That was quick. Mom usually didn't reply to my texts for hours, if not days. I squeezed through the cluster of passengers who were refusing to move along the bus, pulling my phone out of my purse.

It wasn't from Mom.

> *BEN CELL*
> *Hey, you free tonight? Got 2 tickets to Black Lotus at Howl at the Moon, starts 9pm. Wanna join? I can be there at 8 if yes. :)*

I smiled, and looked up to find myself inadvertently grinning at an old dude who was staring at me from his seat. I blushed, and turned my attention back to the text.

Ben, inviting me to a fun cover-band gig on a Thursday night. We'd seen the band together before, along with Bonnie and Amber, several years ago, and I'd said how much

I enjoyed them. He must've remembered. That was . . . thoughtful of him.

I checked the time. It was 7:32, so I had no time to go home and change first. But I could get off the bus at Grand and walk to the club, and be there just after eight. The satin camisole and tailored pants I was wearing weren't what I'd pick for a gig night, or a date night, but they'd be fine.

Not that it was in any way a *date* night. Not at all. It was only Ben, knowing that I'd probably be available, and the venue wasn't too far from my place. He'd probably bought the tickets for an actual date and the girl had canceled on him last minute, or something.

I replied to his text.

> *Sure, I'm game! I'm about a half-hour away from Howl right now, so I can meet you there just after 8. Thanks for thinking of me! Will be fun. See ya soon.*

I hit send, then instantly second-guessed my word choices. Was that text overly breezy? Like, trying-too-hard breezy? Why in the world had I written "ya" instead of "you"?

I shook my head, and put my phone back in my purse as the bus rattled along Clark. The air was ripe with stale sweat, and a massive guy beside me had his armpit dangerously close to my face. The old dude on the seat was still grinning at me, his teeth crooked and rakish. I gave him a small, thank-you-but-please-don't-talk-to-me smile back and tried to avoid further eye contact, while turning to dodge armpit guy as much as possible, for the rest of the ride.

Off the bus, it was finally cooling down on my walk to the bar, the tall buildings providing shade from the low sun. I made it to the venue and spotted Ben already inside, standing at a small high-top table near the side of the stage, wearing a close-fitting black T-shirt. He beckoned me over with a wave and that wide grin of his.

"Snagged the last table for us." He sipped on his beer, looking very proud of himself. He knew from experience how much I preferred having a table, even at a gig.

I laughed. "Thank you. I appreciate the effort." I ordered a vodka soda from the server. "This was a fun idea. Thanks for inviting me."

Ben nodded, still smiling. "Thanks for coming. I wasn't sure you would."

What did *that* mean?

"Well, I was free, and I'd just finished up with an appointment, so I was already out and heading downtown anyways," I replied, with a false nonchalance that Ben would see right through.

And why was I even trying to be nonchalant with him? It was just Ben.

But it was kind of different, being here with only him. We hadn't really spent that much time together just the two of us — it was almost always the three of us, with Bonnie. And sometimes four of us, before he split up with Amber.

It had taken Ben *way* too long to break things off with Amber. He and I had spoken about how his relationship was at a now-or-never crossroads, over that lunch with Bonnie on her deck, three years ago now. I'd gotten the distinct impression at the time that, because Amber was spoiling for a proposal ultimatum, he was going to end things with her imminently. But it had taken him nearly another two years to finally break up with her. He'd kept saying that he couldn't do it to her, as she'd invested so much time in him. But Bonnie and I knew he was never going to propose. So he'd only ended up wasting more of her time.

Not that I had a leg to stand on, when it came to relationship choices. I was two years into my job at Magnolia, and still swooning over Stephen.

I thanked the server for the ice-cold drink, and took a long sip. At least I was here, on a night out at a music venue, in the company of somebody who had always been there for me. And obviously it didn't hurt that Ben was a very good-looking and entertaining guy to be with. Even more entertaining recently, since he'd finally gotten out of that God-awful relationship.

We chatted easily about the play he was co-directing while writing his own next piece, and about my demanding work projects, and how proud we both were of Bonnie's success at the store. As the roadies were finishing the stage set-up, I was reminded of a thought I'd had on the bus.

"How did you have these tickets available so last minute, anyways?" I asked Ben. "Like, were you supposed to be going with someone else who canceled?" I lifted my glass and raised my eyebrow exaggeratedly at him over the rim. "Did you have a *date* bail on you? Be honest!"

A tiny crease appeared at the top of Ben's strong nose, and the corner of his lip turned down ever so slightly.

"No . . . no." He stopped, his gaze wandering to the stage. The roadie was high-fiving the band's charismatic frontman, who picked up an electric guitar as the other band members settled. "I, uh, bought them a few weeks ago. I remembered you liked—"

"Good evening, all you Howlers!" the singer yelled into the mic, interrupting Ben and drawing my attention back to the stage. "Oh yeah! Let's kick this off with a classic!"

The band soon got both of us bopping along, then fully dancing, bar stools pushed away, with song after song of Americana rock and old favorites. Ben was an easy mover, unselfconscious as he danced beside and occasionally with me, laughing as we amused each other with increasingly silly moves. Turned out Ben's Running Man was quite accomplished, and he looked genuinely impressed at my knee-knocking Charleston.

With the crowd singing along at the tops of their voices, and the stack of speakers probably only ten feet away, there was no chance of hearing my phone dinging. But it was lying face-up on the high-top beside us and, as the audience applauded, I glimpsed it flashing with a text notification.

Probably Mom, replying to my earlier message. With Ben having slipped out to the bathroom between songs, it wouldn't be rude to check.

Once again, though — not Mom. It was a text that had come in about a half-hour ago, but I'd been having such a good time, I hadn't noticed.

STEPHEN CELL [9:29PM]
SOS!! Emergency! Need to fix Actively online ad ASAP, the link is wrong. Do you have your laptop at home? I left mine in the office as I've been out with clients. Heading into office right now, but not sure how to fix it without your login. Can you do it from home, or come in?

My stomach performed a little flip.

Stephen needed me.

But also, crap. I was really having a good night with Ben, and it was nice to be on the arm of a man who made me feel good about myself, for once.

Still, this crisis wasn't an ideal situation. The Actively campaign had been set up in my account, so Stephen probably wouldn't be able to fix the link himself. He'd be almost at the office by now, which meant I'd have to go into the office, too. I'd also left my laptop at work, not wanting to haul it to my therapist's, so I couldn't fix the problem remotely.

> *Ugh, sorry. My laptop also in office, and I'm not home right now. I can be there in 20 and we can fix it. Sorry if your evening with the fam got ruined. See you at 10:20-ish.*

Ben wove his way through the crowd back to our table. "Who are you texting?" he shouted in my ear, over a rousing rendition of "Hotel California."

I turned to speak directly into his ear, our noses almost touching in the movement.

This was probably the closest, physically speaking, I'd ever gotten to Ben.

He smelled *really* good, this close.

"Work emergency — sorry. I gotta run to the office and meet a colleague to fix it." I pulled back and grimaced at him, waving my phone as if to prove the emergency was real.

Ben's face noticeably fell, and his mouth twisted in clear disappointment. He leaned in again. "That Stephen guy?" He drew back, assessing me for a response, his eyes flitting between each of mine.

My stomach did another somersault. I must've mentioned Stephen a few times over the past couple of years, for Ben to remember his name. But all I felt, under Ben's appraising gaze, was embarrassment.

I nodded, and gave an exaggerated whaddya-gonna-do shrug. Ben raised his eyebrows and parted his lips, like he was going to say something, then closed his mouth again. He looked hard at me once more — making some kind of decision.

Then he nodded, just once, slowly.

"See ya," he mouthed at me over the din.

He turned back to the performers before I could mouth anything back. Instead, I put my hand on his lower arm, just for a second, then grabbed my blazer off the bar stool and made my way outside into the warm night.

I rushed through the streets to the office, my stomach churning. I'd *had* to leave the gig — it was a work emergency. I hadn't had a choice.

Had I?

Well, maybe I could have texted Stephen my account login, so he could have fixed it himself. But that would have been a total cop-out, given Stephen was heading into the office at this time of night and he had a young family at home. It would be shitty of me to leave him to fix what was at least 50 percent my mistake.

So why did it feel even more disappointing to have left Ben standing alone in that bar?

JUNE, THIS YEAR

There's nothing at all in the basement this time, and the place is silent.

It's surprising how often this house is left empty and unloved — an ill-used second-home lake house, or some foreign owner's vacant investment. Such a shame.

I drag myself up the steps into the kitchen, exhaustion seeping into my bones. The main floor has been recently renovated, and has a strong fresh-paint smell, with bright white walls, and cellophane wrap still on the appliances. I let myself out of the kitchen door onto the warmth of the deck, checking my pockets once more for clues to my existence.

No keys, or wallet — just an iPhone in a plain black case.

I go straight to Instagram, where I'm in photos with a bunch of people I've never seen before, captioned with names I don't recognize. Nothing with Bonnie or Ben.

On LinkedIn, Bonnie is working at City Hall again, as she almost always seems to be in worlds where we're not friends.

But, weirdly, Ben has no LinkedIn profile at all. And he's never had other social profiles like Instagram, not in any of my worlds — being such a private person — so I can't look him up there.

I scroll through Bonnie's Instagram feed instead. Lots of photos of her with a dark-haired guy I don't know, so she seems to be in a steady relationship. But none with Ben — at all. That's weird. Maybe he moved away, in this life, and they don't see each other much anymore?

Scrolling further back, the images of the new guy disappear, and her posts are fairly infrequent. The further in the past they go, now eighteen months back, the more Bonnie's posts become moody lake and landscape shots, with captions about "healing" and "recovery." About the loss of her parents, maybe? But that was many years previously, even then.

Then I find it.

A photo of Ben, that gorgeous black-and-white one taken by the arts magazine a couple of years previously, and a caption that makes my heart stop.

> *"Dearest friends. For those of you who don't already know, I'm heartbroken to have to tell you that, tragically, I lost my brother Ben in a lighting-rig accident on March 5. As you know, our parents died a few years ago, and Ben was all the family I had left. He was the brightest of lights in an often dark world. Ben was brilliant, funny, talented, loving, and the best imaginable brother. To say that I'm devastated would be an understatement. But I feel grateful to have the love and support of so many of you, my wonderful friends, and plenty of help in taking on funeral arrangements. I hope you will join me in saying goodbye to Ben at a memorial event at The Lookingglass Theatre next week, March 18, at two p.m. Please don't send flowers but feel free to donate in Ben's name to one of the charities linked in my bio. Hugs to you all, Bonnie."*

No.

No, no, no, no, no, no, no.

Ben.

Ben is dead.

I slump against the wooden bar of the deck railing, staring out over Lake Michigan, but all I see is him. Different

238

phases of Ben, different versions of him, across all my lives, all flashing before me in a rapid silent movie. Playing guitar in the basement. Laughing with me on this deck over a thousand dinners. Teaching me to cook with abandon in Bonnie's kitchen. Strolling with me on Chicago's lakefront, too polite, no longer knowing me. Dancing with me to a cover band, knowing me so well. Being a brilliant theater director and playwright.

And in this world, he's *gone*.

I can barely breathe. Every fiber of my being feels like it's on fire.

Grief and horror overwhelm me in a wave that ripples up my body, from my toes to the top of my head.

I drag in a long, deep breath from the depths of my soul, pull back my shoulders, and emit a deafening primal scream across the lake.

It reverberates through the neighborhood around me, over the water, and throughout all the universes in which I have lived and have yet to live.

After, everything is still and quiet.

My body shudders, and my knees buckle beneath me. I crouch down on the decking, my head against the glass barrier, and let the sobs come. Once they start, there's no stopping my tears. They wrack my entire body, and I slump down onto the deck, arms wrapped around my knees. Every part of me is shaking.

And I let it happen. I let the grief consume me.

Grief at the thought of any world where Ben is gone. At the darkness of a universe where his light doesn't shine.

Grief from past lives, lost opportunities, missed chances. Sadness — and, yes, anger — at my parents for not showing me how to allow healthy love into my life. Frustration that no matter how many times I go through that fucking door, I can't seem to get it right — or let myself be satisfied with what I've got.

I weep, and weep, until it seems I have no more tears left.

Finally, eventually, my shuddering stops and I wipe my face on my sleeve. I heave myself to my feet on shaky legs, and try to calm myself with slow breaths once more.

At least one thing can comfort me. Something I can hold onto. A tiny light in the darkness.

The fact that it's only in *this* world that Ben is gone. This awful, nightmare world that's worse than any other I've found.

Because in every other life I've been in, he's been alive. So, presumably, if I reset yet again, he'll be alive again and this horror will be over.

Then that's what I'll have to do. I have no choice but to keep . . . flipping through lives, until I find one where Ben is alive — a life that's bearable. I need to be a lot less picky about what's good enough to stay for.

One thing seems clear, though, and that is that I'm probably never getting back to my original life. Not that it was perfect, anyways. But it was a good life, with Bonnie, and Ben, and my great job. And there *is* no perfect life. I know that. Life can never be perfect, and if I try to chase some kind of utopia, I'll be flipping through universes for eternity.

But the key to finding a good life is surely figuring out what I truly *want*.

Because I already found the life I *thought* I wanted, that life with Stephen, and I couldn't even stick that out. Clearly, it wasn't what I really wanted.

Not for real. Not forever.

So, what *do* I want?

Who do I want?

An image, the *same image* that keeps appearing in my mind's eye, over and over again, returns to me. Now, that picture is the only thing I can see as my gaze skims the blue of the water before me.

Ben, again. It's always Ben.

Ben, many years ago, young, beardless, shirtless, playing a Muse riff on guitar in the basement below where I'm standing right now.

240

And it's suddenly so easy.

I'm such a fucking idiot.

Of course.

Of *course* Ben's the one I want.

I *love* Ben.

I can't live in a world where he doesn't exist. In fact, I can't live in a world where he isn't in my life, close to me.

If I'm *really* honest, digging deep into my soul . . . I've loved Ben ever since I've known him. I just never consciously let myself look at him like that, or admitted to myself that's how I saw him. Because I loved Bonnie just as fiercely, in a different way, and it would be tough to be in love with her brother when she's like a sister to me. I could never bear to make her feel like a third wheel, or as though I wouldn't want her there. Because *of course* I also want her there.

And besides, I've never really known how Ben saw me, so it was always easier to pretend it wasn't a thing.

But, yeah, I've always adored Ben. Kind of worshiped him, even. He's *constantly* popping into my thoughts, and I dream about him more than anyone else. Not necessarily romantically — often he's just . . . there. Present. Fundamental. In my life, as a positive force, no matter what.

Plus, I've always hated his girlfriends, always been so jealous of them.

What's more, I think maybe, just *maybe*, he was jealous of my boyfriends, too.

There was that one night, a while back now, when I thought he maybe liked me as more than a friend. When we went out, just the two of us, to that gig downtown. Maybe something would have, could have, *should* have happened that night. But then Stephen had texted with a work emergency, and I let that get the best of me. I left Ben there at the bar, and I still remember the disappointment he tried to hide.

I really screwed up that night. I should have turned my phone off, and let Stephen deal with it. I should have stayed there with Ben.

But in truth, I didn't leave the bar just because Stephen texted. I hadn't admitted it to myself at the time, but I think I left because I got scared.

Because deep down, I knew if I let Ben kiss me, that'd be it. There would never be any going back from that.

If Ben were to kiss me, even once, I would be his forever.

No wonder I was scared that night. No wonder I messed up, and ran to Stephen. Stephen was a much safer option, because he was never going to be mine, and therefore could never really hurt me.

The only person who has ever had the power to truly break my heart, if he left me or rejected me, is Ben. *That's* why I never let myself think of him like that.

But, oh God, all that has changed now.

Now, he's *all* I want. Him, and of course my friendship with Bonnie. They're all I'll ever need. The rest of life — my career, my home, my relationship with my mother — I can figure those out as I go along.

I just need Ben, and Bonnie.

And they're not in this world with me.

I have to keep looking.

I can reset again, and maybe now I can get it right. Maybe now I know what I truly want, *who* I truly want, I'll have a chance at happiness.

I could search through more new universes, this time seeking a life that has just two things. My friendship with Bonnie, close and intact, and Ben, unmarried and available. In a world like that, I could at least tell him how I feel, and let the chips fall where they may. And if he said no, at least I'd have Bonnie.

There's the beginning of a plan, then. A way forward. In a universe where it seems I have nothing that I care about, it's something.

I wipe away the remnants of my tears.

Right back downstairs to the basement door, then?

That damn door.

Every time I've thought about that door, and wondered why *that particular door* seems to be my own personal portal to the multiverse, that memory of Ben has leaped into my mind.

It was the first time I ever saw him, when I first went through that door. That was the moment I met the man I now realize I love with every part of my soul.

It's so clear now that it's no coincidence it was the same door through which I went and first met Ben, that now takes me into infinite possible lives.

That moment was the big, defining incident of my life.

Maybe *Ben* has been the key to solving the riddle of the basement door all along.

Guess I'm about to find out.

JUNE, THIS YEAR

The basement is warm, well-lit, and fully furnished this time. Strains of music are coming from upstairs, along the creak of footsteps on the floorboards above me. The sliding doors in the basement that lead beneath the deck are slightly open, and a warm breeze drifts in.

There's someone here. I just need to creep upstairs and out the front before they notice me and I unwittingly scare them.

I scan the basement furniture as I tread lightly towards the stairs, and then stop in my tracks.

That couch.

That looks *very* much like the Masons' couch. As in, Frank and Angela's couch that they had in their basement for years, and is still in Bonnie's house in my original life. The very same one that Ben was playing guitar on, that first, pivotal moment.

Above it, the kitschy framed print hangs on the wall. "Home is not a place, but a feeling."

My entire body flushes with goosebumps.

This is clearly still a Mason house. Either Ange and Frank are alive once more, and they live here, or it's Bonnie's inherited house again.

Either way, if I'm also friends with Bonnie in this world, it would be a pretty great place to spend some time, after everything I've been through. Maybe even stay permanently. No matter what else is going on in that world — no matter who Ben might be with.

My heart soars, as a stray tear slips down my cheek. Even just to rest here for a while . . .

But this *might* also be a reality where I'm not friends with Bonnie, maybe even never was, and I might be a stranger to all of them. They might have no idea who I am. I need to tread very carefully here.

I reach to check my phone, and realize I'm clutching a bottle of red wine — the same brand I was bringing to Bonnie's place tonight, in my real life.

Okay. *That's* interesting.

I pat down my back pocket and find a phone in a palm-print case, just like the one I have in my own universe. I flick immediately to Instagram, and there's a ton of photos of me with Bonnie, and us together with Ben, at his play and at the lake — all scenes I recognize. I've posted these exact photos myself in my own life. That means I'm in a very similar life to my own.

I blow out a breath. Thank Christ.

Ben is alive.

And we're all close again here.

I examine the photos further. None of us with Frank or Angela, which must mean this is a world where they are gone once again. So this has to be Bonnie's house, and she's upstairs right now. Because someone is *definitely* in the kitchen.

I check my emails, and both my personal and work inboxes are exactly as I know them. That's even more reassuring. I still work at Magnolia, and on the same client accounts. I even have the eviction notice from my landlord from earlier today, so that's an issue in this world, too.

I turn to my text message app to investigate further, and my heart all but stops.

The most recent texts are *exactly* as I remember my last messages from my real life.

[6:16PM]
Should I get the dim sum ordered?

BONNIE CELL *[6:17PM]*
You know it! Get the usual, and add the new chicken pot stickers they have. Yum. :P

This seems like the *identical* situation I was in, back in my original life — about to spend the long weekend with Bonnie, starting with wine and takeout on the deck, and commiserating the loss of my cute apartment.

Am I *home*? Like, really home?

But I *can't* be, right?

Because in that world, in my own world, Bonnie was running late at the store and I was entering her totally empty house, having to let myself in through the basement. Whereas, in this universe, someone is walking around upstairs. So I guess this has to be a very similar, but ever-so-slightly different, version of my reality.

Maybe the *only* difference is that Bonnie's inventory isn't late in this world? And everything else could be identical. It's possible. In which case, this would be as good a reality as any to make my own, on a permanent basis. Still not truly *my home*, but definitely good enough.

Then again, it's also possible that this universe has all kinds of differences to mine that I just haven't discovered yet. It's likely, even. And it's also possible the person upstairs isn't even Bonnie at all, but a stranger, like maybe she has a boyfriend in this life, and I won't have any idea what to do — except run away again. Reset, *again*.

With my pulse pounding in my ears, I make my way quietly up into the kitchen — which is, as expected, painted in rich cream and fitted out in Bonnie's recent renovation style. The teal wireless speaker I bought her last Christmas is sitting incongruously on the quartz countertop, playing that Grace Potter song about stars.

But the kitchen is empty now, with the patio doors open and letting the evening breeze waft in. Whoever is here, they're now out on the deck.

I pause briefly as I catch myself in the mirror near Bonnie's dining table. I'm in the exact clothes I was wearing when I drove up to Bonnie's in my life — a Ramones T-shirt, denim shorts, and retro Converse sneakers. My hair is styled in its usual slightly wavy, slightly messy bob, with dark-bronze streaks at the front. I seem like . . . myself. Really like *me*, for the first time in many universes.

I look myself directly in the eyes, and take a deep, cleansing breath.

"Let's make this a good one," I say to the Millie in the mirror.

She stares back at me, and we nod slowly at each other.

I turn and step through the open sliding door onto the deck.

And it's neither Bonnie, nor a stranger, sitting at the patio table.

It's Ben.

He turns at the sound of my footfall, and smiles at me, warm and wide. My world falls away.

Oh my God.

I'm *so* in love with this man.

How in all the worlds did I never fully realize this before?

He's wearing the blue linen shirt I bought him a few years ago for his thirtieth birthday, the sleeves rolled up, his arms lightly muscled and tanned. His thick hair is the same as when I last saw it, and his dark-blond beard is neat and trim.

He's looking . . . incredible.

Ben lifts his brows at me, a little quizzically. "You okay? You look like you're about to have a heart attack."

Oh. I'm staring at him. Probably with an expression like an idiot.

"Uh, yeah. I'm fine. I guess I wasn't expecting to see you." I put down the wine I'm still holding, and grab onto the edge of the table for support.

He nods. "Yeah, I wasn't sure I'd make it this weekend. I had to figure out some stuff with Shelley — the woman I went on a few dates with? Anyways, we decided not to keep seeing each other. It just wasn't . . . gelling. But then I was at a loose end, and figured I'd head up to the house, since I knew you'd both be here." He grins at me. "Thanks for bringing the good red. Bonnie running late? I already opened her bottle of white."

My legs wobble underneath me, and I slide into a seat as he pours me a glass.

Ben is single again.

"Erm . . . yeah," I reply, awkwardly. "Yeah, she'll be on her way, any moment. Something about inventory at the store?" Crap, I really hope this is a world where she has her store, otherwise that will make zero sense.

Thankfully, Ben just nods and hands me the glass of cold wine. "I figured. We should get some food ordered, though, I'm starving."

My stomach responds to that comment with an audible growl.

Hold up.

Didn't I already order food? In my original life, before I stepped through the door, I had just ordered an unreasonable quantity of dim sum.

If that delivery is on its way in this world, that's *surely* proof that I'm really back.

I pull out my phone and check the delivery app.

The exact same order is showing, still due to arrive at 7:12 p.m.

With a slightly trembling hand, I show Ben the order on my phone. I don't trust my voice not to betray my emotions.

He nods approvingly, and huffs out a laugh. "Looks delicious. And good thing I'm here to help you out with that — it's enough for five people."

I smile back at him, but still can't find words to say anything aloud.

It's gradually sinking in.

This is my original life.

I'm really home.

Home isn't a place, it's a feeling.

And I feel, I *know*, with every part of my being, that I'm home. And that my ultimate realization of what I truly want in life is what brought me back to my real life.

I could cry with joy and relief, right here at the patio table, except I don't want to freak Ben out. So I control my threatening tears with slow breathing, and let the moment of overwhelm pass.

Ben doesn't seem to notice my emotional rollercoaster. He's leaning back in his chair, stemless glass in his hand, smiling gently at me.

"So, how've you been since I last saw you . . . when was it? Two weeks ago? Three? It's been a bit nuts, with the play."

I almost laugh at this question. How have I *been*?

Well, I've just spent what feels like weeks traveling through the multiverse of my alternate lives — being chased by crazy psychos, being a recovering addict, being a tech billionaire's partner, being a wife, being a mother . . . So, yeah, it's been kind of interesting. To say the least.

"Uh, yeah, fine, thanks," I stammer. "Things are . . . good. I've been . . . err . . ." I flip back mentally to my pre-multiverse week, which seems like a dozen lifetimes ago. "Oh, I've been working on a new ad campaign with Vici. Since, you know, you're such a fan of their sneakers, I figured you'd be into that."

Ben laughs and nods at his huge, Vici-clad feet through the glass top of the table. "That's awesome," he replies. "Very cool. I like their new high-tops, too. Gotta get some of those." He leans towards me, with an almost imperceptible wink. "What's a guy gotta do to get a friends and family discount?"

He has me laughing within moments, and we fall into conversation about our respective work projects and my eviction predicament, until the food arrives and Bonnie shows up minutes later. We take the dim sum onto the deck and dish out dumplings and spring rolls, along with the rest of the white wine.

I'm gradually beginning to relax, to feel fully like myself again.

Except, of course, for the fact that I *can't stop staring* at Ben. We keep catching each other's eyes. Smiling, a little shyly — at least on my part — at each other.

From his perspective, he's probably wondering what the hell has gotten into me and why I'm being so weird, and is just smiling to be kind about it.

Bonnie, of course, is utterly clueless as to my altered state. She's distracted herself, constantly checking her phone — she's getting texts from somebody. She suddenly turns to me, her eyes bright with excitement.

"It's Paul, the pastry chef. He wants to meet me at a bar in Lake Forest, like, in a half-hour. Would you hate me if I went? I really want to see him."

Her lovely face is lit up, as if from within. Wow, she really likes this Paul. I've rarely seen her like this over a guy.

I put my hand over hers and squeeze. "Go for it, honey. He's clearly no fool, since he texted you like he said he would. You wouldn't want to miss this chance, right? You look beautiful. You go get yours."

She beams at me, rises from her seat, and plants a kiss on my temple. "You're the best. I'll be back . . . well, I don't know when. Might be late . . . might be tomorrow morning . . ." She grimaces an apology, and blushes a little as Ben, protective big brother that he is, quirks an eyebrow at her.

"You spend as much time with Paul as you like," I tell her, firmly. "We have the whole rest of the long weekend to hang out. We won't wait up. How about, if you're not back by morning, we meet at Malone's for brunch tomorrow — say, eleven?"

"Perfect," Bonnie replies with a devilish grin. She turns to her brother. "You take care of our girl, you hear?"

Ben responds with a nod and a solemn salute.

As Bonnie excuses herself for her hot date, I help Ben clear the table and clean up the kitchen. We bring the last of the plates inside and load them into the dishwasher.

"Okay," Ben says, wiping his hands on a towel. "That's everything. I wouldn't mind another drink, though. Okay if we open your red?"

My stomach flips.

Me and Ben, totally alone, with no interruptions, on a warm evening?

This is it.

This has to be my moment, to tell him how I feel about him. This is *surely* what I came home to do.

I nod, my tongue suddenly thick in my mouth. My pulse is quickening again as I watch him tug the cork out of my bottle of Shiraz, looking all tall and sexy in his blue shirt.

But, despite my nerves, I know there's nothing that's going to stop me from spilling my heart out to him. I'll tell him that I'm in love with him, and risk everything. And even if he shoots me down, I know he'll be kind about it.

He hands me a glass. "Wanna go back outside?" he asks. "It's still plenty warm." His eyes are on mine, and they're smiling, crinkling slightly at the corners.

"Sure," I reply, my heart racing at his prolonged gaze. Something deep within me is tugging, pulling me toward him. Aching to touch him. To tell him.

But he turns away.

"I'll be out in a second — just need to plug my phone in somewhere. There are no goddam chargers in this house."

I nod, gathering myself, trying not to be disappointed in the loss of a moment that wasn't even a moment. Only in my own head.

Pull your shit together, Millie. You've known this guy for over a decade. You can wait a second to spill your deepest desires to him.

I step back out onto the deck, where the light is waning. The sky above the lake is a rich cobalt, fading to a lighter blue, then a streak of mint green before it hits the watery horizon. At the very highest point, in the deepest indigo, a few pinpricks of stars are pushing their way out.

I take a sip of the deep, fruity wine and place my glass on the flat ledge above the railing. A wishing rhyme my mother taught me as a child springs into my memory.

Mom. I hope she's doing okay. I'll go visit her, make things better between us. She's been a flawed mother, but she's a good person, and she's always loved me.

I mutter the rhyme into the warm evening, toward the heavens.

"Star light, star bright, first star I see tonight. I wish I may, I wish I might, have this wish I wish tonight."

What to wish for?

As a child, I was always wracked with anxiety about what to choose. But now, it's easy.

"I wish . . . to stay in *this* life, my true life, but also have Ben as my partner throughout it."

The highest, brightest star twinkles merrily back at me.

The patio door slides open behind me, and Ben's heavy footsteps tread across the deck.

I don't turn around — not yet.

He comes to the railing and stands beside me. For a moment he says nothing. He might be looking up at the stars, too.

Then he breaks the silence. "So, Millie . . . are you gonna tell me what's going on with you tonight?" He turns his body to face mine. "What's happening here?"

I shake my head, unable to turn to him just yet. He always could see right through me. My vision blurs with sudden tears, and a single sob shakes my frame.

Ben takes a step even closer. "Mill? What's the matter?"

He reaches out and gently rotates me by the shoulders so that I'm facing him. My tears are falling freely now, and he wipes one away with his thumb, tenderly, waiting for me to reply.

I don't even know if I can speak. I part my lips to attempt it, but nothing comes out, except another distorted sob.

"Mill . . . what is it?"

I try again, focusing on the deep indent at the base of his throat, aching to place the pad of my finger there, see how it fits. This time, the words come out all in a rush.

"I just . . . I'm in *love* with you, Ben. I'm crazy about you. I think I always have been. I don't know why I was such a fucking idiot before, because of *course* it was you." I screw up my face, embarrassment warming my damp cheeks, and push through. "But you were almost always with someone, and I've been such a mess, and God, I don't even know how *you* feel . . . I mean, this is probably not something you even want, but I just had to tell you anyways, and I hope it won't stop us being friends, because you mean so much . . ." I'm rambling, probably making no sense to him. I finally manage to lift my gaze to his, biting my lip, trying to gauge his response.

Ben's eyes search mine, and he gives a low, sudden chuckle that reverberates through my body. "Oh, thank *fuck*. I really don't know how much longer I was gonna be able to hold on." He laughs more freely, shaking his head in what looks like absolute relief. The smile fades, and he becomes tender again. With his hands still steadying my shoulders, his gaze roams my face, then meets mine once more. "I'm totally, *completely* in love with you, too, Mill. Have been for . . . well, for a while now. I just didn't think you felt the same."

Then he slides a hand around the nape of my neck, pushes me gently back against the railing, and lowers his mouth onto mine.

Oh my God.

Ben is kissing me.

He's really, *really* kissing me, with a passion and a desire and a love that I've never felt from anybody, not in my whole life. Not in any of my lives.

And I'm kissing him back, through my fresh tears, feverishly, desperately. My fingers are in his hair, as one strong arm pulls my slight frame into his firm body. His other hand is round the back of my head, his grip steady. His lips are warm and fruity, his beard soft on my chin.

His own kissing becomes more feverish, and his tongue explores my mouth — not too much, just gently probing. Promising. Good God, I've never wanted anyone this much, not even in the height of my infatuated lust for Rufus.

I run my hands under his loose shirt, where my palms meet firm, soft skin, and run them over his smooth back. His denim-clad thigh is starting to tease my legs apart, and I push my pelvis into it. Against my lower stomach, through his jeans, his erection has formed, large and hard. A burst of wetness between my thighs accompanies a dark tug of desire, and I let out a small, involuntary moan.

Jesus.

Ben moves his mouth down to my neck, grinding his body against mine, as the deck railing digs into my back. He's fully bending down now, being so much taller than me, and I'm straining on my tiptoes to give him access to my collarbone.

"Holy shit," he mutters into my clavicle, his voice lower and darker than I've ever heard it, "I need to get you into the guest room *right now*, before I fuck you right here on the deck and the neighbors hear us."

I laugh, suddenly, into his temple. "Great idea. Lead the way."

In a moment, he pulls back, contemplates me for a second, his eyes narrow and stormy, then grabs both wine glasses and turns on his heel. He hustles through the sliding door, straight through the kitchen, and into the beach-themed guest room off the foyer.

I follow him through, scurrying to match his pace, and shut the bedroom door behind me.

A low, bedside light is on, and the mood is cozy and inviting. Ben is sitting on the edge of the large bed, hurriedly pulling off his sneakers and socks.

"Lock the door, baby," he says.

Baby.

Is that what he'll call me?

I love it.

I turn, and flick the metal latch at the top of the door handle. Now we won't be disturbed, even if Bonnie makes it home tonight.

Now, Ben is all mine.

I kick off my sneakers, and step over to where he's sitting on the bed, standing directly in front of him. Without saying a word, I ease his legs apart with my knees, stepping closer as he grabs my butt cheeks and pulls me toward him. He presses his face in the dip between my small breasts, and lets out a sigh of what sounds like total contentment as I stroke his hair.

I run my fingernails lightly over his scalp, mussing up his dark-blond locks, and he's entranced for a moment. Then he lifts his face toward mine, gives me that wide smile, and this time it's my turn to lower my mouth onto his.

As he kisses me, his wide hands roam freely over my body — first my butt, with generous squeezes, then under my T-shirt and over my back, then moving them round to the front. He pauses in kissing me to lift my T-shirt up and over my shoulders, and I take it all the way off, dropping it on the floor. He kisses my breasts through the cotton of my turquoise bra, and my small nipples harden into aching points that he teases lightly with his teeth. He deftly unclasps my bra with one hand, pulls back for a second to let me drop it to the floor, then swiftly takes a breast into his mouth, sucking on it and swirling his tongue around the nipple, his fingers teasing my other breast at the same time.

I think I might die.

I'm *definitely* in my best life.

And it was my own life, all along.

Still driving me wild with his tongue, he unzips my denim shorts and pulls both them and my lace panties off in one swift, firm move.

I'm now totally naked in front of him, while he is still fully clothed.

I stand perfectly still as I let his eyes wander up and down my body. The way he's drinking me in tells me everything I need to know about how he feels.

He puts a hand in the small of my back, and pulls me close again, this time taking the other breast into his mouth. The other hand, he slips between my legs, into the moisture, and I gasp with the agonizing pleasure of his touch. He explores me with his fingers, rubbing faster and firmer in the perfect spot, his tongue and teeth still grazing my nipple, until my body buckles and I let out a muffled cry into his hair.

Ben catches me as I crumple, swinging me round and lowering me onto the bed, my butt on its edge, legs hanging off the side. I'm a limp mess, muscles quivering, my entire body a mass of nerve endings.

He gives me a lazy smile as he takes off his shirt, and steps out of his jeans and gray briefs. Finally, I get the full view of what a naked, turned-on Ben looks like. And it's the most beautiful thing I've ever seen.

Kneeling beside the bed, he wriggles his pelvis between my thighs, opening my legs so they are wide and unabashed. He runs his thumb down my wetness and positions himself, then pushes into me with a swift thrust that has me crying out with ecstasy. I grab a pillow from beside me to muffle my noises as he thrusts in and out, faster and faster, until I'm totally losing my mind. We both come at the same incandescent, climactic moment, eyes locked on each other's, and each laugh as he collapses, panting, on to my sweaty stomach.

"Holy mother of God," he says into my belly button. "That was incredible." He's still on his knees on the carpet. With some effort, he lifts himself onto the bed, and pulls me up with him so we're side by side on top of the covers. We've made kind of a mess of the bottom of the comforter, but neither of us cares. That's a Tomorrow Us problem.

He slides an arm under me, and I nestle into the crook of his shoulder, my naked body pressed against the side of him, skin on damp skin.

I'm overwhelmed with a million emotions, but I manage to speak, a little breathlessly. "Absolutely. Incredible. Honestly . . . the best of my life."

He laughs softly. "I always knew it would be, with us. If it ever finally happened."

I pull back a little to see his beautiful face. It's lit with a smile I've never seen on him before. Pure joy and contentment.

"So . . . you've been thinking about me like that for a *while*, huh?" I nudge him gently in the ribs with my elbow. "When did that start? Like, from the very beginning, or . . . ?"

Ben gazes up at the ceiling, remembering. He shakes his head slightly. "Not really . . . I mean, obviously we met and I thought you were totally gorgeous. You just *are* — that's an objective fact. So, sure, I had a bit of a crush, at least to begin with. But you were joined at the hip with my sister, and about to start Northwestern, and making all kinds of . . . questionable decisions. That ridiculous affair with Rufus, for one thing." He shudders. "And then I guess I got used to being around you just as a friend, plus I was with Amber for so long, trying to make that work. I just stopped myself from seeing you that way, I guess.

"But then, it was that night at Howl at the Moon? I was finally single again, and we'd been spending a bunch more time together, and my crush on you had come back in a big way. So I fully intended that night to be a date, but also didn't want to freak you out, so I just made it seem like a casual hang. And you walked in, so cool and chic in your office clothes, totally out of my league, and I was like, *fuck*, I'm so into this girl — it just hit me like a train. But at the same time I felt like, you know, I'm her best friend's brother, she's just here to see the band, she'll never see me that way. So then I'm already backing out of what I went there to do, and then the band started and we were dancing, so I felt kinda off the hook. But, also terrified it would be a missed opportunity. Then you got a text from work, a crisis to deal with, and I knew it was from that married guy you had a crush on, who I was wildly jealous of."

Ben emits a sudden laugh at his own memory, rocking both our bodies with its ripple. "And I totally chickened out. I just threw in the towel and said whatever, go do what you gotta do. But I knew, I *knew* I would be way better for you. Better than any of those guys you'd been with."

He pauses, with a slight shake of his head. "And ever since then, I've been torturing myself, wondering what would've happened if I'd asked you not to go — to stay with me. If I'd kissed you in that moment, right there in the bar."

Ben turns his face down to mine. His warm hazel eyes flit around my features, before settling on my gaze. "What about you?" he asks. "I mean, I never told you how I felt because you've always seemed like you were into someone else. When did it change for you?"

I hesitate, examining the golden fleck in his left iris. Now that he's mine, now that I've come home . . . maybe one day I'll be able to tell him what has happened to me. How I traveled through the multiverse of my realities, and how the journey made me realize how much I loved and wanted him. And how it was this epiphany that brought me home to him. It will sound utterly unbelievable, totally impossible, because of course, it is. But I'll find a way to make him believe me.

Just not tonight.

Tonight I just want to lie in his arms, and for us to love each other.

"It's been . . . more recent for me, in terms of realizing how I truly feel about you," I admit, tracing a finger over his chest. "I've been getting it all so, so wrong. But when I did finally figure it out, I realized I've felt this way for a long time. I just never really admitted it to myself, or let myself go there, because there's just so much more at *stake*, you know? Compared with any other guys. You and I, we're already so close, we already care about each other so much, and there's Bonnie to think about, and what if it didn't work out?" I grimace at the thought. "But I guess it all built up to the point of no return, where the balance was tipped, and it became worth risking everything to tell you. And to where I knew that if you felt the same, if we *did* get together, that would be . . . it. There's no question of it not working out. We already know each other well enough to know that."

Another smile tugs his lips wide, reaching his eyes. "Yep. You're definitely stuck with me." He kisses my forehead. "And sure, there's a lot at stake, that's true. But hey — at least you already know you'll be good buddies with your sister-in-law." He pauses, cringing a little. "I mean . . . you know . . . if we ever get married."

Married.

He's already thinking of *marrying* me.

I chuckle, and lift my face up to reassure him.

"Marriage is definitely something I want one day. And maybe not even that far off. I mean, you and I . . . we're not exactly starting from scratch here." I reach up to push back a thick lock of hair that has fallen over his brow. "And recently, I guess I've realized . . . not just how I feel about you, but also how important it is to fully live how we want to, while we can. Because it's also so fragile, you know? Life, I mean — not how I feel about you. More like, how tiny things can change the course of events so radically. We can never know how much time we have."

Ben nods, deliberate and thoughtful. "Yeah. And I feel like it's probably even more so for you, considering the chaos of your own upbringing, all the shit you've been through with your parents. I know we're the closest to a real family you've ever had."

He's right.

I lift my hand to run a fingernail lightly down his beard. "You and Bonnie, honestly, you two are my whole world. I mean, I love Mom, of course, but I see you two as my true family. You, in a life-partner way, and of course Bonnie is already a sister to me. No matter what I'm doing in my life, what my career is, where I'm living, that's incidental. You two are all that really matters."

We lie in silence for a moment, Ben gazing at the ceiling but seeing something else, me examining his strong profile, the line of his nose, the dip and curve of his mouth. His lips part as he searches for some words.

"I know life feels fragile, but . . . I dunno . . . I feel like you and I can definitely make it work. No matter what happens. And that we'd *always* have found a way to make it. Like, even if you hadn't had the courage to say anything to me tonight, about how you feel . . . We still would've gotten together, one way or another. Eventually. Somehow, you know?"

I smile, and lift my chin to brush my lips to his cheek. "I'm sure there are many universes in which we're together, all in slightly different ways. And many where we're not, through bad luck and circumstance. But definitely more where we are. Or will be, eventually. Somehow, like you say."

He turns his face down to mine. "You're so philosophical tonight." He pauses a second, then adds, "What was it that finally broke for you? What tipped the balance?"

I gaze into his eyes, behind which lie a whole galaxy of emotions.

"I've been on . . . a bit of a journey, recently. And I guess it's led me to recognize and respect that fragility. Realizing I don't want to live a life of what-ifs. What if I never told you how I felt, what if we never got together? What if we had never even met? What if we had totally different lives. It's all so circumstantial. I realized I had to *choose* my life, and be true to what I want. Grab it while there's the chance."

Ben nods, deliberate and thoughtful. "I get that, sure. You need to secure what matters, create as much certainty as possible in an uncertain world. So do I, if I'm honest. For me, after what happened with Mom and Dad . . . you're right. We need to live every day how we want to live. Starting today." He smiles at me, softly, tracing his thumb along my temple. "Your studio lease is up next month, you said?" I lift an eyebrow in affirmation. "Okay, then . . . so, I know this is really fast, but . . . how about you move into the loft with me? I mean, we should probably live together for a minute before I go ahead and, you know, actually *propose*. You can see what it would feel like to be married to me. Now that we're fully stuck with each other, and everything."

260

I laugh, and stroke his cheek. "Yes, Ben. I will live with you. I'll live with you for the rest of our lives."

He grins, and squeezes me tight. Then he kisses me once more. And again. And again.

THE END

AUTHOR'S NOTE AND ACKNOWLEDGMENTS

How do you follow a pair of novels in which each protagonist finds herself in an alternate version of her life? By giving your next protagonist *multiple* alternate versions of her life, I guess!

After my first two books, in each of which there are dual parallel universes, I wanted to write a thematically similar novel to appeal to the many wonderful readers who have supported my work so far. But, of course, it was crucial to take the concept to the next level. Which is to say, something like the first two books, but on steroids!

For this story's concept, I was inspired by Matt Haig's *The Midnight Library* and the original inspiration for my debut, Kate Atkinson's *Life After Life*, as well as the Oscar-winning movie *Everything, Everywhere, All at Once*. In all three of those incredible stories, the protagonist tries on many different lives, as opposed to merely splitting their life in two, as in *Sliding Doors*.

I wanted to take that true *multi*verse idea into my next novel, which I chose to set in Chicago as one of my favorite US cities, and where I was able to take a fantastic research trip to get my locations right. I came upon the idea of an incongruous basement door (which would somehow have a significant, life-altering history to my protagonist) as a personal portal to all her other lives. Initially, the house of this door was going to be some kind of student accommodation at a Chicago-based university. But I soon changed the door location to a family home near the city, when I started building out my characters and realized how crucial the Mason family would be to Millie's story.

Once that device was in place, it was a whole heap of fun to imagine the infinite possible paths Millie's life could have taken, some of which could be pretty extreme. After all, we're arguably all just a hair's breadth away from ending up as billionaires or on the poverty line (or anything in between); being in a relationship with a loving partner or an abusive narcissist; living in desperate sadness or incandescent joy; and anything else. It takes only the tiniest of butterfly-wing-flaps to cause seismic changes in Millie's reality, further down the road — she's even the unwitting creator of a futuristic technology that creates a sci-fi-like alt-reality. (And, for me, it only took one overly vivid dream to turn me into an author — for more that story, see my blog, link below!)

People often ask me about my process, and to be honest, I've only just figured it out. I've always been a plotter, and will set out the story from start to finish in chapter-sentences before I start — that hasn't changed. But *The Love I Never Knew* was the first novel I've written in what I'd call a regular, repeatable way. After all, my debut novel took several years and incarnations, given that I was new to all this and made many horrible errors. Conversely, the second book was written while I was furloughed from my day job in 2020, and the first draft only took five weeks, writing full-time. Whereas this third one, written at a steady pace on the weekends while working full-time at my new job, was completed in just under a year, start to finish — January to November 2023. The initial draft was complete by the end of May; the rest was my own editing and rewriting, then back and forth with beta readers and my agent, and then to the publisher and some more changes, all of which took another six months. So I now feel like I can complete a book in a year, which is reassuring. By the way, anybody curious about my writing process and publishing journey can follow my blog at cjconnollybooks.com.

Helping me along the way, as ever, have been my fabulous agent, Victoria Skurnick of Levine Greenberg Rostan in New York, and the whole team at my publishing house in London, UK — Joffe Books — especially their wonderful publishing director, Kate Lyall Grant. Warmest thanks to all of them for making me a happy and well-taken-care-of author, in an industry where I know that isn't always the case!

I remain so grateful to the community of writers and readers who support each other, and have bolstered me in creating this novel, as well as others. Particular thanks this time to my NY Writing Gals group — Jen McGuire (a brilliant memoirist and essayist, and you should read her memoir *Nest* immediately), Erin Ortiz, and Heather Jacobsen — I really appreciate you all feeding me wine and chips in the Catskills to help me get "draft zero" across the finish line! And to my small but mighty group of beta readers, who challenged everything that was wrong with draft three — Jemma Wood, Shona McGlashan, Jackie Estacio, and Melissa Senger — this is a much better novel because of you.

My unending gratitude, as ever, to my personal support system who help so much just by being there, loving me, and being excited for this publishing ride I'm on. Special love to my girls Shona, Sarah B, Libby, Becky, Jo, Rach, Sarah J, and Nic A, who are spread far and wide, so I always have besties wherever I am. Love forever to my brother Rich and his family, and my sister Alice and her family, especially the boys, Oscar and Felix — my great loves in any life! And, of course, to Mum and Ian, who took their chance and made their own reality the best possible version of itself. Thanks for inspiring me every day with your own love story.

THE JOFFE BOOKS STORY

We began in 2014 when Jasper agreed to publish his mum's much-rejected romance novel and it became a bestseller.

Since then we've grown into the largest independent publisher in the UK. We're extremely proud to publish some of the very best writers in the world, including Joy Ellis, Faith Martin, Caro Ramsay, Helen Forrester, Simon Brett and Robert Goddard. Everyone at Joffe Books loves reading and we never forget that it all begins with the magic of an author telling a story.

We are proud to publish talented first-time authors, as well as established writers whose books we love introducing to a new generation of readers.

We won Trade Publisher of the Year at the Independent Publishing Awards in 2023. We have been shortlisted for Independent Publisher of the Year at the British Book Awards for the last four years, and were shortlisted for the Diversity and Inclusivity Award at the 2022 Independent Publishing Awards. In 2023 we were shortlisted for Publisher of the Year at the RNA Industry Awards.

We built this company with your help, and we love to hear from you, so please email us about absolutely anything bookish at feedback@joffebooks.com

If you want to receive free books every Friday and hear about all our new releases, join our mailing list: www.joffebooks.com/contact

And when you tell your friends about us, just remember: it's pronounced Joffe as in coffee or toffee!